Intercepting LOVE

by

L. P. Dover

Printed in the United States of America

Intercepting Love
A Second Chances Novel

Copyright © 2014 by L.P. Dover
Cover design by Regina Wamba of Mae I Design
Edited by Melissa Ringsted
Formatting by JT Formatting

ISBN-13: 978-0990396413
ISBN-10: 099039641X

Prologue

Kate

"So how does it feel to be done with school for the summer?" Evan asked.

With my phone propped up on my shoulder, I shoved the last of my belongings into the back of my Jeep and smiled. "It feels amazing, but I'm having a hard time believing that I'm actually done ... well, at least for the time being. It went by so fast," I replied.

It was like one minute I was a freshman struggling to make ends meet, and now I was about to do my hospital rotations, making my way to graduating with a medical degree. My rotations, however, weren't going to be in Raleigh—where I'd spent the last few years at Chapel Hill—they were going to be back at home in one of our local hospitals in Charlotte. Luckily, I already had a job lined up to be one of the private physicians for my hometown NFL team, the Carolina Cougars. I had my brother to thank for it since he was their star wide receiver and it was his idea that I apply for the job. I couldn't wait to get my medical degree and get started. I'd be able to travel with the team and see new places, all while doing what I loved. It was a dream come true.

"Yes, it did fly by," my brother agreed. "Hopefully, I have a few good years left on the team before I have to retire. Oh yeah, just to give you a heads up, I already warned the guys to keep their hands and eyes to themselves when you start coming around. The last thing I want is for one of them to break your heart."

Chuckling, I started up my Jeep and pulled out of my apartment parking lot. "Yeah, I don't think that's going to be a problem. I'm taken, remember?" I hesitated for a second before adding, "Or ... at least, I think I am."

"How long do you think it's going to last, Kate?" he asked. "Your boyfriend does know that you'll be travelling everywhere with the team, right? You two will never see each other. I'm sorry, but I don't see it working out for very long."

"I know that, Evan," I murmured sadly. "I think Scott knows it, too, but we'll take it one step at a time. I'm on my way to see him now to drop off some things he left at my apartment. I'll see you at Mom and Dad's house for dinner tonight, okay?"

I knew he could hear the trepidation in my voice because the phone went silent. My brother was younger than me by only eighteen months, but ever since we were little he had always been more of a big brother to me. I had a strange feeling I was going to see that side of him a lot when I started working with the football players.

"All right," Evan muttered, finally breaking the silence. "Just be careful on your way home."

"Will do." I hung up the phone, setting it in the center console of my car.

The closer I got to Scott's house, the more the pain in my chest grew; I knew nothing was going to help the ache go away. I'd always known that leaving was going to be an issue, and when I tried to talk to Scott about it over the past couple of months he would always change the subject. Being the coward that I was I never pressed the issue; I let it slide knowing I had more time to address it. That time swiftly approached and here I was on my way to say good-bye.

Even though Scott never wanted to talk about it, I could see it in his eyes that he wasn't happy. Maybe I wasn't good at relationships. I had no clue how to make things better between us or how to make him smile again. Something was wrong with him, but I had no clue what it was.

I'd met Scott during my first year of college, and we went out on a few dates every now and again. He was always busy with baseball and I was busy studying, so we never got too serious. At least, not until he became my patient after a torn rotator cuff put him out of commission for a while. It was then we were able to actually spend time together, and it wasn't long after that when I fell in love with him. I had to believe things would work out between us, even with the distance.

Pulling into Scott's driveway, I parked my car and blew out a nervous breath. He lived in a moderately sized, brick ranch style house in a nice little neighborhood not far from campus. I basically lived with him and only ventured to my apartment when I needed something of my own. Squeezing my eyes shut, I desperately tried to hold back my tears, but I couldn't. *Come on, Kate, pull yourself together. Scott and I love each other and that's all that mat-*

ters.

The box sitting in my passenger seat had a few of his shirts, a pair of his sneakers, and his laptop. I was tempted to keep it all just so it wouldn't feel like we were breaking up. Opening the car door, I threw my blonde hair into a ponytail—so that it wouldn't stick to my shoulders from the summer heat—and grabbed the box beside of me. Box in hand, I waltzed up to the front door and pressed the doorbell.

The sound echoed through his house and as I waited for him to get to the door, my heart literally felt like it was being ripped out of my chest. I didn't want to leave him.

After about three minutes of silence, I rang the door-bell again and knocked as loud as I could. "Where are you, Scott?" I mumbled to myself. *Surely, he'll want to see me before I go, right?*

Setting the box down, I marched over to my Jeep and grabbed my phone from inside. I dialed Scott's number and could hear it ringing inside his house, but no one picked up.

"You better not be ignoring me," I grumbled.

Even if he was pissed at me for leaving he would never intentionally ignore me; he wasn't the type of person to do that. Blowing out an angry breath, I placed my hands on my hips and stalked over to his garage. I knew I shouldn't do what I was about to do, but I had to see him. No one was around to see me punch in the five digit code to Scott's garage and sneak inside. His shiny, black Ford Mustang was in its usual place, and normally my Jeep would be beside his ... but not today.

Taking a deep breath, I slowly walked past his car and opened the door that led into his kitchen, nervously biting my lip the entire time. "Scott," I called out hesitantly. "Look, I'm sorry for barging in, but I didn't want to leave without saying good-bye. Will you please talk to me? I know things haven't been the best between us, but I want to see you. I don't want to leave without knowing we're okay."

I waited for him to speak, but there was no answer … only silence, except for the sound of the television coming from the living room. "Scott," I called again, standing awkwardly in the kitchen. "Please, talk to me."

When no reply came, I decided to seek him out. If he was that angry with me for leaving then he needed to say it to my face so we could work things out. He had always told me how he felt, but for the past couple of months he'd kept his feelings and his anger bottled up. I didn't know how to get him to talk to me, so I buried myself in my school work and figured it would all work out in the end. I had a feeling it wasn't going to.

The living room was vacant when I peeked around the corner, so I slowly made my way down the hall, looking into each room as I passed. *Nothing.* All that was left was his bedroom, and immediately I faltered, freezing in the middle of the hallway. Dread crept up my spine and my skin broke out in chills. It almost reminded me of the feeling you get when you're watching a scary movie and something's about to jump out at you.

I didn't like closed doors, especially, when you didn't know what you'd find behind them. Licking my dry lips, I wrapped my hand around the doorknob and twisted it gently, so afraid of what I was going to find on the other side of the door. Was he with another woman? *Is that the reason why he didn't want to answer the door?*

Please, God, don't let there be someone else, I prayed.

However, another woman in his bed wasn't what I found. He was alone and asleep in his bed. *No wonder he didn't answer his door,* I chided myself.

"Scott," I chuckled, "it's time to wake up, sleepy head." I opened up the window to my right so the sun could shine in and light up the room. When that didn't wake him up, I went to another one and opened it up as well.

"I wanted to say good-bye to you before I left," I continued. "I was thinking maybe we could alternate weekend visits. How about this upcoming weekend I come back here and stay? Does that sound good?"

When he didn't answer, I turned around and placed my hands on my hips. "If this is your way of getting me to stay, you know it's not going to work, Scott. I really want this to work out, but I'm going to need your help. Please talk to me."

I stared at him, lying in his bed, and waited on him to move or speak … or do something. Instead, he just lied there with his back to me. Swallowing hard, I took a step closer, and another. His chest wasn't moving and there was no sound coming from him at all; everything was silent.

"Scott," I pleaded. "You're scaring me."

My breaths came out in shallow gasps as I turned the corner of his bed and got a good look at him. Gasping, I closed my eyes and fell back against the wall, trying to mute the scream that escaped my lips by covering my mouth with my hand. Nothing was going to take away the image of Scott's lifeless body permanently ingrained in my mind. His unseeing hazel eyes were open, staring straight at the ceiling with no shred of life. And there, lying beside of his motionless body, was a pill bottle … and it was empty.

"Oh my God, Scott, what the hell did you do?" I screamed, my voice unfamiliar to my own ears. Frantically, I touched his face and immediately burst into tears when all I felt was cold skin … death. "Why?" I cried, searching his face angrily. "Why would you do this to me?"

It was only just yesterday that he was alive and telling me he loved me. Why would he want to kill himself? Backing away from his cold, lifeless body, I closed my eyes and shook my head back and forth vigorously. "I don't understand. It has to be a bad dream. Oh, please let me open my eyes and it be just a bad dream."

As soon as I opened my eyes, the tears blurred my vision. Unfortunately, it didn't stop me from seeing something that would forever haunt me for the rest of my life. With shaky fingers, I picked up the piece of paper that was on his nightstand and read the words inside.

I was too late.

And it was all my fault.

Chapter 1

Kate

Two Years Later

"Am I doing okay, Dr. Townsend?"

Chuckling, I rolled my eyes and tilted my head back only to be met by Luke's mischievous green gaze and sardonic smile. "I think you're doing more than okay, but something tells me you might have known that a couple of weeks ago," I told him slyly, getting to my feet.

Luke Collins was my brother's best friend, and for the past four months I'd been helping him recover with physical therapy after he broke his leg during a motocross race. From the looks of his progress I'd say he didn't need me anymore, but he swore up and down he did.

He was twenty-five years old—the same age as me—and sexy as hell with tousled dirty blond hair and piercing green eyes. The last thing I needed was to get involved with my brother's best friend; especially since he was the same guy that had women falling all over him everywhere he went. Still, it didn't stop me from admiring the view of his well-toned, tanned abs as I slowly got to my feet. His dark blue gym shorts hung low on his hips, showing off that sexy 'v' that women loved so much on men and all I wanted to do was run my fingers through the indentions.

Luke had always come on strong with me, and in turn I'd pushed him away, knowing that all we would have was a relationship based on sex. We were completely different; I was reserved and responsible … he wasn't. He was wild and full of life; the way I wished I could've lived. However, it wasn't exactly my style to be promiscuous and party all of the time like him. There were moments when I wanted to give in, to let loose of my inhibitions and have fun, but I hadn't given in to the temptation … yet.

I was on the border of it though.

Clearing my throat, I bit my lip and reached for my bag. "In fact, Mr. Collins, I'd say you're more than ready to start racing again. However, I humored you and stayed on for an extra two weeks per your request."

Luke grinned and moved closer, wrapping his arms around my waist from behind. I tensed at first, but then melted into his touch. It had been so long since I'd felt the arms of a man around me. Was I stupid to give in to him when I knew it wouldn't mean anything to him? Closing my eyes, my skin broke out in chills as his warm breath tickled the side of my neck and even more so when his dark chuckle echoed in my ear.

"Oh, I know you knew, sweetheart, but I wanted to have you all to myself for a little while longer. The agony of having your hands on me and not being able to do anything about it was the best fucking torture ever. It makes me jealous to think about your hands all over those football players," he said, his voice just above a whisper in my ear.

I scoffed and smacked him on the arm, bumping him with my hip so I could wriggle out of his hold. "You're insane," I teased. When his arms loosened, I turned around to face him; his lips achingly close. "I think you were in too much pain in the beginning to enjoy my touch, and for the most part, so are the players when I'm evaluating them. Besides, I'm sure you had plenty of women here to help you in your time of need."

"Is that really what you think of me?" he asked. "Do you think messing around with women is all I do?"

I expected him to joke around with me like he always did, but surprisingly, he didn't. Instead, his smile vanished and he stepped closer, minimizing the distance between us and gazing down at me with somber green eyes.

Sighing, I shrugged my shoulders and smiled, hoping to lighten his sudden change in mood. "I don't know, Luke. I know you're a great guy. You're talented, funny, a wonderful athlete, and you're extremely good looking. I also know your ways. I've been to your races, and I've seen how you are with women … and how they are with you. You're a ladies' man and there's nothing wrong with that. It's just the way you are. Why do you care what I think about you anyway?"

I had a feeling I already knew the answer, and by the skeptical look in his eyes he could see right through me.

"Really, Kate? You honestly have no idea? Have you not listened to anything I've said to you the past couple of months?" When I averted my gaze, he grasped my chin and gently held me in place. "Why won't you answer me?"

"Fine," I gave in, glaring up at him. "Yes, I've lis-tened to you, but you were so subtle I didn't think anything about it."

He scoffed incredulously, "It's because I didn't want to come off too strong. With some people it works, but with you ..." He paused to take a deep breath. "With you it's different."

Surprised by his words, I just stood there and stared. He didn't even sound like the Luke I knew. It almost made me think he and my brother were playing a joke on me. Luke was the type of guy you took home for the night and had wild, passionate monkey sex with ... nothing else. I never pictured him as a serious relationship type of guy, and if I was honest with myself, I had no clue if I even wanted that.

"Luke, I'm flattered, really," I admitted truthfully. "On one hand, I would love to go out with you and have fun, but on the other, what if it changed things between us? What if one of us wanted more than the other could offer? It would ruin our friendship."

Smirking, he tapped me on the chin with his fingers. "No, it wouldn't, Kate. I want just you, but if you wanted something casual then that's fine with me, too. I can offer you whatever you want and more if you just give in to me. Trust me, it'll be fun."

Actually, what he offered didn't sound like a bad idea, I thought.

For so long, I thought of others well-being above my own and never allowed myself any shred of happiness, especially with a man. I craved the intimacy, but I couldn't let go of the guilt from my past in order to attain it. After what had happened two years ago, I felt like I didn't deserve it; like I wasn't worthy.

Luke gazed at me expectantly, his eyes twinkling

with delight as he waited on my answer. Grinning, I gave in and nodded my head. "Okay, fine. I'm going to give you a chance. I honestly don't think you'll hold up the end of your bargain anyway. One date is all you get."

Guffawing, Luke scooped me into his arms and held me tight. "I knew I could wear you down, sweetheart. You won't regret a second of it."

Both of us laughing, he set me down and cupped my face in his hands, his smile boyish yet completely sexy. *What have I gotten myself in to?* He leaned down ever so slowly and placed his lips to mine, kissing me gently. His hands caressed my back, pulling me closer, and he deepened the kiss by opening my lips with his tongue.

"Don't leave, Kate," he begged. "Stay."

Before I could give in to the temptation of his touch, my phone began to ring in my bag.

"Ignore it," he whispered, trailing his lips down my neck.

Groaning, I moved back and reached for my bag, which was sitting on the table beside us. "Luke, you know I can't. It could be an emergency with the team." Reluctantly, he nodded and stepped back to give me my space, his gaze heated.

Luckily, it was just my brother when I pulled out my phone. Breathing a sigh of relief, I sat down on the arm rest of Luke's black leather couch and answered it.

"Evan, what's up?" I asked.

"Hey, where are you? Have you left Luke's yet?"

Trying to sound as innocent as I could, I looked up at Luke and replied, "No, I haven't left yet. We just finished the last of his … therapy session." Grinning from ear to ear, Luke winked and bit his lip, squeezing my ass as he pulled me back to him.

"Okay, good. Coach Harris wanted me to call and see if you could come to the stadium in the next hour or so."

Trying to hold in my snicker, I looked over at the clock on Luke's wall and cleared my throat. "Yeah, of course. Is everything all right? I thought he didn't need me until tomorrow."

"That *was* the plan," he replied. "It seems our new quarterback is coming in early, and Coach wants you to look him over before practice starts tomorrow."

Inwardly, I groaned. When I found out our team had taken on Cooper Davis as our new quarterback, I just knew they had made the worst mistake ever. He used to be the best quarterback out there, and I had to admit I was impressed with him when I read a ten page spread on him in the *Physique Sports and Fitness Magazine.* He definitely went downhill after injuring his shoulder.

Our team needed guidance, but bringing in someone who clearly needed help of his own definitely wasn't going to facilitate a win for us. Not only had he been injured and traded to our team, but the guy had serious issues with being reckless, even getting into trouble for misusing drugs. I wasn't looking forward to working with him.

"Okay," I grumbled into the phone. "I'll be there in about thirty minutes. Will you be there, too?"

"No, I just left, but I'll see you tomorrow morning. Oh yeah, and tell Luke there's a party this Saturday night with the team and that I want him there."

Glancing up at Luke, I held the phone away from my ear and said quickly, "There's a party my brother wants you to go to on Saturday night."

Luke nodded and grinned. "Okay, but he's going to

have to wait until after my date. Unless you want to go with me to the party as well."

Jaw dropping, I glared at him as my brother cleared his throat, choking in surprise. "I heard that! Please tell me he's joking, Kate."

I groaned and hung my head. "No, it's no joke, and it's not that big of a deal, Evan."

"Yeah, for him," he scoffed. "I don't think I like this, Kate. He's my friend, but the guy's a serious player. I don't want to see you get hurt."

He didn't have to worry about that. Having fun with Luke was one thing, but I knew how to control my feelings. I wouldn't get hurt unless I wanted to, and that wasn't going to happen.

"Believe me, Evan, you have nothing to worry about. You have to trust me on this," I told him.

Evan groaned. "Okay, but don't say I didn't warn you."

"Duly noted. I'll see you tomorrow."

As soon as the call ended, Luke pursed his lips and followed me toward the front door. I had a little less than an hour to get to the stadium and I wanted to get there early so I could look over Cooper Davis' file again.

"What does your brother need you to do?" Luke asked.

When we got to the door, I stopped and turned to face him, exasperated. "Our new quarterback, Cooper Davis, is coming into town today and Coach wants me to evaluate him. I'm really not looking forward to having this guy on the team. Do you know who he is?"

Leaning against the wall with his arms crossed at the chest, he scoffed and curled his lip in disgust. "Yeah, who doesn't know him? The guy seriously went to shit after his shoulder gave out. I'm surprised he hasn't been kicked out of the league with all of the problems he's been causing. I wish you luck though. He's a time bomb waiting to explode."

"Great ... thanks," I remarked sarcastically. We had a couple of problem players on the team, but nothing like Cooper. We deserved to win, and I was afraid that wasn't ever going to happen if we couldn't get reliable players.

Luke walked me to my Jeep and opened my door for me before leaning his arms inside my window. "So ... Saturday you'll go on a date with me, right? Then afterwards we can go to the party together?"

Reaching for my sunglasses, I slipped them on and smiled. "Sounds like a plan. Give me a call sometime this week and we'll figure everything out."

Slowly, he leaned forward, keeping his gaze on my lips before gently touching his to mine. "I look forward to it. I just hope you're ready for me."

"Please," I scoffed incredulously.

Kissing me once more, he winked and sauntered back to his front door while I started up my Jeep. Tomorrow all hell would break loose, and I had a feeling this season was going to be the most memorable one yet ... and not in a good way.

Chapter 2

COOPER

I didn't see a reason to delay the inevitable, so I made an earlier flight and flew across the country to North Carolina, especially since everything I owned was already there. There was nothing keeping me in California now that I screwed everything up and basically got kicked off of my team. What looked to be a simple trade wasn't exactly so. The real reason was too fucking embarrassing, and thankfully, money talked or else the story would be publicized in every magazine and tabloid in the United States.

How did I fall so low so fast? I had everything going for me until it was all taken away in one single game. Who would've thought that one injury could destroy everything? I wasn't going to get back what I lost.

Finally, after several hours of listening to the guy beside me talk about his marketing plan for selling cat food, the plane landed and it was time to go. By the time I got out of the terminal, Coach Harris was there dressed in a black polo shirt and khaki pants, waiting for me with a smile on his face. It had been years since I'd seen him, but his once dark brown hair was now covered in gray, giving him the salt and peppered look that was very prominent with the men in my family.

You see, Joel Harris wasn't just my coach … he was my uncle. If anyone found that out, I was pretty sure speculation would suggest that the only reason I got on the team was for that fact alone. No one else wanted me, except him. Sometimes I wish I'd have just given up on football and let it go, but it was in my blood. It was all I had.

"Cooper, it's so good to see you again," Joel said, extending his hand. "How's the family back home?"

Nonchalantly, I shrugged and shook his hand. "They're fine," was all I could say. I didn't want to say that they were disappointed in me and could care less what I did with my life since I was an utter failure. Thankfully, my uncle could sense I didn't want to elaborate so he moved on.

"Do you have any more luggage other than the bag you're carrying?" he asked, letting go of my hand.

"No, this is it. Everything should've already been delivered to the house. I have a lot of unpacking to do this week."

"I'm sure you do, son. How about we get out of here and head over to the stadium for a few minutes? I want one of our physicians to look at your shoulder and get to know you since you'll be joining our team. How is the shoulder anyway?"

I subconsciously rolled it in a circular motion; I didn't have pain per se, but there was always a constant ache that never seemed to go away. My addiction was what I thought about the most. Every time the pain would become too much, I knew what I had to do to make it disappear. It was a place to escape where no one else could judge me; a place where I honestly didn't give a fuck.

Shrugging, I kept my gaze straight as we walked through the airport. "The shoulder's fine. I'm just ready to get back into the game." Out of the corner of my eye, Joel pursed his lips and I knew he wanted to say something, but he kept quiet until we got outside.

"Look, Cooper, I'm sure I don't have to say this twice, but the shit you got into out in California with the drugs, alcohol, and the reckless behavior won't fly here. I'm putting my neck on the line for you, and I expect you to work hard and get along with the team. They already have their doubts about you and I want you to show them that you can lead them."

Talk about pressure.

"You used to be the best quarterback in the NFL, and I know you can be that way again. You have one chance to redeem yourself, son. My guys work hard and they need someone like you to help get them to the top. Except, the first time you screw up you're out of here, understand?"

Closing my eyes, I blew out a frustrated sigh and turned to my uncle. All I'd heard from my family for the past eight months was how much of a screw up I was. I was so goddamned sick of listening to it.

"Yeah, I understand," I mumbled.

The only time I felt like I was worth something was when I was on the field, and thankfully, I spent the summer in a drugged and drunken haze to not notice that it was off season. I was afraid that might've been why I spent a few nights in jail. Now, however, wasn't the time to be like that. I had to prove to everyone that I *could* be the winner I used to be, that I wasn't going to screw up again. All I had to do now was convince myself.

Unfortunately, that was easier said than done when I had bigger problems to deal with.

Chapter 3

Kate

Pulling into the team's designated parking area, I saw that Coach Joel Harris' white Range Rover was in its usual spot. Otherwise, the stadium was quiet. *I guess Cooper hadn't arrived yet.* My hair was windblown from the ride over in my Jeep, and unfortunately, I didn't have time to put on something presentable since Joel wanted me at the stadium within the hour.

Thankfully, Joel was more down to earth and I knew he wouldn't mind what I wore as long as I did my job. I liked that about him, and it made working for him and the team that much more enjoyable.

Once inside, but before getting to his office, I pulled the tie out of my hair and ran my fingers through my wavy, golden locks in hopes that it wouldn't look so messy from the ride. After looking at my reflection in one of the windows I knew it was hopeless; the hair was going back up into a ponytail.

Joel's office was just up ahead, and taped to the door was a yellow piece of paper. The closer I got, I could see it was in Joel's handwriting and addressed to me. Peeling it away from the door, I read it out loud.

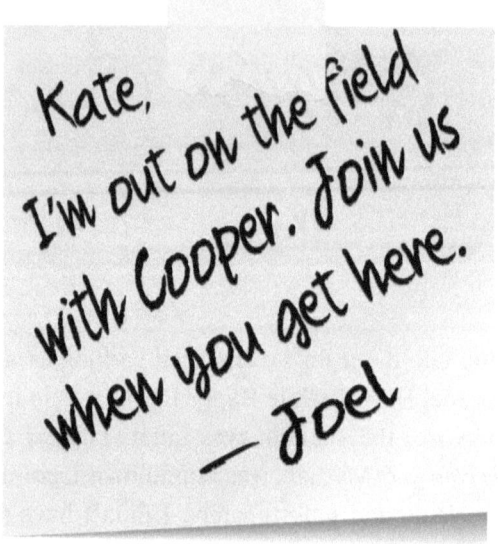

Kate,
I'm out on the field with Cooper. Join us when you get here.
— Joel

"On my way," I muttered, turning around.

Walking through the empty hallway, it didn't take long to get to the door that led onto the field. Joel's loud, booming voice echoing through the air caught my attention, praising Cooper on how great he was doing. Slowly, I edged closer and stayed out of view so I could watch. As much as I didn't like the guy, he sure could throw a football. One after the other, and with exact precision, Cooper didn't miss one single pass through the holes in the practice net. Our last quarterback couldn't even do that. When he was done, Joel grinned. I had never seen such a big smile on his face as I did in that moment. He had faith in our new quarterback … I could see it.

Out of the shadows, I sauntered onto the field so Joel would know I was there. Cooper had his back to me, but the second Joel saw me, he clapped Cooper on the shoulder and turned him around. For a split second, my steps faltered and my stomach fluttered when Cooper's gaze met mine. I hated to admit it, but he looked amazingly different in person than in the newspapers; his hair was a little longer on top and the arrogance I could see in his pictures didn't show on his face now. He almost looked … lost.

They both stopped in front of me and surprisingly it was hard to tear my eyes away from the hypnotic, ocean blue color of Cooper's gaze. There was no smile on his face, just the intensity of his stare. His dark brown hair looked almost black, and his sweat glistened skin—which had the golden glow of the California sun—was bare except for the pair of denim jeans he had hanging low on his waist.

Stop staring, Kate, I scolded myself.

"Ah, Kate, thank you so much for coming," Joel greeted warmly. "I'd like you to meet Cooper."

Cooper held out his hand, and for a moment I just stood there, still staring mesmerizingly at the bluest eyes I'd ever seen. It wasn't until the corner of his lip turned up in a smirk that I snapped out of my trance.

Shaking my head, I grasped his hand and said, "It's nice to meet you, Cooper."

Mine looked so small wrapped inside his warm, rough hand, but I tightened my hold and shook before abruptly letting go. "The pleasure's all mine … Kate," he replied amusingly, his voice dipping lower when he said my name.

Smiling, Joel put his arm around my shoulder and squeezed while looking over at Cooper. "Actually, this is Kate Townsend. She's one of the physicians for our team. She'll be the one taking care of you today. I want her to look over your shoulder."

Cooper's eyes went wide in disbelief, and finally a smile spread across his face when he looked me up and down. I'd seen that look plenty of times before and it never failed. Each time I told someone that I worked for the team they immediately thought I was one of the cheerleaders. It didn't make me mad, but I had a lot of people underestimate me … and that was what I hated the most.

"Is there something funny, Mr. Davis?" I asked pointedly.

He shook his head and grinned wider. "No, not at all. I just didn't expect you to be a young woman. You must have a trying time dealing with a bunch of football players. I don't see how you do it."

If it wasn't for my brother, it probably wouldn't be as easy as it had been, but I had to believe I could handle it all on my own if I had to. "I think I manage pretty well on my own," I informed him dryly. "Are you ready for me to take a look at your shoulder?"

Cooper nodded. "I'm ready when you are."

Once he grabbed his shirt off of the ground and bottle of water, I turned on my heel and marched out of the arena so we could go inside to the locker rooms where I had all of my medical supplies. Joel and Cooper strutted along behind me—talking about random things—but I couldn't help but overhear Joel's warning to him.

"I'm warning you, Kate can be a pistol, especially when she has to deal with certain players. Oh, and to give

16

you a heads up, she has her own protector on the team that makes sure no one messes with her. I'm sure you understand what I mean."

Quickly hooking a glance over my shoulder, I glared at Joel before turning to Cooper. His gaze never wavered from mine when he responded, "Yeah, I understand ... loud and clear."

I could only imagine the things my brother was going to say to him tomorrow. If any of my family and friends thought I got any action from the players they were sorely mistaken. Not that I had any interest in any of the guys, but if I did, I knew my brother would never let me live it down.

When we got to the locker room, I turned on the lights and took a deep breath. My stomach was jittery and I couldn't tell if it was because I hadn't eaten anything yet or if it was Cooper making me nervous. *Why would Cooper make me nervous? He's just a damaged football player that let fame go to his head. Just overlook his sexy as hell body, his gorgeous eyes, and that smile of his that makes everything in my body tingle.* I could feel his gaze on me the entire time I moved about the room, searching for my notebook and pen, and his file.

With my gaze looking down toward the notes in my hand, I pointed to one of the medical benches. "Cooper, if you wouldn't mind sitting down for me I'd really appreciate it. All I'm going to do is ask you some questions and do a couple of mobility exercises with your shoulder."

Joel reached out and took Cooper's shirt and bottle of water and set them both on the small wooden table that I used to hold my ointments and bandages while I tended to the players. The temperature in the room spiked as I watched Cooper's muscles flex before he sat down in the chair, but it didn't stop him from making eye contact with me first. Immediately, I averted my gaze back to my notes.

I had the sudden urge to fan myself, but the last thing I wanted was for Cooper to think I was going to fawn all over him. That wasn't going to happen ... ever. Thankfully, I wasn't alone with him since Joel stood off to the side of the room; at least, until his phone rang and he excused himself. Once he left, an awkward silence filled the room, and all I could hear was the pounding in my ears as I slowly walked up behind Cooper.

I usually didn't get nervous being around men, but unfortunately, there was something about the tall, dark, and handsome quarterback that lit my body on fire. Licking my lips, I was about to ask him questions about his medical history when Joel came back into the room.

Glancing at both of us, he held up his phone and said, "I'm sorry you two, but I need to get out of here. Something's come up." Then he looked specifically at me. "Kate, do you mind giving Cooper a ride home? He moved two houses down from you, so it shouldn't be an inconvenience." He smiled quickly and waved good-bye. "Thank you and I'll see you both tomorrow."

Before I could even protest, he disappeared around the corner, his footsteps racing down the hallway. What the hell? Since when was chauffeur added to my job description? Not that I wouldn't help out someone on the team, it's just I didn't want to help the man sitting in front of me. He already made me feel uncomfortable. When we could no longer hear Joel's voice echoing down the hallway, Cooper spoke.

"Dr. Townsend, don't worry about taking me home. I

can call a cab once we're done here. I don't want to cause any problems with your husband," he stated, sounding tired ... almost weary.

Mouth gaping open, I froze in place and tried to hold back my snicker. The husband part was kind of funny, and I was pretty sure my brother would get a kick out of that ... especially when Cooper found out that my protector was really my brother. However, I had to hand it to him, he actually sounded sincere. I knew for a fact that a lot of the guys on the team wouldn't have cared if I was married.

"Actually, Cooper, I'm a PA, not a doctor, so you don't have to call me Dr. Townsend. Andrew Sawyer is the real team physician, but he's on vacation right now. You'll see him around in a couple of weeks."

"I see," he replied.

"Also, just so you know," I added, "I don't mind taking you home. It wouldn't make any sense for you to call a cab when you live two houses down from me."

He peered at me over his shoulder. "Thank you, I appreciate it. The last thing I want is there to be more tension when I know no one wants me here."

Setting down his chart, I circled around the chair and faced him, gently taking his elbow and lifting his arm so I could check his mobility. He winced just a tiny bit when I raised his arm higher, his muscles tensing.

"Do you really think that? That no one wants you here?"

It was sort of true, but we were only worried that he would screw up and bring bad publicity to our team. Shrugging his shoulders, he smiled even though I could see the sadness in his gaze. "Hey, it wouldn't be the first time no one wanted me. You get used to it after a while."

When he averted his gaze, I moved behind him and kept my hand on his shoulder while I rotated his arm in a circle. He must've been talking about his old team. I hadn't realized what kind of impact that would have on him.

"It's not that we don't want you, Cooper. I think we've all seen the newspaper articles on your ... issues. It's just we don't want to be in the crossfire of bad publicity. I'm assuming you've given up your bad habits?" I asked, trying not to sound like an accusatory mother.

With my hand on his warm skin, I could feel his chuckle through my fingertips. "And what exactly would those bad habits be, Kate? There are too many to count."

Rolling my eyes, I snapped, "Do you still do drugs? Drink heavily? Those kinds of bad habits." Done with his evaluation, I faced him head on with my arms crossed over my chest, waiting on him to reply.

Cooper got to his feet and smiled while slowly reaching over my body—brushing his own against mine—so he could retrieve his red T-shirt that was draped over the table. Breathing in deeply, he slowly rubbed his arm against mine, making my skin tingle with the contact. He was pushing my buttons, and I didn't know if I should be pissed off or enjoy those forbidden moments.

Leaning down toward my ear, he murmured, "You don't have anything to worry about. I'm perfectly fine. I know what's at stake if I fuck up."

For some reason, I wasn't sure if I believed that or not. I did know that Joel wouldn't put up with him if he messed up, and if he did it'd be game over. There was nothing I could do about that, but deep down I really did pray he would be what we needed to win.

Putting his file back in the cabinet, I took a deep breath and turned back to him. "All right, I believe you," I claimed halfheartedly. "I have faith that you'll do your best. Now let's get you home so you can rest up before tomorrow. Just because you're new to the team doesn't mean the guys are going to go easy on you."

He grinned and started toward the door. "I wouldn't expect anything less.

Chapter 4

Kate

It was a fifteen minute drive from the stadium to my neighborhood, and I had a feeling it was going to be one of the most awkward rides of my life, but Cooper surprised me by talking nonstop. At first, it was just questions about Charlotte and about the team, but then it moved on to questions about me. I was afraid to get too personal for fear it would cause problems. I needed to make sure I kept my distance.

"So how old are you, Kate?" Cooper asked.

"I'm twenty-five," I answered.

"Well, I'm pretty sure you know everything clinical about me from the size of the file you had in your hands earlier. It doesn't have *everything* about me in it, does it?" he asked, waggling his eyebrows.

Laughing, I shook my head. "No, it doesn't have everything about you in it. However, I do know you're twenty-nine years old, six foot four, you were born in California, and that you have issues with your shoulder. Other than that I think you're safe."

With his body turned my way, he kept his gaze on me. "Good, I don't know if I want you knowing everything about me. Although, I can't help but wonder … why didn't you want to finish your degree and become a doctor? Surely, you didn't have much more to go through."

And right there was the one question I hated having to answer. Keeping my eyes on the road, I clenched my teeth and tried desperately to keep my mind from wandering to that time years ago. Everything was perfect and I was one of the top in my class, but I was too distraught over everything that had happened with Scott to concentrate on it. I was a mess back then.

"Kate, are you okay?" Cooper asked, placing his hand on my shoulder. His fingers touched the bare skin of my arm and I shivered.

Nonchalantly, I plastered on a fake smile and nodded. "Yeah, I'm fine. So much was going on in my life, and I never got the chance to complete my year. It's no big deal, though. Maybe one day I'll go back and finish."

"So you were in your last year and quit?" he asked incredulously.

At the time, I felt like I had no other choice. I didn't exactly quit, but when I had my breakdown and missed my mandatory exams there was no other option. My mind wasn't in the right place to take them, so I settled with being just an assistant, even though I was qualified to be an actual physician.

"Um … do you mind if we talk about something else, or nothing at all? I don't want to think about that anymore."

"Yeah, of course," he replied, his voice softening. "So, how long have you been with the team?"

Now that was something I could talk about. "Only one season. I've enjoyed it, especially going to the away games and getting to see places."

I could see him smiling out of the corner of my eye. "I like that, too. I honestly thought it would be over after my shoulder got messed up. My whole life has been nothing but football."

"Surely there's more to you than that," I said in disbelief. "What did you go to college for? I mean, if you didn't play football what would you be doing? You have to have a backup plan."

"I do," he said. "I studied Architecture at UCLA while I played football there. As soon as I retire in a few years, I'm going to get a job doing that. I'm actually good friends with a guy who owns the West Coast branch of M&M Architectural Design."

I gasped. "Wow, that's amazing. I'm not really knowledgeable in architecture, but M&M is pretty huge in Charlotte. How did you manage that?"

Chuckling, he shook his head. However, when he suddenly sighed, I could tell his laugh was anything but humorous. "The guy who owns the West Coast branch is good friends with a girl I used to know."

I guess it pays to know the right people, I thought to myself.

"Was she a girlfriend?" I asked curiously. For some reason I couldn't imagine him being serious about a woman.

His blue gaze turned angry for a second before leveling out. "Her name was Claire, and for a long time she was more than my girlfriend. Is that so hard to believe?"

"I didn't say that," I replied, holding my hands up in

defeat, but wanting to know more. "What happened to her?"

With a devilish smirk on his face, he focused those gorgeous blue eyes of his on me. "I'll tell you what. If you tell me why you didn't finish medical school, then I'll tell you all about Claire. You see, I don't like to think about her so if you want to know, you need to give me something in return."

That wasn't going to happen.

"Never mind then," I snapped. "I don't want to know that badly." I *did* want to know, but I wasn't going to tell him about my past just so that I could.

In no time at all, we pulled into his driveway, leaving our last few minutes in the car together with nothing but silence. There were still things I wanted to ask him, but I figured we'd spoken enough for the day.

"Thank you for the ride home," Cooper announced gratefully, reaching for the door handle, "and for the talk."

"You're welcome. Do you need a ride to practice tomorrow?" I didn't see a car in his driveway, so I figured I'd better ask.

His hand stalled on the handle and he turned back to me, his blue gaze curious and alit with humor. "You wouldn't mind?"

"No, of course not. You live two houses down from me. Why would I mind?"

He shrugged. "I don't know, maybe because when we were in the locker room I saw your reflection in the mirror when Joel asked you to drive me home. Don't get me wrong, the ride home was really nice, but I'm pretty sure you're capable of plastering on a fake smile. You don't have to pretend with me."

25

I had to give it to him ... he was blunt and to the point.

Although it was true that I didn't want to drive him home at first, it was actually kind of enjoyable on the way home.

"Look, Cooper, at first I didn't want to drive you home, and I'm sorry if you thought I was being a bitch. It's just I've had this notion that you were going to be an arrogant jackass, and I wasn't too thrilled about having to be around you."

"Have I come off like that at all?" he countered seriously.

"No, you haven't, which really kind of shocked me," I confessed. "Anyway, you're part of the team now, and I know the guys are going to give you hell tomorrow, so the last thing you need is someone else igniting the flame."

Surprising me, Cooper's expression changed and he chuckled while hopping out of my car. "You're concern is touching, Kate, but I'm going to have to pass on the ride tomorrow. I don't want to get kicked off the team because I pissed off your husband. I know I definitely wouldn't want you spending time with another man if you were *mine*."

Instantly, my body tightened when he said the word *mine*. I hadn't belonged to anyone in so long I forgot what it felt like to have someone hold me and touch me ... to make love to me. Was it wrong of me to wonder? *Yes, you idiot. You've already ruined one person's life, the last thing you need to do is destroy someone else's.* It was too dangerous thinking of things like that. I destroyed a life long ago, and I refused to do it again, especially to Luke and Cooper. There was nothing wrong with being friends though.

"Wait," I exclaimed before Cooper could shut the door. With a smile on my face, I laughed and said, "You're not going to get kicked off the team by pissing off my husband. My brother, on the other hand, is a different story. So if you want a ride tomorrow it's perfectly fine for you to come along with me."

"Your brother?" he questioned with a slightly confused look on his face. "So you're not married?"

"Hey, I can't help it if you assumed my so called protector on the team was my husband. I'll be here tomorrow morning at eight. If you're not ready, I'm leaving without you."

Tilting his lip up in a seductive smirk, he backed up toward his front door, keeping his ocean blue gaze on mine. "Goodnight, Kate. I'll see you in the morning."

With those final words, I pulled out of his driveway and drove the short distance to my house. I was actually curious to see how well he handled the other players. There was something different about him that I hadn't seen in any of the guys on our team, except for maybe Evan. It wasn't arrogance—because our players had their fair share—it was more like … confidence. Underneath Cooper's mask of failure he still had that spark of confidence that made him a winner, a leader. Hopefully, he let those sides of him be seen.

Chapter 5

COOPER

After falling asleep to the sound of the television, I woke up at precisely six in the morning like I did every day. Everything in my life moved like clockwork. My body knew when it needed a fix, and as soon as my eyes opened every morning I was happy to oblige it. I had hundreds of those little white pills ready to take their place in my body. They could do wonders on the muscles and the soul.

By the time seven o'clock rolled around, I was geared up and ready to go. What Kate didn't know was that I actually didn't need a ride to the field. A few weeks ago, when I'd flown into North Carolina, I had bought a silver Mercedes G-Class and it was sitting in my garage, all shiny and brand new.

In my mind I kept telling myself to keep the ruse up and let Kate offer to drive me every day, but my conscience wouldn't let me. As much as she intrigued me yesterday with her stubborn glares and sexy southern belle accent, I didn't want to deceive her. She wasn't the type of woman you could mess around with and escape unscathed. From what I could gather in the little time I'd spent with her, pissing her off would be a huge mistake. Which was why I was on her front porch, waiting on her to answer the door.

I hadn't realized it was only a few minutes after seven until I looked down at my phone. To my surprise, she answered the door with a smile, fully clothed in a pair of black pants and a pink lacy top that hugged her breasts perfectly. Instead of in a ponytail, her blonde hair was left loose down her shoulders, falling in soft curls. My fingers ached to grab a handful of it and hold her to me as I claimed her lips with my own. She was so goddamned beautiful.

"Good morning," I greeted her. "I'm on time even though I know you didn't think I would be."

Smiling, she opened her door further. "Yes, but now you're too early. I'm almost ready, but you can come in if you want."

As I walked past her into the house, I noticed it smelled exactly like her. Even though we were in her Jeep riding home with the top down yesterday, I could still smell her skin as the breeze blew her scent my way; it was almost like apples, and her house was enveloped in it.

I followed her into her kitchen, where she hastily finished her cereal and placed her bowl in the sink. "Did you want anything to eat?" she asked politely, rinsing out her bowl. "I'm sure I can find something around here that you'll like."

When she looked back at me, I shook my head. "No, that's okay. I already ate this morning." It happened to be in the form of a couple of white pills.

After she grabbed her purse and keys off the counter, she nodded toward the door in the kitchen and opened it. I knew once she pressed the button for the garage door to open she was going to see my car in her driveway. As soon as she did, she lifted her brows and did a double take before turning to me with pursed lips.

"Is there something you failed to mention to me yesterday, or did you go out early this morning and buy yourself a new car?" She walked out the door and I followed her to my car.

Sheepishly, I held up my keys and smiled. "If you want the truth, my conscience got the better of me. If you'd like, I can drive us since you drove me around yesterday. I bought the car a few weeks ago and it's been in my garage. I think it only has fifteen miles on it."

Kate whistled. "Wow, I think my Jeep has over one hundred thousand miles on it now. I probably need to get a new car soon. It's hard to get rid of things you've grown attached to."

I knew that all too well.

Strolling past her, I opened the door to my car and waited for her to get in. "I can let you drive if that'll get you to ride with me. I need to get used to the roads here and I figured you could show me around again."

She slid in, and when I was about to shut the door she held her hand out to halt me. "Oh, wait, I have a problem. There's somewhere I have to go to today, so I was planning on dropping you off at practice and coming back later. I'll need to drive my car so that I can leave."

Moving her hand, I shut the door and hopped in the driver's side before she could say anymore. I didn't want excuses, and if she rode with me she had no choice but to ride back. It was a win-win for me. "No worries, you can take my car wherever you need to go, and then come back to get me. I know you drive safe because I was about to fall asleep when we were on the highway yesterday."

"Hey," she scoffed, smacking me in the arm. "I do not drive slow if that's what you're implying. However, if you insist on me driving your brand new car, I'll be happy to do that. If I wreck it, don't say I didn't warn you."

Putting the car in gear, I backed out of her driveway. "I'm pretty sure I know where to find you to collect for damages. Besides, this thing is a lot safer than your Jeep."

"That might be true, but my Jeep has been through a lot with me over the past few years."

We both chuckled, but then the car went silent. "So," I began, "if you're not married, are you dating anyone?"

Crossing her arms over her chest, she narrowed her gaze and studied me. "Why do you want to know?"

"No reason really," I said nonchalantly. "Just asking since it looks like we'll be spending a lot of time together."

"Well, as of right now, I'm not officially dating anyone."

"Is that because you don't want to be, or because you haven't found someone you want?" I inquired curiously.

She laughed nervously. "My God, you ask a lot of questions. Maybe a little bit of both, I guess. I got hurt a couple of years ago and it kind of stuck with me." Pressing her lips together, she looked down at her clasped hands, her eyes sad and distant. She wasn't the only one in the car who had been hurt.

"You're not asking me out on a date are you?" she blurted out, lifting her head to face me.

"Would you say yes if I did?"

Sighing, she rested her head against the seat and smiled halfheartedly. "Oh, Cooper, I'm the last person you'd want to get involved with. I don't think I'm your type anyway. Besides, we work together, so if anything were to happen it would be very awkward."

It was all excuses, but if I was anything, it was persistent.

"We're adults aren't we, Kate?"

"Yeah, the last time I checked."

"Well, then I'm sure there's a way we can mix business with pleasure without causing problems. We don't even have to tell anyone on the team if that helps. However, the real question here is why do you say you're not my type?"

She scoffed. "I've seen pictures of the girls you date, Cooper. I'm not a fashion model or some glamorous movie star. I'm just a normal girl that lives in a small town in North Carolina, earning probably a quarter of what you're used to. We're from two different worlds."

"Do you honestly think that?" I asked, clenching the steering wheel tight. "You have no idea where I'm from or what I want. Why do you think I picked a house in your neighborhood, Kate?"

She paused, eyes wide, and shrugged her shoulder in reply.

"Okay, I'll tell you. When I lived out in California, I didn't have the opulent mansion like my friends. Yeah, my parents are all about the money, but I chose to live in a smaller place out in the middle of nowhere because that's what *I* liked. I didn't want to show off what I had. Forget what you've seen in the tabloids and newspapers, and find out who I am on your own. I'm so goddamned sick of everyone judging me when they have no fucking clue."

"Hey," she said softly, placing her hand gently on mine. "Look, I'm sorry for being presumptuous, but with your record how could I not be? People change, I get that, and I can tell you're a great guy, but you also have to see where I'm coming from. I have to be careful what I do, because if I let something happen between us it could not only cause a hardship between me and you, but also with the team. I don't date the players, Cooper."

"Things change, Kate," I told her. "When you want something bad enough, it's hard to just let it walk away. Over the past year, I gave up because I was too fucked up to even try. Not anymore, though. When I want something I'm going to go for it, and when I see it I'm going to take it."

We pulled into the parking lot of the practice field and I shut off my car, the tension in the air crackling like fire. When I turned to look at her, it was like her stormy gray gaze could see right through me. There were a shit ton of things I wanted, but nothing as much as leaning forward to kiss those lips of hers.

With her breaths coming fast and low, she licked her dry lips and shook her head. "Cooper, we can't."

Bending over the center console, I glanced down at her lips and murmured low, "Yes we can, Kate, and I'm going to make sure we do."

She didn't move, only stared wide-eyed at me as I came closer. Something over my shoulder caught her attention and she abruptly backed away, fidgeting in her seat. "Okay, now's definitely not a good time to discuss this. The others just showed up, and the last thing I need is to explain what I was doing in your car, about to kiss you."

So she *was* going to let me kiss her.

Almost immediately, she opened her door and slid out, racing over to the others who all smiled and surrounded her. *I wonder how many of them tried to get with her, too.* Grabbing my bag out of the back seat, I took a deep breath and opened my door.

Kate waved me over, and I assumed the guy standing beside of her was her brother; he had the same blond hair and gray eyes as her. Kate nervously glanced back and forth between us. "Evan, this is Cooper. Cooper, this is my brother, Evan. I trust that you all will play nice."

I held out my hand and Evan firmly gripped it with a sly smile on his face. "Of course, you have nothing to worry about. I'm sure me and the guys will make him feel … at home."

I bet, I thought to myself.

Shaking her head, Kate lifted her brows and rolled her eyes. "I'm sure you will," she mumbled sarcastically before walking away. "Okay, well I hope you all have fun, but I have some things to do. Try not to get hurt today."

Glancing at me quickly, she strolled off across the field toward my uncle. "Kate," I called, catching up to her.

Nervously, she turned around. "Yes?"

Taking her hand, I opened her fingers and placed my keys on her palm, closing her hand around them. "We can finish up our conversation later."

"Cooper, I don't know if that's such a good idea," she whispered. "The guys are already watching you like a hawk. It wouldn't end well for you."

"I think I'll take my chances."

Putting my keys in her purse, she held up her hands in

defeat. "I can see it now … you're going to be a bad influence on me, aren't you?"

When all I did was wink, she turned on her heel and groaned before marching off toward Joel. "You know you're wasting your time, right?" Evan remarked, coming up beside me. His arms were crossed at the chest as he glared protectively at his sister. "She has strict rules about dating the guys on the team; she doesn't do it. She's broken many hearts by turning them down, and I know she's not changing her ways for you. Sorry, dude, but you might want to consider another female if all you want is to score a touchdown under the sheets."

"That's not what this is about."

Clapping me on the shoulder, he scoffed, "I don't believe that for a second. Now come on and show us what you got. We have a lot of work to do."

Yes, I do, and it doesn't involve playing on the field.

Chapter 6

Kate

Driving Cooper's car was almost like driving my Jeep, except his was a lot nicer. I felt strange leaving in his car, but he smiled at me when I left while my brother looked on in confusion. I was going to have a lot of questions to answer when I got back.

Today happened to be the anniversary of Scott's death; it was exactly two years ago. Trying to keep it together in front of everyone wasn't easy, but I was trying. I prayed that things would be different this year, and so far I was in the clear. You see, Scott wasn't the only one who haunted my dreams ... his family did as well. They liked to give me reminders that it was my fault Scott was gone.

Last year, the anniversary landed on a Sunday, so I was able to stay at home and drown my sorrows with a bottle of vodka. At least that way, when I got the threatening phone calls I was too oblivious to even care. *I wonder what they'll say to me this year.*

My friend, Lara, was a good distraction, which was why I wanted to meet her. She accepted my invitation for lunch at this quaint little tea room that I loved going to with my mother when I was a child. They had the best poppy seed muffins and strawberry butter, along with the best chicken salad I'd ever tasted. All in all, it was a ploy to get my mind off of everything.

When I walked into the restaurant she was already seated and looking through the menu. "Hey, girl," I said, bending down to give her a hug. I took the seat across from her and smiled. "Thank you for meeting me for lunch."

"It's my pleasure. Besides, I know what today is and I figured you could use all of the happiness you can get."

"You got that right."

Lara was my age, and also my neighbor; I had no idea she lived alone until we ran into each other on the street one day. She had long, golden blonde hair with dark hazelnut streaks so that people could differentiate between her and her twin sister, Summer. I didn't talk to her sister much, but they both moved from Atlanta, Georgia and started up a restaurant, The Carolina Tavern. It was my absolute favorite place to eat.

"So is there anything you want to talk about? I know you don't discuss much about Scott, but I know today the emotions are running high."

I took a sip of water and cleared my throat. "Yeah, they are, and you know I'm bound to get some kind of crazy phone call from his family saying how if it wasn't for me their son would still be alive. Every time my phone rings I cringe, Lara. I don't know how long I'm going to be able to handle it."

"Have they called you today?" she asked.

"Not yet, but it's only lunch time."

Reaching for my hand, she squeezed it tight and huffed. "Kate, listen to me, the next time they threaten you like that you need to call the police. It's been two years. It wasn't your fault, and with them contacting you like that it's considered harassment. You don't deserve to have to listen to it."

Taking a deep breath, I clenched my teeth together to keep my chin from trembling. If I could erase everything in my mind I would. I didn't like seeing images of Scott on the day I found him. To this day, I still kept the letter he wrote to me; it'd been a year since I read it.

"What if I do deserve it?" I whispered. "If I'd been there for him, I could have picked up on the signs. I could've stopped what happened."

Lara's melancholy gaze glistened with unshed tears. She knew how hard it was for me, and how hard I tried to keep my emotions to myself. "There's nothing you could've done to prevent it," she murmured. "He had his mind set and he did what he wanted to do. He made his choice in life, not you. You can't keep blaming yourself."

We both sat in silence while the waitress came by and placed a plate of poppy seed muffins and strawberry butter in front of us. After we ordered our food and started eating, Lara gazed up at me with a sly expression on her face, staring at me in amusement.

"You know, I saw you through the window last night with our new neighbor. Care to tell me what's going on? Did you make him brownies as a homecoming gift?"

I rolled my eyes; I knew eventually she'd make me smile. "Do people actually do that?" I asked curiously, taking a bite of my chicken salad.

She shrugged. "I don't know, why? Do you want to

try it or something? From the way he looked at you when you drove off, I'd say he would be happy to have some hot, delicious chocolate to eat off your body."

"Not going to happen," I gasped.

"Why not? Talk about a yummy distraction if I might say so. You need to get out there and have some fun! But, hey, if you don't want to make him brownies I sure as hell will. He can eat them off of me anytime."

She batted her eyelashes, trying to get a rise out of me, but it wasn't going to work. All I knew was that she better not make him brownies.

"I really hope you're kidding, Lara," I said. "Anyway, changing the subject, he's our new quarterback. The last thing I need to do is get involved with him. I have a date with Luke this Saturday, and being with two men isn't smart. Someone will end up getting hurt."

"Someone always gets hurt," Lara countered. "It's just the way of life. If you have chemistry with the football player then go for it. You can't deny your heart what it wants."

"What about you? Do you think you'll ever find the time to date? I'm starting to think you live at that restaurant."

Lowering her crystal blue gaze, she smiled and shrugged her shoulders. "I'm sure one day I will when I meet someone that blows me away. Right now I'm just focused on helping my sister get her restaurant off the ground. Now that business is booming, she's a lot happier. It's hard to think about myself when all I want is to see her happy."

Lara worked hard every day at the restaurant, and I could tell she was lonely sometimes. Her twin sister had lost her husband last year and that was the reason why she moved to North Carolina. It shocked me that they didn't live together, but Lara said she wanted to give her sister space. I could understand that. After Scott died, my family constantly badgered me and wouldn't leave me alone. I couldn't breathe with them around constantly.

After we ate lunch and were about to get into our cars, Lara smiled wide when she noticed the Mercedes I approached. "New car?" she asked.

Sheepishly, I smiled and opened the door. "It's Cooper's. We rode together this morning and he let me drive it."

Lara gasped and spoke hurriedly, "Cooper? Oh my God, is it Cooper Davis that's playing for our team?"

"Yeah, why?"

She grinned mischievously and bit her lip. "You know, I thought he looked familiar, but I don't usually keep up with football. Summer is the one who's told me a lot about him. When I saw you with him, I didn't even think that it could be the same guy. I had no clue he was coming to play for our team."

"Oh wow, I didn't know your sister was a football fan," I said.

"She's not, but she's really good friends with Cooper's ex-girlfriend. They talk about every week. You should know who she is, Kate. You met her … her name is Claire. Her husband, Mason, is the detective from Charlotte who solved that huge MMA case out in Las Vegas last year. You know, the one where Summer's husband was murdered."

Holy hell, how could this be possible? I thought, wide-eyed.

"Oh my God, this is a small world," I marveled. "The connection is uncanny."

"Yeah, tell me about it. So needless to say, Claire broke Cooper's heart when she left him for Mason. After that he got hurt and started getting into trouble."

"So that's why he didn't want to tell me," I mumbled to myself. The love of his life left him for another man, and it just so happened that I'd met them. *It's so strange how paths cross like that.*

When Cooper mentioned Claire's name, I had no idea that it could even remotely be the same Claire I met a few months ago. She was amazing and we had such a good time together talking about her vineyards and about wine.

"I tell you what, Kate. Since you don't need to be alone tonight why don't you bring Cooper to the restaurant? I'd like to meet him and it'll also get your mind off of everything," Lara suggested slyly. "I'm pretty sure he'd be more than willing to accept."

Getting in her car, Lara winked and waved at me as she pulled out of the parking lot. By the look in her eyes she knew she had sparked an interest in me. Okay, so maybe Cooper could be serious about women. Claire was a successful woman, beautiful, and down to earth; not like the other types of women I'd seen him in the papers with. It didn't matter, though ... I was only going to ask him out for a one night distraction and that was it.

Hopefully, I could hold up that end of the bargain.

Chapter 7

Kate

By the time I got back to the field, the guys were taking a break and sitting on the side lines. I watched as Cooper bantered back and forth with the other players and how he seemed at home with them. At first, I thought he'd keep his distance and be an ass, but every time I turned around he surprised me. I guess it showed me how little I actually knew him.

When he saw me watching him, he came over to his car and I rolled down the window. He was dirty and drenched in sweat, but it didn't make his smile any less sexy. The heat outside was probably in the mid-nineties, and with the sun blaring overhead I knew it had to be miserable for the guys in their pads.

"Did you have fun at your meeting?" he asked, leaning his arms in through the window.

"It was nice. I ate lunch with a friend."

Cooper lifted a brow. "Was it a girl friend or a guy? Please tell me I didn't let you borrow my car to meet up with another man."

"No," I laughed, "it was with our neighbor, Lara." I didn't know if I should tell him that I knew who his ex was. However, I figured if I mentioned it, it'd be best if I waited until he was done with practice.

"Ah, I haven't had the pleasure of meeting her. I'll have to stop by and visit."

Visions of her making him brownies and him eating them off of her went through my mind at that exact moment. *Damn you, Lara, for putting those thoughts in my head.*

"No you don't," I blurted out. "She actually asked if I would bring you to her restaurant tonight after practice. You can meet her then."

Cooper's lips pulled up into a sly smirk. "Why, Kate Townsend, is this your way of asking me out on a date? I didn't think I'd break you down so easily."

"You didn't," I scoffed halfheartedly. "This isn't a date, and I'm only doing this because Lara asked me to bring you. Now do you want to go or not?"

"Fine, I'll go. Even if it's not a date, I'd be more than happy to go with you. I'll just have to take a shower first, but you're more than welcome to join me. My shoulder's been giving me some trouble, and I heard that those exercises you showed me work better in water. You up for that?"

"They work better in a pool, Cooper, not a shower. You might want to consider a cold one while you're at it."

Shaking my head, I rolled up the car window to cut him off. He thought it was funny and laughed the whole way back to the team. My body didn't think it was funny; instead, I had forbidden thoughts of touching his bare body in the shower running through my mind. I felt wet all over with sweat already pouring down the back of my neck, moistening my skin. Even the spot between my legs tingled with the thoughts of a rendezvous under the heated spray of the dual headed showers.

My God, it's been too long.

After practice was over, Evan stayed behind with me in the parking lot while Cooper disappeared to the locker room to take a quick shower. "How you holding up today?" he asked hesitantly. "Any contact from Scott's parents?"

"Not yet," I replied, releasing a heavy sigh. "It's been a year since they last contacted me, so maybe they've moved on."

Evan shrugged. "There's no telling, but if they give you problems you need to let me deal with it, okay?"

"I can handle my own problems, Evan."

"Kate," he warned, glaring down at me, "don't start with me. I'm only looking out for you."

"I know," I murmured softly as he put his arm around my shoulders.

"So what's up with you and Cooper?" he asked. "Everyone was giving him hell about you today, but he claims nothing's going on. Does Luke know you two are getting close?"

"It's not like that," I assured him. "Cooper's the one who moved into the house two doors down, and we figured since we live beside each other it made more sense to ride together."

He stared at me as if he didn't believe a single thing that came out of my mouth.

"Okay, Kate, whatever you say. You're still going out with Luke on Saturday, right?"

I nodded. "Yep, I wouldn't miss it."

"Good, because he's pretty stoked about it. Go out with him at least once before you break his heart. I swear I always thought it would be the other way around."

"Evan, me and Luke haven't even gone on one date. There's no breaking hearts here. We have a date, and I'm sticking with my plans. Cooper and I are just friends, and to be honest, he's actually not that bad."

"Oh, I know he's not," Evan admitted. "He kicked ass out there today. I just don't want you getting in over your head with him … or Luke for that matter."

I groaned and bumped him with my shoulder. "I don't plan on it, and even if I did it's my choice. You'll just have to get over it."

When Cooper emerged from the locker room, his hair was still damp and mussed from the shower, and even from the distance I could see the devilish smirk on his face. His heated gaze followed my body up and down, and without thinking I smiled and bit my lip.

"Oh hell, this isn't good," Evan groaned, snapping my attention back to him. "So help me, if he hurts you I'm going to kick his ass. I can see it now that you two aren't going to behave."

"Everything okay?" Cooper asked, glancing back and forth between me and my brother.

Evan sighed and glared right at him. "It is for now, and it better stay that way." Squeezing my arm, he sent one last warning glare to Cooper before strolling over to his truck.

"I'm assuming that was directed at me?" he asked.

"Of course," I groaned, "but you were warned before getting mixed up with me."

Taking my elbow, Cooper guided me to his car and opened the door. "I'm not worried about your brother, Kate. I'm not going to do anything to you unless you ask me to."

"Like what?" I asked coyly.

Shielded from view by the car door, Cooper leaned in and brought his lips closer to mine, opening them slightly. I couldn't move, but then again … I didn't want to. Instead of kissing me, he murmured across my lips, "I'm sure you'll figure that out when the time comes. If you want me to kiss you, I'm not going to do it until you place your soft lips on mine first. If you want me to touch you, I'm not going to unless you beg me for it. It's all on you now, love."

Breathing hard, I pulled back abruptly and cleared my throat. "Good," I blurted out, "I agree. Now there won't be any complications."

"Exactly," he agreed.

Exactly, I repeated in my mind.

Smirking, he shut the car door and ambled over to his side. From the look on his face he didn't believe me, and even worse … I didn't believe myself.

Chapter 8

Kate

Cooper had a grin on his face the entire way to the restaurant, and the whole time I felt like an idiot as I scowled out the window. My evening only happened to get worse when my phone buzzed in my purse. I was afraid it would be Scott's family, but it wasn't; it was Luke.

"Hey," I answered, sneaking a glance over at Cooper.

In the past two years, I went from a completely desolate love life to now having two very hot and extremely sexy men interested in me. If anything, I needed to stay far away from Cooper. Luke would be the better option if I had to make a choice.

Yeah, keep telling yourself that.

"Hey, babe," Luke replied excitedly. "So listen, I know we have our date on Saturday, but there's something I wanted to tell you. I thought maybe we could meet up tonight so I could give you the good news."

"Oh, Luke, that sounds great, but I'm actually headed over to The Carolina Tavern to eat dinner. Lara wanted me to stop by. Do you want to meet up afterwards?"

"Actually, I'll just meet you there. I'll see you in a minute." He hung up so fast that I didn't even have time to call out his name and stop him; he was already gone.

"Great," I muttered sarcastically, sliding my phone back in my purse.

"What's wrong?" Cooper asked. "And who's Luke by the way?"

Sighing, I blew out a nervous breath. "He's my brother's best friend. He asked if he could see me tonight, and before I could stop him he said he'd meet me at the tavern."

"I thought you said you weren't dating anyone."

"I'm not," I replied truthfully, keeping my gaze on the road. "We have our first date this Saturday."

Cooper chuckled and immediately I glared over at him. "What's so funny about that?" I asked.

"Nothing really," he said between laughs, "it's just, I should've known something like this was going to happen. No worries, though. I can play nice. It's always good to meet the competition."

"Cooper, that's not what this is about. There's no competition!"

"Sure there is," he added. "He wants you and I want you. You're not promised to either one of us, so that right there makes us competing for you."

"Did you have to compete for Claire?" I asked softly. I knew he didn't want to talk about her, but I also didn't want to put him in the same situation that hurt him.

Tensing in his seat, he gripped the steering wheel tight and released a heavy sigh. "No, that situation was completely different."

"How is that?" I asked.

"Because I didn't have a chance with her, Kate. I wanted to believe that I could make her happy … but I couldn't. I saw it in her eyes."

"And what do you see in mine?"

Patting me on the knee, he turned to me with his mischievous blue eyes and grinned. "In your eyes I see exactly what I want. You're not here with me because of my money or because of what I do. You actually see the people you're around and the goodness inside of them. That is what gives me hope."

"Hope for what?" I asked breathlessly, mesmerized.

He brushed my hair away from my face and smoothed his thumb along my jaw. "Hope that one day you will see in my eyes what I see in yours. There's a craving deep inside of you that I can see each time I touch you. It burns brighter every single time. I've never seen that with anyone, and that is how I know I have a chance."

"Now," he continued, staring out at the road, "where exactly am I going? I'm curious to know what I'm up against. Care to enlighten me?"

Closing my eyes, I laid my head against the seat, my stomach in knots. "If you take a left at the next light, you'll see a sign for the restaurant. You'll be enlightened soon enough."

When we pulled into the restaurant parking lot I saw Luke's blue and black Suzuki GSX-R1000 sitting in the front. I was hoping we'd get there first so I could get Cooper seated, and then find Luke to explain. The last thing I wanted was for there to be a problem at my friend's restaurant. Quickly, I pulled out my phone and texted Lara.

Me: I need you to make sure Luke sits at the bar ASAP.

Lara: Already done. I knew when he said he was meeting you that there had to be some sort of mix up.

Me: Thank you. We are coming in now.

Cooper and I got out of his car and walked side by side up to the door. For some reason, I didn't believe him when he said he'd play nice. *Please don't let them fight.*

"Why are you fidgeting?" Cooper asked. "I mean, it's not like there's something to hide, right? Maybe you should ask him to join us?"

Narrowing my gaze, I froze in place as he opened the door. "Are you serious?"

He's testing me, I can see it. Better yet, I'll just test him. "You know what," I said, smiling innocently up at him, "I think that's a great idea. Thank you for letting me include him."

Annoyance flashed in his gaze for only a second, but I caught it. He didn't want Luke joining us, but if I didn't have anything to hide then it wouldn't matter. They could both sit at the table and I'd be perfectly fine because they were both just my friends.

Yeah, right.

When we walked in, Lara met us at the door with a big smile on her face and her blue eyes twinkling with mischief. "Hello and welcome," she announced, glancing back and forth between us.

She had on a soft, yellow sundress, and her hair fell perfectly straight, slightly past her shoulders. Lara was such a people person; she was perfect at talking to the customers and making them feel at home. All of the locals who came in every week loved her.

Holding out her hand, she said, "You must be, Cooper. I'm Lara. It's nice to finally meet you. I've heard a lot about you."

"Really?" Cooper took her hand, but then lifted a brow at me and said, "What have you said about me?"

I rolled my eyes and shook my head. "Don't look at me. Apparently, Lara knows more about you than I do."

"Actually," Lara cut in, glaring at me, "I think we know some people in common. I'll tell you all about it later, but right now I have your table all ready for you."

We followed her to the back, where there was a private room that was used for special guests or when people requested it. I should've known Lara would put us back there, or maybe she put us there in case Cooper and Luke made a scene.

"Thank you, Lara," I said sweetly before turning to Cooper. "If you want to get a drink, I'm sure Lara will keep you company while I go talk to Luke. I'll be right back."

Cooper nodded and took a seat while Lara winked and shooed me off. The bar was on the other side of the restaurant, and when I finally made it there I instantly saw Luke, dressed in a pair of jeans and a red T-shirt, his blond hair tousled from his helmet. He was talking to Grayson—who was the co-owner of The Carolina Tavern—and the brother of Summer's deceased husband. Grayson was a good looking man with closely cropped auburn hair and green eyes, and the sweetest personality of any guy I knew. He could also talk your ear off, so it wouldn't surprise me if Lara asked him to keep Luke occupied until I got there.

Luke must've seen me approach because he immediately turned my way, smiling and getting to his feet. Grayson also looked my way with a sly smirk on his face. Oh yeah, Lara recruited his help.

"Well, there she is," Luke announced, passing me a glass of white wine. "I went ahead and ordered your favorite."

Smiling, I took it from him and gulped it down, earning a wide-eyed stare from both he and Grayson; I needed more to get me through the mess I was about walk into. "Thank you," I gasped. Grayson took my glass and filled it up with another round. I held it up and tapped it against Luke's beer. "Thank you, again."

Chuckling, Luke sat down and pulled out a bar stool for me to sit in. "Hard day?"

Downing the other glass of wine, I nodded and pushed the chair back in. "No, but it's about to be. Come with me. I have a table in the back."

Grayson took my glass and chuckled. "Have a nice evening you two. Don't get into trouble back there."

Luke's devilish grin grew even wider. "You reserved the back room for us? I must be special to get that kind of treatment."

"I wouldn't exactly say that," I mumbled, hating that I was about to ruin the night.

With a hand on his arm, I stopped him and pulled him to a vacant corner. "Actually, we're not going to be alone back there," I remarked as fast as I could. "When you called I had plans to come here with someone else."

There, I said it.

"I thought you said you were meeting Lara. Who are you here with?" he asked, furrowing his brows.

Sheepishly, I squeezed my eyes shut and groaned. "Cooper Davis," I answered.

And just as I expected … he snapped. "You're kidding me, right? Why the hell would you be here with him?"

"Lara wanted me to bring him, and since we rode together to practice …"

Eyes wide, Luke's mouth dropped open. "You rode with him to practice, too? What the fuck, Kate? I thought you didn't like the guy. I seem to remember the other day you said you couldn't believe your team actually wanted him, and now you're spending time with him. Please tell me you're not falling for the guy."

"Look," I snapped impatiently, "I'm going to tell you exactly what I told him. You're my friend, Luke, and believe it or not so is Cooper. I'm still going on our date Saturday and we're going to have fun. He knows that I'm going out with you and that's all that matters, but right now I'm getting ready to eat dinner with him. You're more than welcome to join us."

Groaning, he hung his head and blew out a frustrated breath. "All right, I'll join you. At least he won't make any moves on you while I'm there."

I wouldn't put it past him.

My head started to feel fuzzy and it felt like I was moving in slow motion. It was probably stupid to drink two glasses of wine on an empty stomach; however, it felt good … relaxing. Everything I'd been stressing about, such as Scott's death, was finally slipping away.

Luke lifted his head when I stated, "You don't have

to worry about him making the moves on me, Luke. He said he wouldn't touch me unless I asked him to. I think we're both safe."

Placing his hands against the wall, Luke trapped me in and murmured in my ear, "Hmm … he's better than I thought. You know he's just playing games with you, right?"

"Everyone plays games in their own way, Luke. Even you do, but it's not going to change anything," I told him.

"Good," he murmured huskily. "Although, I'd have to say that's where me and him differ." He trailed his finger down my cheek and past my neck to my collarbone. "I'd be afraid you would never ask me. That's why I have to take what I want until you tell me no."

Backing up to give me space, he smiled and took my hand in his. His skin was warm and rough, most likely from riding hard all day in motocross training. "Okay, let's get this dinner going. The sooner it gets started, the sooner it can be over."

I couldn't have said it better myself.

Chapter 9

COOPER

"So tell me how you know about me? Who do we know in common?" I asked. Leaning on her chin, Lara smiled and looked down at the menu. "Well, from what I hear you're probably not going to be happy with one of the friends we have in common, but at least all I've heard about you is good things."

My uncle lived in Charlotte, but I knew she couldn't be talking about him. Other than that there was only one person I knew, and it was the one person I loathed more than any other. He was the same person that took the only girl I'd ever loved away from me.

"You can't be serious," I said, curling my lip incredulously. "There's only one person I know from around here, and you're telling me that after I packed my shit up and left California I still can't escape from him?"

"Kind of," she answered sheepishly. "I know Claire chose him, but don't you think it was for the best? I mean, now you have Kate."

"I don't have her," I grumbled. "And I'm not the only

55

one who wants her."

"Yeah, but you're the one she needs."

That got my attention. For a long time, I thought Claire needed me, but she didn't. We were independent from one another, but we always found our way back to the other. I couldn't see Kate being like that. With her, I wouldn't want to go my separate ways all of the time. I would want her to depend on me. Claire didn't want me to fight for her because it would've been a losing battle. Kate, on the other hand, needed to know I wouldn't go down without a fight.

"I know it has to be a shock to come here and be reminded of everything," Lara explained. "I don't talk to Mason and Claire, but my sister does. When Mason moved to California, he let my sister move into his house. Summer and Claire talk to each other a lot, and my sister usually tells me what they talk about. Although, I will admit I had no clue you were moving to North Carolina."

I scoffed. "Well, it wasn't by choice."

Lara's head snapped up and she glared at me. "Hey, it's not that bad here. I think our team has a shot at winning this season. Besides, you came here with one of my good friends, who was hesitant on bringing you until I persuaded her. I believe a thank you is in order."

Smugly, she crossed her arms at her chest and pursed her lips. "Thank you," I said with a smile.

"You're welcome." Grinning, she uncrossed her arms and pointed to the menu. "And just so you know, Mason and Claire were the ones who helped me and my sister get this restaurant running. We get all of the wines from Claire's winery, and we also had her give me some ideas as far as entrees. Do you recognize any of them?"

Scanning the menu, my eyes went wide when a couple of the dish selections popped out at me. "Holy shit," I said. "You have some of my ideas in here."

The selections were Cooper's Calamari, and Cooper's Grilled Chicken. The descriptions were exactly the way I used to cook them. Claire wasn't the best cook, so I always made our food when I was in town.

"This is amazing," I remarked in awe. "She never told me she did this."

"Well, it's not like you two really spoke after you broke up. You kind of went on a downward spiral after that. This time, however, I'm rooting for you," she added slyly. "I know Kate is a hard person to crack, but if you're anything like Claire says then you'll have no problems winning her over."

"Speaking of Claire, I can't help but wonder … if she's been in here several times and Kate's your best friend, have they by any chance met?"

Sheepishly, Lara stood from the table and pushed in her chair. "Actually, they have," she confessed. "Kate knows everything about Claire, Cooper. We talked about it today when she told me who you were. She just didn't realize until today that her wine buddy was your ex-girlfriend."

So that's why she asked me questions about Claire today.

"Oh, and to give you a heads up, Luke has been trying to get Kate for months. He's already worn her down enough for a date this weekend. Trust me, it hasn't been easy for him. Don't get me wrong, I like Luke, but I honestly don't see them working out." Pausing, she bit her lip and sighed before saying, "Whatever happens just bear with her, okay? She's had a rough two years and it's taken its toll on her. She may not know what she wants now, but she will if you show her the right way. I think you both have been through enough to understand each other."

She smiled one last time and strolled out of the back room. To get to Kate, I needed her to open up to me and vice versa. We weren't going to get anywhere if we didn't. *I wonder if she trusts Luke. Does he know her intimate secrets? Does he know what happened to her in her past?*

Over the rim of my glass of water, I watched as Kate walked in with Luke, her gaze unreadable. Luke, however, was ready to play the game by the smug expression on his face. *Bring it on, cocksucker.*

Lara waltzed back in with a bottle of wine and set it on the table, along with some wine glasses, acknowledging Kate and Luke with a smile. She winked at me and nodded before walking off. I was glad to have her support because I knew her opinion would matter to Kate.

Kate took the seat across from me, and Luke took the one to my right. She almost looked pale, but brightened as she grabbed the bottle of wine and poured herself a glass. After she took a large gulp, she motioned from me to Luke. "Cooper, I'd like you to meet my friend, Luke, and Luke, I'd like you to meet Cooper."

Extending my hand, Luke shook it firmly and said, "It's nice to meet you."

Wish I could say the same, I thought. Instead, I said, "Same to you."

We both knew that was a fucking lie. "So how is it playing for the team?" Luke asked. "It must suck coming from a bad ass one to ours."

Kate's head snapped up and she glared at Luke before

turning to me. Our team needed a lot of work, but even then, Kate had great pride for her team and she didn't like anyone saying they sucked. I hadn't known her very long, but even I knew not to say anything like that.

"Actually," I informed him, "it's not that bad. The guys are really smart and quick on their feet. With a little more team work, I feel that we'll be just as good as any of the top teams out there."

In all honesty, I did believe that. A few days ago, I didn't, but being with the team and working with them made me see them in a whole new light. They had what it took to win.

Satisfied with my answer, Kate smiled and turned to Luke. "So what was the good news you wanted to tell me?"

Moving his chair over, he put his arm around the back of hers, and smiled wide. "I just got a sponsorship with Red Bull. They're one of the top motocross sponsors in the world, and they want me. Can you believe it?"

Kate squealed and wrapped her arms around his neck. "Oh my God, that's great." Smugly, he smiled at me over her shoulder, but I knew better than to let him get to me.

"Congratulations," I said. "So with racing you'll be travelling all over the States, right?"

Luke narrowed his eyes. "Yeah, the supercross races start in February. Why do you ask?"

"Well, I thought it would be kind of cool to come watch you race. I've never been to one before. Since we'll be busy with all of the games this fall, it works out perfectly. You travel to the away games, don't you, Kate?" I asked, tilting my head in her direction.

Pouring another glass of wine, she nodded and took

another gulp. "Yeah, I go to all of them. Unless, of course, I absolutely have to stay home for some reason."

Either she was too engrossed in her wine to notice the jab I made at Luke or she didn't care. I was starting to think it was the former. Luke, however, snarled his lip and rolled his eyes. While he was at home, Kate would be with me and the team every single weekend until the season was over with. Right now, the ball was in my hands.

"Do you all know what you want to eat?" Lara asked, coming into the room. "I figured the ice had to be broken by now."

The room fell silent until Kate handed Lara the menu and said, "You know what I want."

Lara laughed. "Of course, that's nothing new," she quipped. Turning, she smiled at me and Luke. "And for you two?"

I ordered the Cooper's Grilled Chicken because I had to see if it tasted anything like what I used to make back at home. Once Lara got our orders, she disappeared and came back with a basket of bread. From the looks of Kate she needed to eat something; at least to soak up the amount of alcohol she'd consumed.

"Kate, are you okay?" I asked. "Maybe you should eat some bread."

She laughed just once before downing the rest of her wine. "Trust me, that's not going to help, but if you'll excuse me for a moment I'll be right back."

After shakily getting to her feet, both Luke and I stood to help her, but she lifted a hand to halt us. "I'm fine, guys. It's just been a while since I've drank this much. I didn't realize how fast it would hit me."

She seemed a little preoccupied earlier, but I didn't

want to pry and ask her what was wrong. My whole summer was spent drinking my problems away, and I recognized that look in her eyes as the same one that used to be in mine. When she disappeared from sight, I turned to Luke and asked, "Does she normally drink like this?"

Shaking his head, he kept his concerned gaze on the doorway. "No, never. I don't know what her problem is tonight. She's not acting right that's for sure."

"Well, for starters, you don't have to make me look bad to get her to choose you. Kate has more pride in the team than any of the players combined. I'd be careful what you say about them."

Luke scoffed. "Please, I don't have to try and make you look bad because you do that yourself. She knows what you are and what you're like. There's no competition here. She's mine and that's it."

What a cocky bastard.

"We'll see about that," I said, "so just keep playing your games. I must warn you though … I don't ever lose."

Getting to my feet, I marched past him and out of the room. Kate might not have said it out loud, but I could tell when someone needed help, and she definitely did. For the first time in months, it wasn't me that required it.

Chapter 10

COOPER

On my way to the restrooms, I passed Lara. "Hey, have you seen Kate walk by? She left a few minutes ago and I know she's had a little too much to drink."

"No, I haven't seen her. Do you want me to check the bathroom?" she asked worriedly.

I nodded and followed on her heels when she rushed off. Slipping into the bathroom, it only took her about two seconds later to burst out. "Cooper, I need your help," she exclaimed. "Now! I need you to help me pick her up."

Rushing inside, I found Kate splayed out on the floor, unconscious, and her phone scattered into a million pieces. She must have thrown it to cause that much damage. Quickly yet gently, I picked her up and held her in my arms.

"You care to tell me what's going on?" I snapped. "What's wrong with her other than being drunk off of her ass?"

Lara picked up the shattered pieces of Kate's phone and threw them in the trash before running cold water over a handful of paper towels. Placing them on Kate's fore-head, she sighed and explained, "Cooper, I would love to tell you, but it's not my place. Right now she needs to go home. I should've known better than to make her come out tonight. I thought it would help, but obviously I was wrong. I'll pack up your food so you'll have it when you take her back."

"Does she take any meds? Is there anything I need to do for her when I get her home?"

Sadly, she gazed down at Kate, and then back up to me. "Yeah, don't leave her alone tonight. I would take her myself, but I won't be able to lift her if she needed help. She's going to be pissed in the morning when she realizes I let you take care of her instead of me. Are you sure you want to be on her bad side tomorrow?"

"If it means making sure she's safe and taken care of, then I'll do anything. She can be mad at me all she wants."

Lara smiled warily and gently brushed the hair off of Kate's forehead. "Okay, then. Just so we don't have any-one asking questions, take her out the back door and put her in the car. I'll have your food out to you in two minutes."

"What about Luke?" I asked.

She waved me off. "Oh, don't worry about that. I'll take care of him."

Opening the bathroom door, Lara motioned for me to come out and led the way to the back door. As soon as we got out, I carried Kate over to my car, gently laid her in-side, and buckled her in. It was literally two minutes later when Lara came out with our food and handed it to me.

"Here's your and Kate's food, even though she's most likely not going to eat tonight. She's kind of a lightweight when it comes to alcohol. Most of the time she doesn't drink a lot; it's only during stressful occasions when she does."

"Trust me, I know the feeling all too well," I mumbled. "Thank you for the food."

Lara nodded. "Anytime. Just get her home," she commanded, handing me a little slip of paper with a phone number on it. "Here's my number in case something happens. Call me anytime if you need anything. The key to her house is the one attached to the keychain with her name on it. I'm sure they're in her purse."

"I'll find them … and again, thank you."

Once in my car, I double checked that Kate was securely buckled before we left. Her blonde hair draped over her face, hiding her behind a veil of gold so I gently pushed it to the side and tucked it behind her ears. She was so beautiful, but asleep she looked vulnerable and scared. What was going on in her life that would drive her to break down?

Carefully, I drove the few minutes it took to get to Kate's house, constantly peering over at her to make sure she was all right. Once we were in her driveway, I reluctantly searched through her purse to find her keys. It felt like I was violating her privacy, but I had no choice. After finding them, I lifted her out of the car and took her inside, only I did not know which room was hers. Sure enough, it was the last room I looked in; I knew it had to be hers because the room smelled like apples. Gently, I laid her down on the soft, yellow and light blue striped bedspread and turned on her bathroom light so it would give her room a little glow.

Her room was very feminine with a certain southern

charm, consisting of floral arrangements with soft yellow walls. She had a couple of paintings depicting meadows and farmlands, along with horses running through the fields. It all showed a softer side to her, but I had yet to see it for myself.

As I was taking off her shoes, she started to wake, or at least I thought she was waking up. Whimpering, she curled into a ball and whispered, "I'm so sorry. Scott, I'm so … so sorry."

Who was Scott? I wondered.

Carefully, I climbed onto her bed and wrapped my arms around her. "It's okay, love."

Kate shook her head hard. "No, it's not. He's gone and it's all my fault. They tell me it's all my fault."

"Who does?"

I knew I shouldn't pry while she was drunk, but she was obviously upset about something, and if I could help I was sure going to try.

"They say I killed him. They want me to suffer like them," she cried. "And I do. I suffer all of the time because they won't leave me alone."

"Who are they? What do they do to you?" I asked quickly.

She was so completely out of it that I didn't know if she was speaking the truth or if it was just drunk talk. Shaking her head quickly, she sat up and put her hand over her mouth, stumbling out of bed. "I think I'm going to be sick," she sobbed.

As fast as I could, I jumped up and helped her to the bathroom just in time for her to dispel every ounce of wine she drank for the night. Rubbing her back with one hand, I held her hair in the other to keep it out of the way. When her body started to sag toward the floor, I picked her up and carried her back into her room, feeling her tremble against my chest. She began to shiver and shake uncontrollably so I pulled the blankets over her body and mine to keep her warm, holding her tight against me. I wanted her to talk some more so I could find out what was wrong, but instead, her breathing became heavy and deep. She was asleep. For the rest of the night, I held her in my arms but was woken up several times to her whispered words.

"I'm sorry," she would say. "I'm so sorry, Scott."

I needed to find out who Scott was.

Six-thirty had finally arrived and my shoulder screamed at me to take my pain pills. I wasn't at home so I couldn't do it, but I'd make sure to take one as soon as I got there to get ready for practice. As quietly as I could, I slipped out of Kate's bed and sauntered into her kitchen to make her some coffee before I left.

Pulling out Lara's number, I dialed it and prayed that she wouldn't get pissed from the early wake up call, but I had to tell her Kate was all right. "Hello," she answered groggily.

"Lara, it's Cooper."

"Hey, how did everything go last night? I was going to stop by, but by the time I got away from the restaurant it was late and I figured you two would be asleep."

"Everything's fine," I told her. "I'm making her some coffee, and then I'm going home before heading to practice. Do you think she'll stay home today?"

"Of course not," she laughed. "Kate doesn't let anything keep her away from work. She may be late, but she'll be there. Don't worry about her though, this has happened before."

"Does it involve someone named Scott?"

The line went quiet.

"Lara? Are you there?"

Nervously, she cleared her throat. "Yeah, I'm here. What did she tell you?"

"She just said she was sorry. Over and over she kept saying his name and that she was sorry. She also said that they blamed her. Who are they?"

Lara sighed and blew out a nervous breath. "Okay, I'll tell you what's going on, but I'm not giving you all of the details. Kate would kill me if I told you. Two years ago yesterday she found her boyfriend dead in his bed. He'd overdosed on pain pills. Needless to say, his family blames her and they won't leave her alone about it. Every year on the anniversary they come around and do something to her so she's reminded that he's dead. I have a feeling they called her and that's why her phone was shattered."

"Why doesn't she change her number?"

"She has, but they always find it somehow. I wish I knew of a way to help her."

We might not have a way to help her, but unfortunately, we both knew of someone who could. I never thought there would come a day when I wanted advice from the man who stole Claire from me, but I guess there always came a first time for something.

"I'm going to call Mason," I told her.

Lara gasped, "What? Why?"

"Lara, you know what he's capable of. As much as I

don't like the guy, I can't deny that he used to be one of the best undercover detectives out there. He'll be able to find these people and put a stop to whatever they're doing to Kate. If he can't do it then I'm sure he has connections here to people who can."

"Okay, fine, but don't you dare tell Kate I told you anything. She worries too much and I don't want her drinking like she did last night ever again. She only does it once a year on the anniversary of Scott's death and that's more than enough."

As soon as Lara and I hung up, I finished the coffee for Kate. It was four in the morning in California, so I knew I needed to wait a few hours before I called. She may not want my help, but by lunch time I was going to have a plan in motion. Since she was still asleep in her bed, I wrote a note to tell her that if she wanted to see me later to give me a call. It was closing in on seven-fifteen and I needed to leave so I could make it to practice on time; there were penalties if we were late.

After shutting her front door, the moment I turned around, Luke Collins pulled up in the driveway. When his gaze found mine, he snarled and jumped out of his truck.

"What the fuck are you doing here?" he growled, slamming the door to his metallic blue Ford Raptor.

"I could say the same to you," I replied coolly, ambling over to my car. He eyed me up and down, and I knew he didn't like what he saw. I wore the same clothes from last night and they were wrinkled. All night I was in the bed with Kate, but it wasn't what he thought.

"Lara told me she was taking her home and that Kate didn't want to be bothered. Why would she lie to me for you?" When all I did was shrug in reply, it pissed him off even more. "You told her to, didn't you? You told her to lie to me. So help me if I find out you took advantage of Kate while she was drunk I'll kill—"

"Relax," I snapped, cutting him off. "I would never do that to her, and I sure as hell didn't get Lara to lie to you ... that was her own doing. Why don't you just shut the fuck up and make yourself useful. I made Kate some coffee, but she was still asleep when I came out here. Also, she's probably going to need something for a headache, too."

Luke glared at me for another second before rushing to the front door. I was worried about Kate. I wanted to do anything and everything I could to help her, even if that meant calling my number one enemy and getting his help.

I would do it for her.

Chapter 11

Kate

My mouth was dry and tasted absolutely horrible. It might've been because I remembered vomiting in the middle of the night and not brushing my teeth. How could I have been so stupid to drink as much as I did … and in front of people? I wasn't worried about what Luke thought of me because he already knew me, but Cooper probably thought I was a lush.

"Why am I so stupid?" I groaned out loud.

A masculine laugh belted out from the doorway, making me jump. "Well, good morning to you too, sweetheart. Also, just so you know, you're not stupid. You just happened to get a little too wasted last night."

My eyes burst open and I shot up in the bed, my head pounding with the sudden movement. "Ow," I cried, putting a hand to my forehead. "That doesn't feel too good."

Luke sat down beside me on the bed, handing me a couple of pills and a glass of water. "I would say not," he teased. "Especially after the night you had last night. Why the hell did you drink so much?"

Putting the pills in my mouth, I drank them down with the water and laid back on my pillow. "You know why, Luke. August is a bad month for me."

"Yeah, I kind of thought that might've been why, but I didn't know for sure. I guess I thought you would've moved on by now," he uttered sadly.

He didn't understand.

Lowering my gaze, I blew out a frustrated breath. "I wish I could, but it's hard when Scott's family calls to harass me about it every damn year. Last night, before I passed out in the bathroom, Scott's sister called my phone. When I saw that it was her I threw my phone against the wall and broke down. I don't remember much after that."

"Kate, you can't keep putting up with that shit," he said, lifting my chin so I'd look at him. "These people have some serious issues, and if you don't do something about it who knows what they'll start doing."

I nodded. "I know."

It was then I looked down and noticed that I had on the same clothes from yesterday. Someone had to have carried me because I couldn't remember how I got there. I vaguely remembered rushing to the bathroom and throwing up, and then someone holding me during the night to keep me warm.

"Were you here all night? Was it *you* that helped me? I remember someone helping me."

Tucking my hair behind my ears, he smiled and nodded. "Yeah, it was me. I didn't want to leave you alone."

"What about Cooper? Where was he?"

Luke scoffed. "He bailed exactly like I thought he would. I told you he was only playing games with you. When things got rough he left."

"But how did you get me home? I couldn't have ridden on your motorcycle."

"Oh, Cooper brought you back, but he didn't want to stay. I left early this morning to get my truck and come back. I thought maybe we could spend the day together if you weren't feeling up to going to work."

Cooper didn't want to stay, huh? Not that I expected him to stay all night and take care of me, but I at least figured he'd show *some* concern. As much as I hated to admit it, I was hurt … and pissed. I guess it was better I realize what he was like before I let myself get too involved.

"So, how about it? Do you want to spend the day together?" he repeated.

"Luke, you know I'm not a slacker like you. I have to go to work, even if I don't necessarily feel like it. You can come over for dinner tonight if you want."

Mischievously, Luke grinned and leaned in closer. "That sounds like a plan. If you want I can drop you off at the practice field and come pick you up when you get off."

That wasn't such a bad idea because then Cooper could see that I didn't get hurt by him dismissing me last night. "Yeah, that would be great, Luke. I'll be ready to go in thirty minutes."

Kissing me on the cheek, he smiled one more time before getting up and leaving me to my peace. Yesterday was a complete whirlwind of emotions and I was glad it was over. Although at some point during the day, I needed to get a new phone … and a new number. Why couldn't Scott's family leave me alone?

Turning on the shower water, I waited for it to get warm and waltzed back into my bedroom. In my nightstand, I had a collection of letters that I'd kept over the course of my life, including the one I found on the floor in Scott's room when he killed himself. I never got the chance to read it yesterday.

My Dearest Kate,

I love you.

And it's because of those three words that I can't continue on with the way I've been living. I know you don't understand this now, but you will later. My reluctance to open up to you was not because of you, but because of me. A person knows when their time is up ... and my time is up. You have so much to live for, and the last thing I want is to drag you down. I can see that I am with the way I've been treating you. I'm sorry for causing you pain, and one day I hope that you can forgive me. I'm going to miss you, Kate. Your heart and soul is what I fell in love with, and of course, your smile. No matter where I go in the afterlife that will be the one thing I'll take with me ... the memory of your smile.

I love you always and forever,

Scott

"Dammit," I hissed, swiping angrily at the tears on my cheeks. "You said one day I would understand, but it's been two years and I still don't."

Folding the letter up, I stashed it underneath all of the others in my drawer and slammed it shut. Every time I read the letter, I kept thinking I would understand why he did what he did, but I didn't. I was starting to think it'd be a mystery for the rest of my life.

After drinking a couple of cups of coffee, I was ready to go. Luke drove me to the field and I was only a few minutes late, but everyone was there, stretching and warming up before the hard day, including Cooper.

"All right, sweetheart, I'll pick you up around five-ish, right?"

Unbuckling my seat belt, I reached to the back and grabbed my bag. I planned on working out hard and sweating all of the toxins from the wine out of my system.

"Yes, around five will be perfect. Then we can head to my house."

Luke grinned and leaned in, touching my lips lightly with his. "Maybe we can enjoy that pool of yours tonight. I've always wanted to skinny dip."

He kissed me one more time, this time a little slower and deeper. When he pulled back, I laughed. "You expect me to believe you haven't skinny dipped. I'm not that na-ïve, Luke."

"Hey, I didn't say I hadn't skinny dipped before, I just meant that I've always wanted to do it with you. Why don't you forget everything that happened yesterday and concentrate on me and you? I can offer you so much more than Cooper ever could."

"You don't have to worry about Cooper," I told him.

"Good, then there's nothing holding you back to-night."

There's nothing holding me back tonight, I chanted over and over. Why did it feel like something was? When I turned my head, I figured out why I had that feeling of dread in the pit of my stomach. Cooper was there watching every single move Luke and I made. He saw the kiss, the bantering back and forth, and he wasn't happy. In fact, he stared at me in utter disbelief. He had no right to look at me like that when he was the one who left me.

Opening the truck door, I slid out and smiled up at Luke. "I'll see you later."

I shut the door and walked right across the field past Cooper, who tried to reach for my arm, but I pulled away. "Really? That's how you're going to be to me? You're joking, right?"

"I'm sorry, but I don't know what you're talking about. Have a good day at practice, Cooper," I responded cheerfully. I didn't want him to know that not only was I angry, but it hurt that he didn't want to be there for me. The only thing I could do was pretend; I was used to act-ing like everything was okay anyway.

In the girl's locker room, the cheerleaders were changing so they could start their day with a workout and then practice their routines. All of them had on tank tops and really short shorts that always attracted the guys' at-tention when they ran around the track. Most of the time I exercised with them to get my morning run out of the way.

"Hey, Kate," Brianna called, "how are you today?"

Even though I felt like shit, I still put on a smile. "I'm

doing okay. How about you? How's the ankle?"

Brianna was twenty-one years old—the youngest on the team—and one of the sweetest girls I knew other than Lara. Pulling her long, chestnut colored hair into a pony-tail, she hopped up and down on her bad ankle before answering, "I think it's okay. It hasn't been giving me any problems now that I do those exercises you showed me."

"That's great," I said. "Just make sure you do those every day. Your ankle might feel better now, but if you stop stretching it, some of the pain might start coming back."

She'd fractured her ankle several months ago, and had only been running for the past few weeks. It was great having her back. She was my running partner and I'd missed her.

Since I already had on my tank top and running shorts, all I had to do was put on my shoes, which I always left in the locker room. As I sat down to tie them up, Lindsey—whom I really didn't care for—took a seat beside me. It wasn't that I didn't like her, but she cheated on my brother last year when they started dating. He didn't seem too hurt by it, but it still bothered me that she did it. Not to mention she was completely self-involved and only talked about herself. I usually tried to avoid her at all costs.

"You know, I couldn't help but notice the icy interaction between you and Cooper just a few minutes ago. Does this mean you two aren't seeing each other anymore?" she asked curiously.

"What are you talking about? We were never seeing each other in the first place. He's only been here for three days," I claimed incredulously.

"Yes, but you two were looking kind of cozy the other morning in his car, and then we all saw you with Luke this morning. Does this mean that Cooper's available? The girls want to know."

Lifting a brow, I pursed my lips and stared at her. She wasn't asking for the other girls, she was asking for herself. Her innocent emerald gaze wasn't fooling me as she sat there batting her lashes at me, her platinum blonde hair in braids. Except, what could I say? Cooper *was* available, and as much as I loathed the idea of him hooking up with one of the cheerleaders, there was nothing I could do if he did.

"I think he's available," I said blandly. "You'll have to ask him."

Squealing, she jumped to her feet and grinned wide. "Great! I'm going to ask him to be my date this Saturday for the party. Thanks, Kate."

Once all of the girls were out of the locker room, Brianna stayed behind to wait on me while I stretched. "You like him, don't you?" she asked.

My head snapped up. "What? No. It's not like that."

She lifted a brow and smiled. "Don't lie to me, Kate. I could see it in your eyes that you hated the thought of Lindsey asking him out. What happened between you two? I can definitely tell he's into you."

"Yeah, he's into me, Brianna, but I'm pretty sure that's because he wants to get *in* to me, if you know what I mean. He's not a stick around type of guy, and that's not what I want. Lindsey is more his type. Besides, I'm seeing Luke now."

Brianna laughed and put her arm around me. "Oh, Kate, I can see it now. You are going to be in so much trouble. I wish *I* had two men fighting over me."

She giggled the whole way to the field, and as soon as Cooper came into view, I stopped mid-step. He was smiling at Lindsey, who batted her eyelashes and brushed her fingers along his arms. Gritting my teeth, my stomach twisted into violent knots as I watched them, hating the fact that I had no right to go over there and tell her to fuck off.

Yes, I was in trouble because I knew what I was feeling. That urge inside of my body to run right up to them and tell Lindsey to back off was something I had never felt. It wasn't jealousy per se, but it was something similar to it. All I knew was that I didn't like it.

Chapter 12

COOPER

Watching Kate during practice and not being able to talk to her was fucking torture. I wanted to know what the hell her problem was and why she was being such a bitch to me this morning after everything I did for her. Unfortunately, she had left with Luke before I had the chance to speak with her.

My shoulder throbbed, but then again my whole body pulsed in anger. I knew I needed to calm down, which was why I stayed behind while everyone left. Lounging on the field didn't exactly give me the peace I needed like it would back home, but it was a start. I had to get used to the heat, humidity, and the sound of traffic all around me whereas at home I didn't have to worry about any of that.

"Are you going to be ready for the game this Saturday?" Evan asked, standing over me.

My response was immediate. "Hell yeah, I'll be ready."

"What about the party? Do you think you're ready for that?"

I scoffed, "Please, I bet you guys don't even know what a real party is like."

Evan chuckled and sat down on the grass beside me. "Yeah, you're probably right. We're nothing but a bunch of country boys out here."

"Believe me, I was the same way out in California. I didn't want to live in the big cities. I enjoyed having my land and being in the wine country."

Evan's eyes went wide. "Really? I never would've pegged you for a country boy. I guess there's a lot we don't know about you."

"Yep, including your sister," I mumbled low.

"You know, if you want to make my sister jealous I wouldn't do it with Lindsey. I saw her with you today."

"Trust me," I said, "the last thing I'm going to do is mess around with Lindsey. She asked me to the party Saturday night and I said yes. Kate's going with Luke, so I figured it was fair game."

"Okay, so you have a point there, but in all seriousness, don't play games with Kate. I don't know what's wrong with her today, but she's not herself."

Opening my eyes, I sat up and slid my sunglasses on. "She didn't tell you what happened last night?" I asked curiously.

"No, what happened?"

"Well, I guess it's a good thing you're here. There's something I want to do and I'm going to need your help. Last night, Kate got extremely drunk and passed out. According to Lara, she doesn't do that very often except on a certain day of the year."

Evan sighed and hung his head. "Yes, I know. I knew she was upset, but I had no clue she was going to get wasted because of it. What else did Lara tell you?"

"Not much, but I do know Kate was dating that Scott guy when he killed himself and his family likes to fuck with her. I think they called her last night," I told him.

"What the hell?" he growled. "I wish they would leave her alone. I don't know why she doesn't do anything about it. What happened after that?"

"Well, last night Kate and I went to the tavern because Lara wanted us to. She started drinking a lot, and when she went missing we found her passed out on the bathroom floor with her phone shattered. I took her home and stayed with her until this morning. Now she won't talk to me and I don't know why."

Evan blew out an angry breath. "I'll talk to her. She's not exactly the most rational person in the world and she's always been too hard on herself. If she doesn't want to get a restraining order from those psychos then I'm going to make her."

He turned to leave, but I stopped him. I didn't want to pry into her life if she didn't want me there, but I couldn't stand to see her suffer. "There's someone I know that can help, and I was actually planning on calling him today. If you give me the names of Scott's family that have been harassing Kate then I can get him to investigate."

"Oh, that would be great. Who's this person you're going to call?"

"His name is Mason Bradley. He used to be an under-cover detective," I grumbled.

Evan's eyes lit up. "Oh yeah, I know him. Good guy and one hell of an MMA fighter. How do you know him?"

Chuckling, I got to my feet and brushed the grass off of my clothes. "It's funny you should ask that. Mason was the guy who took someone away from me, someone I cared a whole hell of a lot about."

"And you want his help even though you don't like him?" he asked incredulously. "Wow, you must really want to help Kate."

If he only knew how much.

After I grabbed my bag, Evan and I started off toward the parking lot. "I do, but I also figured that Mason owes me one. Even if Kate wants nothing to do with me, I want to know that she doesn't have to put up with that bullshit anymore."

Slapping me on the shoulder, Evan shook his head and grinned. "You know, I never thought I would say this, but you're actually an okay guy. I honestly think you'd be better for her than Luke. Don't give up on her."

I wasn't planning on it.

When I got home I wanted to talk to Kate, but Luke's truck was in her driveway. Was that fucker always going to be in the way? Instead of storming over there, I did what I always did when things pissed me off. In my bathroom, there were plenty of bottles with those little white pills that made everything better; this time I swallowed three.

Before they could hit my system, I picked up my phone and dialed Mason.

"Yeah," he answered.

"Mason, it's Cooper," I replied.

"Ah, Cooper, so what can I do for you? Do you want permission to speak to Claire or something?"

"Smart ass," I growled. "If I wanted to talk to Claire I would've called her. I don't think I need your permission to do that. Besides, this call isn't about her. It's about someone else, and she's having some trouble."

"Her, huh? Are you seeing this woman?" he asked curiously.

I huffed, "Not exactly. Can you help me or not?"

"That depends. What's going on?"

"Okay, let's see. My neighbor, Kate, found her boyfriend dead in his house two years ago. He committed suicide, and now his family blames her. For the past two years, they've tormented her by saying it was all her fault and basically harassing her. Last night was the anniversary of his death and she broke down, bad. I don't want her like that again."

"Do you have the names of the family members and those involved?"

"I do," I said. Taking the piece of paper out of my pocket, I read off the names that he would need.

"Okay, I got it. I'll see what I can do. Can you give me a few days?"

"Yeah, of course. Just call me back as soon as you hear something."

By the time we hung up, I was already starting to feel good from my pain meds; the haze making everything feel less complicated. Grabbing a bottle of vodka from my refrigerator, I marched outside and headed straight for Kate's house … except I didn't get that far.

"Cooper, are you okay?" Lara asked, walking to her mailbox. "Why do you look stoned off of your ass?"

"It's because I am. I'm going to talk to Kate."

"Oh, no you're not," she shouted, rushing to step in

my way. Placing her hands on my chest, she pushed against me, backing me up toward her garage. "The last thing you need to do is go over there like that and start a fight. What did you take?"

"It's just my prescription, Lara. It's nothing illegal," I stammered. "Anyway, Kate won't talk to me so I'm going to go over there and make her."

"Has she not been talking to you? Why would she do that?"

Chuckling, I lifted the bottle of vodka and took a long, hard gulp. I haven't had alcohol in days, and it felt fucking amazing. "How the hell should I know? After last night she blew me off and started spending time with that fucker," I hissed, pointing over at his truck.

"Well that doesn't make any sense." Sighing, she looked at Kate's house and then back to me. "Okay, I want you to go into my house and wait. I'm going to get Kate to come with me, and that way you can talk to her without Luke interfering. When you go inside, turn to the left and there will be a hallway. Go down to the second room on your right and wait in there. As soon as she gets into the room with you, I'm going to lock the door from the out-side so she can't walk away."

"Why are you doing this for me?" I asked.

Lara grinned mischievously and winked. "Oh, I have my reasons. Don't get me wrong, I like you and all, but for once I don't want to see Luke get the girl. He deserves to be put in his place."

With those final words, she turned on her heel and marched off to Kate's house. Kate wasn't going to like getting locked into a room with me, but at least I'd get my answers.

Chapter 13

Kate

Kissing his way down my neck, Luke slowly lowered the strap of my tank top down one shoulder. "Why do you keep pushing me away, Kate? You have no idea how bad you're killing me right now."

His fingers glided down my arm and then back up to cup my breast. "Am I supposed to make it easy on you?" I asked. "Besides, I'm not just going to jump in bed with you, Luke."

Picking me up in his arms, he laid me down on the couch and covered me with his body, spreading my legs with his knee.

"And why not?" he growled, thrusting his hips up and down between my legs. His emerald gaze burned with desire as he leaned down to kiss my lips.

As much as I wanted to deny it, my body craved a man's touch. It had been so long since I felt an ounce of pleasure, and with Luke touching me in all the right places I couldn't help but want to submit. Luke was there and he wanted me, but why couldn't I give in?

Before we could go any further, the doorbell rang. Agitated, Luke rested his head on my chest and groaned, reluctantly sliding off of me. "Why is it that we always get interrupted by something?"

Maybe it was a sign, I thought.

Straightening my tank top, I fixed my shorts and headed to the door while Luke stayed on the couch and adjusted his pants to hide the bulge. When he was ready and decent, I opened the door to see Lara standing there, looking overly excited with a big grin on her face.

"Lara, what's wrong? Why do you look like that?" I asked, laughing.

"You have to come look at this new painting I got. It's absolutely gorgeous."

"Do you want me to look at it now?"

Her smile grew brighter. "Yes, but is it a bad time? I know Luke's here."

"No," I claimed, breathing a sigh of relief. "Your timing was actually perfect." It saved me from making a decision I didn't know if I was ready to make.

Over my shoulder, I called out to Luke, "Luke, I'll be right back. Lara wants to show me a new painting she bought."

"You have to go now?" he asked.

Lara lifted a curious brow and I laughed it off nervously. "Yes, so just sit tight."

Quickly, I shut the door and sighed. "Thank you for saving me. I swear he knows how to push a woman's buttons."

When we got further away from the house and into her yard, she leaned in and asked, "You haven't slept with him, have you?"

"No, of course not! Trust me, I've been tempted, but I know better."

It'd been so long since I felt what a real orgasm was like. I wanted it like I wanted air to breathe. The longer I was around Luke, the more I wanted to give in, especially now that Cooper proved to be exactly what I thought he was.

"Why do you say that?" Lara asked as we stepped up on her front porch. "Don't you like him?"

"I do, but something's holding me back."

A wide smile spread across her face as she led me through her house to one of the back bedrooms. "Are you sure it's not a *someone* instead of a *something*?"

I shrugged. "Does it matter?"

She opened the door slightly and put her hands on my shoulders so she could look at me. "It makes all of the difference in the world, Kate. You're not scared of Luke, but you *are* of Cooper because you know he can be the real deal. Stop running and look at what's in front of you."

"Lara, what are you talking about?"

She pushed open the door to reveal Cooper sitting on the navy blue bed with his elbows resting on his knees and gazing straight at me. Arms crossed, Lara nodded toward the room. "You two need to talk. Deny it all you want, but I know you want to talk to him, too."

I did want to talk to him to tell him what a worthless douchebag he was for leaving me. Turning my back on Cooper, I glared at Lara and gritted my teeth. "Fine, two minutes, and that's it."

Lara winked over her shoulder at Cooper and shut the door, the sound of a lock clicking into place. When I tried the handle, it wouldn't budge. "Lara, you can't be serious!

Unlock the damn door," I shouted, banging on the door.

"Nope, not until you and Cooper talk. This is for your own good."

I banged on the door some more, but it was no use because I could hear her footsteps echoing down the hall. "Lara! Lara, get back here!"

"Is it so bad to be locked in here with me?" Cooper asked. "You know, I thought things were going great with us the past couple of days. What happened?"

Leaning against the door, I sighed before turning around. "Look, Cooper, it doesn't matter. We work together, that's it. We need to keep our relationship on professional terms."

"Professional terms?" he sputtered, slurring his words. "So you're saying we can't even be friends?"

It was then I smelled the remnants of liquor in the room. His dumbass was drunk, and here I was trying to talk to him. He probably wasn't even going to remember what was discussed anyway.

As I walked past him I said, "Yes, that's exactly what I'm saying." Suddenly, he grabbed my arms and turned me around, holding me close to his body with both hands on my biceps.

"Cooper, let me go."

"No, not until you give me an explanation. Even if it takes all night, you're not going anywhere."

"Fine," I snapped, finally having the courage to look him in the eyes. "The sooner I get this over with the sooner ..."

I stopped mid-sentence the second I got a good look at his eyes; something wasn't right, they were mainly pools of the magnificent blue of his irises with only a tiny pinpoint showing of his pupils. It wasn't normal, especially since the darkened room we were in would make anyone's pupils larger … and it wasn't the alcohol that would do it either.

"Son of a bitch," I hissed. "You're on something, aren't you? Tell me!"

"Why are you switching the subject?" he countered. "Why don't you tell me what I did wrong? Are you mad about last night, or embarrassed that I saw you at your worst? You don't have to hide that stuff from me."

Narrowing his gaze, he pulled me closer and I could feel his heart pounding in his chest. Everything about his arms felt familiar, like I'd been in them before. How could that be?

"Why don't you answer *my* questions first and then I'll answer yours," I murmured breathlessly. "I promise to be honest and tell you the truth, but *only* if you do the same."

Closing his eyes, he lowered his forehead to mine and sighed, his voice low and pained. "Okay, love, you want the truth … here it goes. I still take my pain killers every day. I've tried to stop, but I can't. I've at least cut my pills down from six to four a day."

I gasped. "And you've done this for how long?"

"For four months."

"Has your shoulder been giving you that many problems?" I asked. "Or are you taking them for the hell of it?"

Cooper ran his fingers through his hair and blew out an angry breath. "I don't know, both I guess. I love the way I feel when I'm on them because I never care about anything. At least, not until I met you. I've taken five of them today, and I still find myself thinking of nothing other than you. If I'm addicted to anything it's not those fucking pills … it's you."

My breath hitched in my throat and I froze. He was addicted to me? "Cooper," I murmured, taking his face in my hands. His blue gaze stared back at me—so deep—that I almost forgot to breathe. "You need to tell me when you're in pain. It's my job to help you. Taking pills like you're doing is a serious problem. Starting tomorrow you're going to cut down the amount of four to three and you're going to work with me. I'll show you some exercises that are great for pain management. Then the next week we'll cut down to two and finally to one."

"What about withdrawals? Will I experience that?"

"Unfortunately, yes. That's why you need to slowly cut back until you can wean yourself off of them. It's not going to be easy, but I'm not going to let you go through it alone."

Not like you left me alone last night when I needed help. I knew he was going to need help and my heart couldn't let him do it alone even though I was angry as hell at him.

"Do you only want to help me because it's your job?" he asked huskily. "Or do you actually care? And don't lie to me. You promised to tell me the truth."

I glared at him for a few seconds before throwing my hands in the air. "Fine, that's not the only reason. At first, I thought there was something between us, but I was wrong. You see, a friend wouldn't have abandoned me last night. Yes, I'm embarrassed and I handled my problems in the wrong way. As much as I hate to admit this, I was actually kind of pissed that you dumped me on to Luke last night and left."

Slowly stepping back, Cooper's eyes went wide and his jaw tensed. "Kate, I never left you last night. What made you think I'd leave you when you needed help? The only time I left was when seven o'clock rolled around and I needed to get ready for practice. Luke didn't tell you?"

Dumbfounded, I stood there gaping at him. "No, he didn't," I said through clenched teeth. "He made it sound like you didn't want to bother with me."

"You have got to be kidding me! What a lying cock-sucker. I should've known he wouldn't tell you I was there. However," he slowly began with a mischievous smile, "I think I should be offended that you don't remember being in my arms all night. I have to admit, even though I didn't get any sleep, I loved being able to take care of you."

So that's why it felt familiar being in his arms; I spent all night in them.

"Why are you smiling? Aren't you pissed that he lied?" I asked incredulously. "I know I am."

"Yes, I'm angry, but he probably only said that to get me back. After Lara and I found you in the bathroom, I snuck you out the back door and brought you home. Lara lied to Luke so I could be with you and not have him interfere."

"So what you're saying is that you're both at fault? I should be mad at both of you?"

Grinning, he took a step closer … then another. "Not exactly. I think you can say we're both determined." Tilting my chin up with his finger, he gazed down at me, his lips so close to mine. "I'm not a bad guy, love. I have my issues, and you have yours. I think in time we'll be what each other needs. You may not see it now, but you will.

I'm still waiting on you to ask me."

"Ask you what?" I breathed.

"To kiss you, touch you … whatever it is you ask of me. When that time comes, I don't want you to only *want* me. I want you to need me like I need you."

Finally, the door to the room unlocked and opened wide as Lara set us free. Closing my eyes, I felt Cooper's finger leave my chin and the brush of air as he walked past me and out the door, completely silent. Lara's voice was what I heard next.

"Kate, if you don't want him, can I have him?" she teased. "I couldn't help but listen, and boy, did he have my heart racing."

"Mine too," I whispered, and it was still racing.

Now that I knew the truth, I couldn't deny what was in my heart any longer. I just had one more thing I needed to do.

By the time I got back to my house, I was so angry with Luke for lying that I could barely see straight. Playing games was one thing, but outright lying and saying he was the one who took care of me when he didn't was something on a completely deceptive level. I couldn't ignore it.

Slamming the door shut, Luke jumped to his feet and approached me. "Well, it's about time you got back," he chimed, putting his arms around my waist. He bent down to kiss my neck and whispered in my ear, "Where were we?"

"I think we were at the part where you lied. Does that

ring a bell?"

His lips froze on my skin and he slowly pulled back to gaze down at me. "What are you talking about, sweetheart?"

I scoffed and walked past him to the living room. "I'm talking about last night, Luke. I'm talking about you lying to me and saying it was you who stayed with me when it was Cooper all along. You made me believe it was you. How could you do that? How could you lie to me like that?"

Coming up behind me, he tried to put his arms around me again, but I moved away. If he thought I would give in to his charms he was sorely mistaken. When he realized I wasn't going to buckle, he sighed and backed up toward the couch, putting his head in his hands when he sat down. "Fuck, Kate, what was I supposed to do? Cooper had Lara lie to me and say you didn't want me around. I only wanted to pay him back for deceiving me. I would've stayed with you and taken care of you if I'd only known. I never got the chance."

I could see the sincerity in his gaze and slowly my anger started to dissipate. However, it still didn't change the fact that he lied. Sitting beside him, I sighed and took his hand in mine. "Luke, I know you would've stayed with me and I'm sorry that Lara lied to you, but Cooper didn't have anything to do with what she said."

"How do you know that?" he asked, furrowing his brows.

"Because," I murmured, "he just told me and I believe him."

"He just told you?" He peered over at the door and then back to me, his eyes narrowed. "So that's the reason why Lara came over here to get you? To talk to Cooper?"

When I didn't say anything, he let my hand go and jumped off of the couch to his feet. "Don't you see what they're doing, Kate? They're working against me. How the hell can I compete with that?" Angrily, he ran his hands through his hair and started for the door.

"Where are you going?" I shouted, rushing after him. I stopped him by plastering myself on the front door.

"I'm going to talk to Cooper. He's not going to come into town and take you away from me when things are just starting to happen for us."

Exasperated, I lifted my hands in the air and snapped, "Nothing has even happened with us, Luke. We've kissed and fooled around some, that's it. I don't understand why you're getting so upset when we don't even have a commitment. All you have to do is walk down the street and you'd have at least five women jumping all over you."

Immediately, he tensed and blew out an angry breath. "So is that what you want me to do?" he asked. "Are you saying you want to let me go and run straight to Cooper?"

Taking a deep breath, I slowly walked up to him and looked into his weary green gaze. "I didn't say I was going to do that," I hissed, "but at least he didn't lie to me. It's because of Cooper that I'm not ripping your head off for doing what you did. This isn't a competition, and you of all people should know I don't like playing games. I'm trying not to be angry with you, but I don't think I can do this right now."

I opened the door and stood back, my heart pounding out of control. "I need some time to think, Luke."

I hated turning him away, but after everything that had happened I knew what I wanted, but I also knew what

I needed.

"Some time," he repeated dryly. "I don't like the sound of that, but it looks like I have no choice." Taking a deep breath, he put his hands on my waist and bent down to kiss me on the cheek. "I'll give you what you want, Kate, but all I ask is that you don't give up on me. I'm sorry for what I did. Please believe me."

I watched him walk out the door, but before getting into his truck his gaze met Cooper's across the street. They stared each other down as if in a silent standoff, but then their gazes met mine. Why couldn't things just be easy?

"How do you feel?" I asked as I got into Cooper's car.

Everything about him seemed normal, but again it was the first day of his detox and only seven-thirty in the morning. Anything could happen at any given time. It was a gamble with him being around the guys because the last thing we wanted was for anyone on the team to know that he was addicted to pain meds. If Joel found out that I kept this information from him, I didn't want to imagine the kind of trouble I'd be in, much less Cooper.

With a smile on his face, Cooper shrugged and backed out of my driveway. I loved seeing him smile, especially now that the truth was out and things were better between us. Riding to the field together was going to be interesting, considering that just yesterday I rode in with Luke. *My how things have changed.*

"I actually feel fine," Cooper said. He wouldn't look

at me when he said it, so right there I knew he was keeping something from me. However, he did turn to look at me when he asked his next question, his gaze guarded … concerned. "When do the withdrawal symptoms start?"

Sighing, I reached over and rubbed his shoulder soothingly. I knew he was worried, even if he didn't admit it to me. "That all depends. You might not have any symptoms since you're taking it slow, but if you do have them it could happen in the next couple of hours or days from now. It's different with each case. Are you worried about it?" I asked.

Shaking his head, he squeezed my hand that I had lying on his shoulder and smiled. "No, as long as I have you with me I'm not worried. You'll see me through it, right?"

"I promise," I murmured wholeheartedly. "I'll be right by you until it's over."

When we got to the field and separated ways, I prayed that he would be okay, knowing very well he was going to have a tough time. As the day went on, I noticed a few changes in him. He didn't realize I was watching him from the stands, but I wrote down every single thing I noticed that was different with him. *Come on, Cooper, you can beat this.*

Over the next few days I decided to keep notes on his behavior and symptoms so I could keep track of his progress and get more of an idea on the detox process. In school, I only studied the effects, but I had yet to see it all in person.

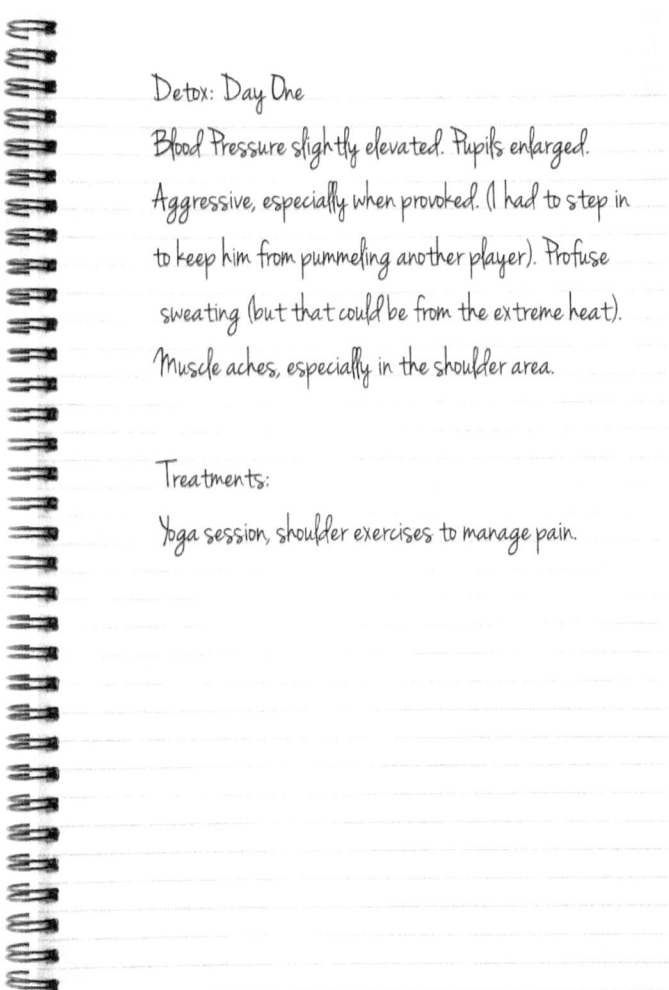

Detox: Day One

Blood Pressure slightly elevated. Pupils enlarged.
Aggressive, especially when provoked. (I had to step in
to keep him from pummeling another player). Profuse
sweating (but that could be from the extreme heat).
Muscle aches, especially in the shoulder area.

Treatments:

Yoga session, shoulder exercises to manage pain.

Detox: Day Two

Loss of appetite (I still made him eat). Blood pressure slightly elevated. Anxious (can't stay still). Irritable (especially when I made him eat). Aggressive (but that could've been because another player asked him if I was good in bed. Thankfully, Evan stepped in).

Note to self:

> He's either very protective or that reaction was because of the pain meds … or both. Muscle aches (a little worse than the day before). Runny Nose.

Treatments:

Meditation, shoulder exercises to manage pain.

Detox: Day Three

Blood pressure was normal. Rapid breathing (could be from working out in the heat). Sweating. Loss of appetite. Muscle aches (pain getting better). Slightly irritable (only during practice). Overall: symptoms showing improvement.

Muscle aches, especially in the shoulder area.

Treatments:

Yoga session, shoulder exercises to manage pain.

Chapter 14

COOPER

Three Days Later

So far, taking one less pill a day hasn't bothered me too much; or at least that was what I told Kate. Yes, I've been a little short-tempered and irritable, but how the hell could I not be when it was so fucking hot and I had to deal with some of the cocksuckers on my team?

The idiot who asked me if Kate was good in bed shouldn't have been so goddamned stupid to think I wasn't going to lay into his ass. I mean, who in their right mind would ask something like that and not expect to get their ass kicked? Even Evan had a hard time keeping his restraint.

Kate wasn't stupid, though; she knew I was keeping my true feelings and concerns to myself, but didn't seem to think it was an issue. So for the time being I kept my weaknesses to myself. However, by the end of the day, the exercises she did with my shoulder really seemed to work. By the time she was done with me it was only my cock that was in pain. I respected her and kept my hands to myself even though it took a fucking miracle. That was another thing that had changed; my whole body had a new craving, and it wasn't for those damn white pills … it was for her. Each time we were alone and her body would brush up against mine, it took all I had not to rip her clothes off and fuck her. Needless to say, my right arm got a good workout each night in the shower.

Much to my dismay, I was sure it was going to be like that again now that we were on our way to her house. Waiting for her to ask me to kiss her and touch her was outright torture. I could see it in her eyes that she wanted me, but she held back. I had no idea how to get her to let me in. I knew it wasn't Luke because she'd told me she let him go, and I witnessed that the other day when he left her house pissed off. Unfortunately, the game still wasn't over.

With Kate's arms crossed at the chest, I couldn't help but notice the mounds of her breasts pushing up through her pink tank top. She even had on short shorts for the first time since I'd met her. Usually she wore yoga pants or capris, but now she showed off those gorgeous, tanned legs of hers and all I wanted to do was feel how smooth they were wrapped around my waist. Maybe one day she'd give in, but until then I had to be patient. Unfortunately, I wasn't exactly a patient man.

"What are you thinking about?" I asked, glancing over at Kate who kept her gaze directed out the window. "Are you thinking about how good it's going to feel to get your hands all over me this afternoon?"

Kate perked up and laughed. "No, but I'm sure you are. Actually, I was thinking about a lot of things: you, the game, and—"

She didn't get to finish her sentence because my cell phone started ringing nonstop in my bag. I wasn't going to answer it, but Kate fetched it and handed it to me. It was Mason. *Shit, I need to answer it.* I didn't want to do it in front of her, but I had to know what he found.

Taking a deep breath, I answered it, "Hey, what's up?"

"Cooper, it's Mason. Do you have a minute?"

Hesitantly, I peered over at Kate. Thankfully, she was too busy fiddling with her phone to pay attention. "Yeah, go ahead," I told him.

"All right, I've looked into everything and let me tell you it's pretty fucked up. You already know that Kate found Scott after he overdosed on pills. Apparently, Scott's mother, Marianne Easton, had gone a little crazy after that. She vandalized Kate's car and spray painted the word murderer on it. She also had friends and family follow her around, and even show up at the hospital where she was doing her rotations at. It took a toll on Kate and she ended up having a nervous breakdown that landed her in the hospital. After that, she completely dropped out of school and moved back home to Charlotte."

What the hell? I had no clue she went through all of that shit. No wonder she was screwed up over it. If Scott's family tried to mess with her like that again I was going to step in and do something about it.

"And that's all? Nothing else as far as recent or the past year?" I asked.

"Nope, nothing at all. If your friend feels like she's in danger, we can get a restraining order. Until then, that's all I can do. I hope this helps."

"It does. Thank you for calling me back. If something

happens do I need to call you or is there someone local that I should speak to?"

"Yeah, I'll text you his number. His name is Sam Lennox. He used to be my partner, and is one hell of a good detective. I gave him the heads up already, so if you have issues he'll be there to help you."

"Thank you," I added again.

"You're welcome, and good luck with the game tomorrow. I have a lot of money riding on it so you better make sure you win."

"Don't worry, we will."

After we hung up, Kate turned in her seat to face me, furrowing her brows. "Is everything okay? You looked a little worried there for a moment."

"No, everything's fine," I replied, turning my gaze to the road. "So back to my question earlier … you said you were thinking about me. What exactly were you thinking about? My good looks? My charm? What?"

Chuckling, she smacked me on the arm. "All of it, actually. I just wanted you to know that I really admire what you've done over the past couple of days. I know it hasn't been easy cutting back on the pain meds, but I can see you're working through it as hard as you can. I really admire you for that."

She reached over and grabbed my hand, clasping it with hers. "You're going to be great at the game tomorrow. I can't wait to watch you play."

With my other hand, I traced along her fingers with my own. "You'll be there, so I know I'll do fine." Lifting her hand, I gently kissed her palm and watched her shudder.

She kept her body turned to me, watching me with

her sensual gray eyes and biting her lip. If she kept doing that I was going to have to pull the car over and bite those lips myself.

"Cooper," she whispered.

Finally pulling into her driveway, I turned to her and lifted a curious brow. "Yes, love."

She licked her lips and averted her gaze for a moment, taking deep breaths in and out … almost nervously. "Kate? What's on your mind?" I asked. "You can tell me."

When her gaze lifted to mine, I knew without a doubt that things were about to change. All I wanted was to hear her ask me the one question that would change everything. It just so happened that what came out of her mouth wasn't a question, it was a demand.

"I want you to kiss me," she murmured softly. "And don't hold back."

It's about fucking time! She's mine.

Chapter 15

Kate

I finally said it. After days of senseless agony, I gave in and told him to kiss me. However, it wasn't just a kiss I wanted … I wanted all of him.

Everything moved in slow motion, especially when Cooper's lips touched mine. Immediately, my body lit up hotter than the summer sun and I was on fire, burning from the inside out. I grew impatient, needy, as he held me firmly in place with my face between his hands, opening my lips with his tongue and thrusting deep and hard. I wanted to get closer, but I couldn't because of the damn center console of his car.

"Cooper," I moaned breathlessly.

He nipped my ear and groaned low in his chest, "Yeah?"

"Let's go inside."

Immediately, his lips stilled against mine and he pulled back ever so slowly, his gaze heated yet uncertain. "Are you sure this is what you want?"

"Yes," I claimed breathlessly, nodding my head. "I

want this."

I didn't have to say anymore because in one quick move, he opened his door and came around to mine, lifting me in his arms and carrying me to the door. After fumbling with my keys, I finally got it opened and dropped the keys on the table in the foyer as we passed. Shifting me in his arms, he wrapped my legs around his waist and I gasped as he pushed me into the wall. *Holy hell, he's intense ... wild.* He lifted my hands above my head and held me prisoner while he bit his way along my collarbone and down to the mounds of my breasts.

Groaning, he pushed his hard cock between my legs and rocked his hips, sliding me up and down against the cold, smooth wall. I could only imagine what it was going to feel like to have him inside of me. I knew it would hurt since it'd been two years since I'd been with anyone, but I was so damn turned on I didn't even care. I would welcome the pain just to end the relentless throbbing between my legs.

"Where to?" he asked, grabbing my breast with his firm hand. "The living room? Your bedroom? Where do you want me to fuck you?"

He massaged and squeezed them so hard I could barely think, and even more so when he pinched my nipples to get my attention. I cried out as the pain shot through my body on down to my clit; it felt amazing. "Where to?" he repeated more forcefully. "If you don't tell me where, I'm going to fuck you right here against the wall."

Gasping, I bit my lip and rolled my hips, watching his eyes roll back in his head. Two could play at that game. Fucking against the wall didn't sound like a bad idea. My clit pulsed so violently that I could barely speak; I was so close.

"My room," I stammered. "I want you to take me on my bed."

He knew where my room was so as he climbed up the steps, I kicked off my shoes, making them tumble down the stairs along with my socks. Next, was my pink tank top, and with one hand, I lifted it up over my shoulders and threw it off the side of the staircase.

Cooper moaned deep in his chest and chuckled. "Eager, are we? I seem to recall it was your fault for taking so long."

"Yeah, but the tension makes it so much better."

Bursting through the door, Cooper dropped me on the bed and took off his shirt before covering me with his body. "Are you sure this is what you want, love? Once we start there's no going back. I want you to know what you're getting in to."

Slowly, I glided my fingers down his washboard abs and slid my hand inside of his shorts; his cock was so thick and hard I could barely wrap my hand around him. *Oh yes, it's going to hurt.* Holding him tight, I pumped the full length of his cock up and down gently until a strangled moan escaped his lips. Reluctantly, I let go.

"I think I can handle it," I remarked amusingly.

"Well, then you better be ready." With his blue gaze on mine, he reached behind me and unclasped my bra, throwing it across the room before closing his lips over my nipple, sucking it hard … feverishly.

"More," I rasped, arching my back.

Lifting my hips, he slid off my shorts and my underwear and lowered me back down. "I'll give you more," he growled, spreading my legs wide.

He flicked his tongue across my clit, making me jump, and did it again. His breath teased my sensitive flesh as he breathed in and out, licking inside of me. Over and over, he licked and sucked my clit until I couldn't take it anymore.

"That's right, love. Come for me and let me taste you," he commanded.

Doing as he said, I exploded from the inside out, reaching down to grip handfuls of his dark tresses as he tasted every drop of my desire. When he lifted his head and climbed up my body, I smiled and muttered breathlessly, "Cooper that felt amazing."

My body quivered as it came down from its orgasm induced high, and Cooper was all too happy with my reaction. "I think I'm addicted to your mouth," I teased. "I want more."

"Trust me, you'll get more, love. But first, are you…"

He didn't need to finish what he was going to say because I knew what he was going to ask by the way he looked down at my stomach and back up to me. "Yes, I'm protected, Cooper. I'm on the pill so we're safe."

With a devilish smile on his face, he pulled down his shorts and boxers, throwing them on the floor, his cock long and thick between his legs. "In case you're wondering, I'm safe, too."

I swallowed hard and nodded. "Yes, I know. I have access to your medical files, remember?"

Cooper chuckled. "I see. I guess I can't blame you for looking considering my past. I just had to make sure we didn't have any little Cooper's running around anytime soon."

"Oh, definitely, not," I stated wholeheartedly.

I wanted kids, but it was going to be a long time before I even considered having one.

Smirking, Cooper lifted me up in his arms and sat back against the antique wooden headboard of my bed. Straddling his waist, I could feel his cock throbbing between my legs, and I teased him by only letting the very tip of him inside of me.

With short, gentle strokes, I glided up and down until his grip tightened on my hips and he growled, "You're killing me, love. Ride me now or I'm going to take control, and I don't think you're ready for that just yet."

In a way I wanted to see what he would do, but instead, I lowered down inch by inch until he was completely inside of me. "Cooper," I moaned, slowly moving my hips to get used to him. It hurt at first, but I was so turned on and wet for him that the pain turned into a delicious ache.

"Kate, you feel so fucking good. I can't believe how wet you are for me."

With one hand tugging on my hair, he lowered the other one so he could rub my clit with his thumb. "Lean back so I can taste your nipples. I want them in my mouth when I come." I had never been with a man that talked during sex like that. It was a rush and it felt amazing to feel desired, wanted.

His grip on my hair tightened and I arched my back, still moving my hips as he bit down on a taut nipple. "As much as I love you riding me, I think it's my turn now, love."

"Then do it," I moaned.

Picking me up by the hips, we stayed connected when

he flipped us around and collapsed on top of me. I wrapped my legs around his waist and held on tight as he thrust his hips deep and hard. Faster and faster he pumped, his lips still suckling on one of my nipples. The harder he sucked and pushed, the closer I came to losing myself; we were both almost to the edge.

"Cooper," I cried. "I'm so close."

He growled low in his chest and held on tighter. "Me too, love. Oh fuck, you're getting so tight."

Digging my nails into his back, I screamed out my release at the same time I could feel his cock throbbing inside of me and coating me in his desire. Breathing hard, he kissed my neck and held on tight for a few minutes while he rested. When he lifted his head, he brushed the hair away from my face and kissed me gently on the lips, tracing them with his tongue.

"I think this is the kind of pain management I needed all along."

I laughed. "Do you now? So your shoulder doesn't hurt?"

He shook his head and bit his lip. "Not at all. So how about it, love? Do you think you can add a new regime to our pain management every day?"

Slyly, I bit my lip and smiled. "I think we can come up with something. Besides, I don't think we're done for the day. You know, water aerobics is wonderful for people dealing with pain. How about we try it out in the pool?"

"Hey, you're the doctor," he agreed matter-of-factly. "I have to do what you feel is best."

"Oh, believe me," I murmured, wrapping my arms around his neck, "it's definitely for the best."

After our pool exercises were done, Cooper offered to cook me dinner, which I couldn't refuse; especially, when it happened to be spaghetti. Over the rim of my wine glass, I watched the way his muscles worked in his arms as he moved around my kitchen, shirtless and in only a pair of ripped jeans that hung low on his hips.

"So what inspired you to pursue a football career? What is it about the sport you like?" I asked him.

Cooper turned around and smiled, his blue gaze sparkling. "I think a lot of it had to do with my grandfather. I remember being a kid and playing out in the field behind his house, passing the ball back and forth with him. There were pictures with me as a baby with a football in my crib when I slept. I think it had always been ingrained in my mind since I was a little boy that I was going to play. I lived it and breathed it for all of my life. It's all I know."

"That's not true," I countered. "You have your degree in architecture. I'd love to see what you can design. One day I want to have acres and acres of farmland and have a house built on it."

Leaning over the counter, he brushed his lips against mine before gently tracing them with his fingers. "I tell you what. When that time comes, and if you're still putting up with me, then I'll design your house for you. I'll even design your stables for free," he said with a wink.

"How did you know I wanted horses? I never told you that." My whole life I'd wanted to have my own stables with a bunch of animals. Horses were beautiful creatures and I'd dreamed of one day being able to raise some.

"Love, you have no idea how much I pay attention to you. I figured since you had those horse paintings in your room that you had a passion for them. Speaking of keeping secrets, when are you ever going to tell me about what happened the other night? You don't take me for the type of girl to get drunk and pass out in bathrooms."

Lifting his brows, he turned away from me and back to the stove so he could get back to the spaghetti. I had a strange feeling Lara already told him what happened to me considering they had become good friends. I loved her to death, but she had a big mouth on her.

"Do you know already?" I asked curiously. "It's not like it's a big secret or anything. I'm pretty sure if you googled my name you would have all the answers you needed."

Cooper sighed and peered at me over his shoulder, his eyes wary. He was hesitant at first, but then he nodded. "Okay, fine, I do know what happened. I just wanted you to trust me enough to tell me yourself."

"It's not that I don't trust you, Cooper. It's just it was a really hard time in my life and it hurts to talk about it. Did Lara tell you?"

"She told me not to tell you, but yes, she told me a little so I'd understand what was going on." He paused and turned back around. "Did you love him?" he asked softly.

My eyes welled with tears and I hastily wiped them away. "I did. He was a great guy. When I found him, I honestly wanted to believe it was a sick joke. Scott wasn't the type to joke around like that, but I wanted to believe almost anything other than he was dead." Cooper came around the bar and pulled me into his arms. I held on to him tight and let the tears stream down my face. "I think this is the most I've talked about it since it happened."

Smoothing his hands up and down my back, Cooper kissed my head and held on tighter. "It's good to talk things out, love. I'm always here to listen to you. However, there is one thing I want to ask and I want you to be honest with me. After we talk about this, I'll let this whole subject go if you want."

Furrowing my brows, I gazed up at him curiously. "What is it?"

"The phone calls," he stated adamantly, "from Scott's family." Immediately, my body froze. "I know you get them on the anniversary of his death. You received one the other day, didn't you?"

Reluctantly, I nodded. "I did. The first time it was from Scott's mother, and this time it was from his sister. When the call came in that's when I threw my phone against the wall."

"So you have no idea what she wanted?"

I glared at him incredulously. "I think it's pretty obvious, Cooper. They've blamed me for Scott's death, and for years I've carried the guilt from it. I will always carry that guilt, and I don't need them reminding me. I just wish they'd leave me the hell alone."

"Hey," he said, taking my face in his hands. "If they so much as try to contact you again you need to tell me, you understand? I'm not going to let them hurt you anymore."

"And you think you can stop them?"

He kissed me gently on the lips. "I don't think, love … I know. Promise me you'll let me know if they bother you again." When I didn't answer, he held my face tighter. "Promise me, Kate."

I didn't want him fighting my battles, but I nodded anyway. "Okay, I promise."

Ding ... dong.

"Expecting company?" Cooper asked, releasing me from his grasp. "If it's Lara I'll put together a bowl of spaghetti for her to take home."

"You really like her, don't you?"

He chuckled. "How could I not? It must be the southern charm you ladies have. Also, she cares about you. It's not every day you have a friend that will do anything for you."

"You're right," I agreed. "She's amazing." Turning on my heel, I headed for the door, but from the look of the silhouette outside it didn't appear to be Lara. Instead, it was ...

I opened the door wide and gasped, "Luke, what are you doing here?"

Holding his motorcycle helmet in his hand, he sighed and stepped past me. "I thought I'd come by and see how you were. I've missed you, and wanted to see if there was any possible way for you to forgive me."

He kissed me on the cheek and placed his helmet on the foyer table, along with his blue and black leather coat. Dressed in a pair of jeans and a white tank top that showed off his tattoos, he was the epitome of a woman's fantasy. He just wasn't a part of mine.

"Actually, Luke, I was about to eat dinner with Cooper."

His smile faded and he narrowed his eyes. "He's here?" he sneered. "So basically you're telling me it's a lost cause, right? Evan told me you've spent every afternoon working with him. When am I going to get to spend time with you? We used to be friends, remember?"

Cooper turned the corner at that exact moment and crossed his arms at the chest. Both guys stared each other down, and I prayed that neither one of them tried to start something.

"All right, I see what's going on," Luke hissed, glaring at Cooper. "You might have tonight, but tomorrow is mine. She promised she'd spend tomorrow with me and she always keeps her promises. I don't have to fake an injury to get her attention."

Taking my hand, he grabbed his helmet and jacket with the other and pulled me outside. Cooper snarled and was about to come after me until I shook my head, wanting him to stay back. Thankfully, he didn't follow when Luke tugged me out the door. "Luke, what are you doing?" I exclaimed.

"Please tell me you're not going to choose that douchebag over me? Yes, I made a mistake by lying to you, but I said I was sorry. What more can I do?"

"Nothing," I replied, letting go of his hand. "Why do you even want me anyway? Is it because I'm a challenge for you? I know you haven't had to work for the women you've slept with, they all fall at your knees."

"Kate, no, that's not it at all! I don't want those kinds of women anymore. You haven't even given me a chance to show you that I've changed."

Which was true … I hadn't. I just never expected to have Cooper come in and sweep me away. "You're right, Luke, and I'm sorry."

"You are going to keep your promise to me, right?" he asked. "If you decide I'm not the one for you that's fine, but I want you to give me this chance first. That's all I ask."

I knew Cooper would hate me for agreeing to this, but I nodded. If there was one thing I was noted for, it was my promises. I never made one I couldn't keep, and I'd promised him I would go on that one date with him. "Yes, I'm still going to keep my promise. I'll see you tomorrow, okay?"

Luke smiled warily and pulled me into his arms. "Thank you," he murmured. "I promise you won't regret it." I was pretty sure I would once I told Cooper.

Before going inside, I watched him put on his gear and ride away on his bike. I wasn't looking forward to going inside and telling Cooper what I had just done.

Chapter 16

COOPER

The day of my first game had finally arrived. We were playing on our home turf against Tampa Bay. The parking lot was full, and the sound of everyone cheering echoed through the halls, making the guys all pumped and ready to go. It was going to be a great victory.

"Dude, what's wrong with your back? Did you get attacked by a cat?" Derek asked.

The hulking linebacker smirked and waggled his eyebrows before continuing on his way, his gaze alit with humor. His head was freshly shaved, but the scruffy red beard on his chin made up for the lack of hair up top. When I turned my back and looked in the mirror, he chuckled and said, "All I can say is you better hope Evan doesn't see that."

Fuck, I forgot.

Kate raked her nails down my back so hard last night that it drew blood. There were red marks all across my skin. It was a shame Luke didn't get the chance to see them when he came by last night. I didn't even think about others seeing it today.

"See what?" Evan growled, rounding the corner. I turned my back away from him as he glared at me and Derek, who stalked away. "You know what, never mind. I'm sure it has to do with Kate, and I probably don't want to know. How's the arm?" he asked.

My arm was doing a lot better; it was the staying away from the Vicodin part where I had issues. I stared at the bottle for twenty minutes this morning, wanting to open it up and grab another pill. The only thing that stopped me was the thought of Kate. The journey to stopping was about to get a lot harder when I had to lower my dose next week.

"It's doing good," I told him. "Kate worked with me this past week, showing me different exercises to help."

"Speaking of Kate, you know she's out there with Luke right now. That's not going to bother you, is it?"

Immediately, my blood pressure shot through the roof. The thought of Kate with Luke pissed me the fuck off, especially after he threw a fit at her house last night. It took all I had not to kick his ass after he pulled her outside. My jaw still hurt from clenching my teeth as hard as I had. Kate wanted to keep her promise to him, and I respected that she wanted to uphold that, but dammit if it didn't piss me off. I knew that if I demanded she go against her word it would only cause a rift between us. That was only giving Luke what he wanted. So in other words, I bit my tongue.

Evan stared at me, waiting for a response. "You're not going to let your anger about my sister and Luke make you play shitty, are you?"

"What the fuck, Townsend, what's with all the questions? Yes, I know she's out there with that cocksucker.

Trust me, I'm focused on the game and nothing's going to change that."

He chuckled and nodded his head. "All right, that's what I like to hear. Just use that aggression against the other team. I had to make sure nothing was going to bother you out there today. The boys are counting on you to help us win."

"And win we will, boys," my uncle hollered behind me, slapping me on the shoulder. "Okay, everyone, huddle up."

The team still didn't know that our coach was my uncle. One day I was sure they'd find out because secrets always made their way known. Out of all of the coaches in the league, Joel had to be the most driven and down to earth. I'd met plenty of them over the past couple of years, and none of them had the heart like my uncle. At first, I was embarrassed about being on his team, especially since they weren't known for their amazing wins like the other teams I'd been on. They just needed the right element on their team and I think we had it … confidence.

After all the guys huddled around, Joel entered the circle and looked at each player, one by one. "All right, boys, this is the first game of the season. We need to show our fans what we can do and that we're winners. You all have what it takes to kick Tampa Bay's ass, and by God, I better see you kick it … hard. No holding back today. This is our time, boys. This is the season we make it to the Super Bowl, I can feel it. Now let's get out there and show them what you're made of!"

The team's thunderous roars were music to my ears. Rushing out of the room, they hooted and hollered all the way down the hallway, their shouts bouncing off the walls.

Before I could join them, Joel held me back with a hand to my shoulder.

"I just wanted to say that you've been doing amazing in practice. I know we haven't spent much time together one on one since you've been here, and I'm sorry about that. Just so you know, your parents asked about you yesterday. They're flying in tomorrow for a family gathering I'm hosting at my house. I know you could care less, but I want you there."

What the hell? My parents were the last people I wanted to see. "Did you by any chance tell them what you just told me?" I asked. "That I've been doing well?"

He nodded. "I did, and they're really proud of you. So will you come tomorrow?"

I didn't believe that for one second, but I didn't want to let him down. "Yeah, I'll go, but I'm bringing Kate with me. If anyone can help me deal with our family it would be her."

Joel's eyes went wide. "So does this mean you're going to tell her the truth as to why you're here? I thought you spent a good deal of money trying to hide that fact."

"I did," I confessed, "but I trust her. She's not going to say anything to anyone."

"All right, son, it's your choice. Just be careful with our girl. I don't want her leaving because things didn't work out between you two. She's one of the good ones."

Yes, she is.

Grinning, he slapped me on the shoulder and pushed me toward the door. "Now come on and let's go kick some ass. Prove to them all that you're still the best."

Joel sprinted down the hallway and I followed him. The cheering crowd grew louder and louder as the field came into view, and with each step my heart pounded harder. The second I stepped on to the grass, it was as if everything changed inside of me and became clear; I felt at home, and for the first time, I didn't want to win for myself. None of that mattered anymore. All that mattered was the beautiful blonde haired, gray eyed girl whose smile I could see the instant I looked in her direction. *I will win the game for her.*

Chapter 17

Kate

Cooper was on fire and the team loved it.

Every single pass he threw to my brother, Evan caught and sprinted down the field, earning us four touch downs. It was amazing and the crowd went wild.

"As much as I hate the guy, he sure can throw a football," Luke grumbled.

Rolling my eyes, I patted him on the arm but kept my eyes on the field. I couldn't look away from Cooper for a second. I knew we were going to win, but there was still one minute left on the clock. Anything could happen in that one minute, especially since the score was so close.

"Come on, clock, hurry up."

When the guys broke away from their huddle, Cooper turned his head my way and kissed his fingers before placing them on the ball and pointing it toward me. Coach Joel looked back at me and raised a curious brow before grinning and shaking his head.

"I don't know what you've done to him," Joel teased, "but I like it. He hasn't played this good ... ever."

Luke scoffed beside me and mumbled something under his breath. Things were a little weird between us, but I tried to look past his snide remarks and still have a good time. It was hard, but I was doing it.

Once the play was called, Cooper threw the ball to my brother, who caught it at the forty yard line and rushed it all the way to the end zone, deflecting the other team perfectly. The second he passed over the touchdown line, the crowd roared and got to their feet, their screams making the whole stadium shake all around us.

"I'll be right back," I shouted, rushing away from Luke so I could run on to the field toward my brother and Cooper.

Evan got to me first and swung me around in his arms before passing me off to Cooper. "You were amazing," I shouted as he also swung me around.

"It was all because of you, love. You were all I could think about."

Not caring if he was sweaty or not, I wrapped my arms around his neck and kissed him. "I'm so proud of you, Cooper, and I know everyone else is, too. Is your arm okay? Do you need me?"

"Kate, I always need you, but the arm is fine. I would hate for Luke to say I used my arm to take you away. I don't want any unfair advantage when I know how to play fair."

Smiling, I hugged him again and let go. I needed to get back to Luke so we could get ready for the party. It sucked because I knew Cooper had agreed to go with Lindsey, and I definitely didn't trust her to keep her hands to herself. I guess you could say it was my punishment for going on a date with Luke.

"Cooper, I have to go, but I'll see you tonight, okay? Maybe we could get together after the party?"

"You know I'm not going to pass that up," he chimed. "Also, I need to ask you something later. It's kind of important, so make sure you find me."

He grabbed my hand and kissed it before letting go and getting lost into the screaming crowd. We all had a victory to celebrate.

After each and every home game, one of the players would host the after party. It just so happened that my brother was the host for the evening. Since the team had won, I knew he would go all out on the party tonight.

"Kate, are you about ready?" Luke called from downstairs.

"Yes, almost! I just have to put on my dress. Do you mind grabbing my purse out of the car? I forgot to bring it in."

"Okay," he hollered.

Slipping on my white, strapless sundress, I slid my feet into my white wedge sandals and flat ironed the stray pieces of hair that had turned wavy on me from this afternoon. Luke's footsteps echoed off the walls as he climbed the stairs and met me out in the hallway.

He whistled and handed me my purse. "Wow, you look amazing in that dress."

"Thank you," I said, reaching into my purse to find my lip gloss. "You look mighty dapper yourself." Wearing a pair of khaki shorts and a striped navy and white polo shirt, he had his blond hair gelled into spikes along with the devilish smirk he always wore. After I put on my lip gloss and placed it back inside my purse, I smiled and grabbed his arm. "All right, I think I'm ready to go. Have you talked to Evan?"

"Yeah, he says he procured a DJ and for us to be prepared to dance. He also asked if I would race a couple of the guys on the track for fun."

After we got down the stairs, Luke opened up the front door and I followed him out. "What did you tell him?" I asked, locking the door. "Are you going to do it?"

My brother had a whole motocross track built in his backyard. Evan rode for the fun of it, but Luke actually went out there and practiced. "I told him I couldn't since tonight was the only night I had for our date. I didn't want to waste it by riding my bike. Don't you think that would be selfish of me?"

"No," I laughed. "I think everyone would love to watch you race with the guys. I don't mind if you want to. I'd be happy to watch."

He opened the door to his truck and his smile brightened. "Really? If you want me to, I will. You haven't watched me practice in a while. Before I hurt my leg I had gotten a lot faster. I can show those football players what it's like to compete in a real sport."

"Whatever you do, don't let them hear you say that," I stated, laughing.

I'd hate to see what happened if he did.

Chapter 18

COOPER

After watching Kate and Luke leave for the party, I figured it was about time to pick up my date for the night. Even though Kate and I were seeing each other, I wasn't about to go to the party alone. It just so happened that it didn't take long to get to my date's house ... only about one hundred feet.

"It's about time you got here to pick me up," Lara teased, meeting me in her driveway. "I thought I was going to have to go to the party alone. Does Kate know you're bringing me?"

"Nope, she still thinks I'm bringing Lindsey. I told her yesterday after practice that I couldn't take her. She wasn't exactly happy with me after that." While Kate was busy looking over one of the guys, I snuck away and told Lindsey that I had other plans for the party. She wasn't surprised, so that at least made it easier on me.

Lara laughed and took my arm as we walked back to my car. "I bet not. I hope Kate realizes how lucky she is to have you. I figured you would still want to take Lindsey since Kate was going to be with Luke."

"I'm not going to lie, the thought did cross my mind. However, the last thing I want to do is cause problems between me and Kate. I don't like to play games, but I will if I have to."

When we got to my car, there was a small white piece of paper under one of my windshield wipers that I hadn't noticed earlier. Lara waltzed over, slid it out, and unfolded it. "What is that?" I asked.

Eyes wide, she furrowed her brows and passed the note to me. "Well, unlike you, it looks like someone else *does* like to play games."

In big, bold letters the note said:

Glaring at the note, I crumpled it up in my hands but then read it again. "What the fuck! Really? He's going to be like this?"

"Do you think it was Luke?" Lara asked.

"Who else?" I snapped. "It's not a secret that he's pissed off about me and Kate."

What are we ... in high school? The last thing the letter did was scare me away from her. If that was Luke's mission, he failed.

Lara took the letter from me and shook her head. "This is so strange. I've known Luke a long time, and I've never seen him do anything like this. Are you going to show Kate?"

She handed it back to me and I looked at it one more time before angrily putting it in my back pocket. "I don't know. I'm probably going to go straight to him."

"Well, I think you should tell her. If he's actually that psycho over her, she needs to know. Trust me, I know what it's like to have a crazy boyfriend and it's not fun."

Getting in my car, we started on our way to Evan's house in complete silence. The wheels in Lara's head were turning and I knew she was just as perturbed about the situation as I was. She had a point, though; if Luke was being serious about the note then Kate needed to know. My only problem was getting her away from him to tell her.

When we arrived at Evan's house, a majority of the team and their friends were already there and congregating outside. Walking side by side, Lara and I went on our search for Kate and Luke. When we walked past Lindsey, she rolled her eyes and turned her head, but not without Lara noticing with a smirk on her face.

"Was that the girl you were supposed to bring?" she

asked. "She's hot."

Putting my arm around Lara, I briefly squeezed her shoulders and let go. "Yeah, but she's not as hot as you. I'm surprised Kate hasn't set you up with one of the players. Are they not your type?"

"Actually, no," she replied, gazing out in the distance. "I tend to go for the ones who never notice me."

I followed her gaze until I spotted who she was looking at … *Luke*.

"Lara, please tell me you're joking? Is that the reason why you helped me with Kate; to get her away from him so you could go after him?"

"No," she gasped halfheartedly. "I mean, not exactly. I never told Kate I had a thing for him. Besides, I haven't really had much time to date anyway with helping my sister at the restaurant. Also, Kate meshes well with you. You two fit together," she said, and turned to look at them, "… they don't."

"But the guy has some serious issues. You read the letter, Lara."

"Yes, I know, but I've had a thing for him for a long time now. When I look at him, I don't see him as being like that."

"Yeah, well, looks can fool you," I argued.

Kate's eyes went wide when she saw us, and she tapped Luke on the arm and said something to him before starting our way. Unfortunately, he followed, scowling the whole time.

"Hey, guys, I didn't know you two were coming together. What happened to Lindsey?" she asked, glancing curiously from me to Lara.

Luke scoffed and mumbled in her ear, "She probably

changed her mind."

"Actually, it was the opposite," Lara snapped. "Cooper turned Lindsey down because he knew it would piss Kate off if he brought her. So instead, he asked me to be his date and I accepted."

"Also," I added, putting my arm around her. "She's a lot hotter than Lindsey, and a much better date." In her ear, I quickly whispered, "I need you to get Kate out of here for a few minutes."

Lara nodded and hurriedly reached out to grab Kate's hands. "Kate, can you show me to the bathroom? I really need to go."

"You know where it's at," Kate exclaimed incredulously. "You've been here plenty of times."

Lara huffed. "Yeah, but I already forgot. You know how my mind is. Please, come with me. I really have to go."

Exasperated, Kate flung her hands in the air and chuckled. "Fine, I'll go. Just don't pee on yourself before we get there."

As soon as they walked off, Luke glared at me before taking off in another direction. "Not so fast," I said. "We need to talk."

Luke scoffed, "I have nothing to say to you."

Taking the note out of my back pocket, I opened it up and thrust it at him. "So I guess you said it all here, huh? Kind of lame if you ask me."

Narrowing his eyes, he took the letter and read it. "What the hell is this?"

"I was hoping you'd tell me."

He shoved the letter right back at me. "What? You think I wrote it? Why would I do that?" he asked incredulously, eyes wide and full of anger. "If I was going to threaten you, it wouldn't be in a fucking letter. How do I know you didn't write it so you could blame it on me? Then Kate would think I was some kind of psycho."

"Sorry, but that's not my style. I wasn't planning on telling her, but if this shit happens again I'm coming straight for you."

Shaking his head, Luke chuckled and stalked closer. He was about two inches shorter than me, and I had to admit he had some serious balls to step up to me. "Is that supposed to scare me, douchebag? What are you going to do when you find me, *try* to kick my ass?"

It was my turn to smile down at him. "Why don't you write another note and find out?"

We stared each other down for a minute before the sound of Lara's laugh echoed across the yard; we quickly stepped back. Kate knew something was up because she glared at us both as she walked toward us.

"Everything okay?" she asked.

Luke was the first one to answer. "Yep, but now I need to prepare for the race. You ready?" He took her hand and thought she'd follow along with him, but she stood firm.

"I'll join you in just a minute. I need to talk to Cooper for a second."

Gritting his teeth, Luke narrowed his eyes at me and huffed before turning on his heel and stalking off. Over his shoulder, he growled, "Fine, you know where to find me."

"Luke, don't be like that," Kate yelled back at him. He kept walking as if he didn't hear her. I guess I couldn't blame the guy for wanting to sulk; he knew what her choice was because I could see it in his eyes. I'd be pretty pissed if Kate chose him over me.

Looking uncomfortable, Lara backed away from us and waved, heading in the direction Luke stalked off to. "And I'm just going to disappear, too. I'll be around if you need me."

Once Lara was out of earshot, Kate crossed her arms at her chest and grinned. "So Lara's your date for the night, huh? Why didn't you tell me?"

"Why? Are you jealous?" I teased.

She laughed and shook her head. "Maybe. Although, I do have to say that I'm really happy you're not with Lindsey."

Yeah, me too.

"Oh yeah, so what was it you wanted to talk to me about? You said it was important. Did you falter on your meds?" she asked quietly.

Taking her hand, I looked down at her and smiled. "No, I think I'm fine with that. I'm pretty sure I can stop taking them now and be okay."

"Cooper, don't do that," she warned. "You may feel great, but you have to do this slowly. Your withdrawal symptoms are minor right now, but if you stop them cold like that your symptoms will be brutal. I'm surprised you're not having more issues than what you've had."

It's because I have you, I wanted to say. Being addicted to her was a better drug than any pain killer.

"Actually, I wanted to make sure you were free tomorrow. I have somewhere I have to be and I want you to go."

"Where?" she asked curiously.

I looked around at everyone close by and knew it would be risky to even mention it. "I can't tell you here, but as soon as we get you back home I'll explain. Will you be able to spend the day with me tomorrow?"

Mischievously, she smiled and shrugged her shoulders. "I think I could probably say yes if you tell me what you and Luke were arguing about. It wasn't about me, was it?"

Sighing, I moved closer and gazed down into her stormy gray eyes. "Not exactly, but if you want the truth I think your name was brought up at least once."

She groaned and hung her head. "I knew I should've just called off the date with him. He's been my friend for so long, it's hard to say no to him sometimes. When I was still depressed over everything that happened, he was one of the people I could always count on to bring a smile to my face."

"You don't have to explain it to me; I understand," I told her. "But you're not planning on anymore dates with him, are you?"

Shaking her head, she laughed and reached for my hands. "No, no more dates. I wouldn't exactly call what we're doing a date either. I think he knows it's a losing battle."

I wasn't too sure of that.

"Do you think we'll get in trouble if I kiss you right now?" I asked huskily.

She bit her lip and peered at everyone all around us. Luke wasn't in sight, but that didn't mean he wasn't watching. "Probably, so we might want to be careful what we do out here in front of everyone."

Lifting my hands to her cheeks, I swept her golden blonde hair away from her shoulders and smirked. The strapless, white sundress she wore showed off her bare shoulders and it just so happened that she still had a few bite marks on her skin from last night. I smoothed my fingers over them and a raspy moan escaped her lips. My cock got hard just listening to it; it brought back memories of the night before.

"I see you found the marks you left behind last night," she teased.

"They look good on you. How about I put a little more?"

Lifting up on her toes, she put her hands on my shoulders and rubbed her body against my dick while whispering into my ear, "Follow me then.

Chapter 19

Kate

The moment Cooper's eyes found me, I knew … I could feel it. When I turned around and saw him walking toward me—his blue eyes focused solely on me with a smirk on his face, dressed in a pair of jeans and a black T-shirt—I knew I was going to be in some trouble. My insides lit up like fire and immediately my clit throbbed in remembrance of last night. He said he was addicted to me, but I had a feeling I was slowly growing addicted to him. That had never happened to me before.

I had no idea Cooper could surprise me anymore than he already had. Not bringing Lindsey to the party because of me was something I didn't expect. If anything, I figured he'd want to bring her since I was there with another man. You would think most guys would do that … but not him. Luke would have, though. That was what made Cooper different from the rest. All of my preconceived notions about what he was like from the newspapers weren't what he was like at all.

When we got inside of the house, it was pretty much

vacant except for a few people here and there. No one no-ticed me and Cooper sneaking off down the long hallway. As soon as we were out of sight, Cooper trapped me against the wall and quickly lowered his lips to mine, hard and aggressive.

"I wanted to do this the moment I saw you tonight," he growled, biting my lip. His hands came around my back and grabbed my ass underneath my dress, squeezing it tight.

"We can't do it here," I exclaimed. "We're almost there."

I wasn't about to take him to one of the bedrooms be-cause that would be the first place someone would look. Instead, there was a room at the far end of the house that hadn't been finished yet. My brother didn't know what to do with it, so he kept it empty until he decided.

When we got into the room, I shut the door and looked around. Yep, it was still the same; empty with cream colored walls and beige carpet. Once I locked the door that was all it took for Cooper to descend on me again. "We probably need to do this quick," I advised.

With my arms around his shoulders, Cooper picked me up in his arms and I straddled his waist before he pushed me against the wall. "Trust me, love. I can do this hard and quick."

Once his jeans fell to the floor, he grabbed the backs of my thighs and slid my underwear over so he could slip a finger inside of me; he moaned in delight.

"I think you're already ready for me."

"I was ready for you the moment I saw you," I mur-mured huskily.

Sliding my dress down over my breasts, Cooper lowered his lips to one and sucked, moaning deep in his throat. My hips moved against him on their own accord and I tried to lift up so I could get him inside of me.

I didn't have to wait long because he gripped my hips and slammed into me, thrusting hard. I yelped at first from the sheer pain and pleasure of it, but it felt so damn good I didn't want it to stop.

"Harder, Cooper."

He chuckled in my ear and picked up his pace. "Like that, love?"

"Oh yeah," I breathed.

My heart pounded in my ears as the adrenaline of doing something wild and crazy overtook me body and soul. Never have I wanted to do anything reckless or in the spur of a moment. I liked things planned and orderly. Not with Cooper, though. With him I wanted to feel the emotions again … I wanted to feel the pleasure of a man's touch and not feel guilty about it. Most of all, I wanted to feel alive, and with Cooper that was what he made me feel … *alive*.

We needed to hurry, but I wanted to hold off my orgasm for as long as I could. It felt so good I didn't want our tryst to end, but it was easier said than done.

"You're getting tight, love. Let it go so I can come inside of you," he ordered, his voice low and heated.

Gripping his shoulders, I held on tight as my body tightened around his cock and sent me over the edge. To muffle my screams, Cooper closed his lips over mine just as he too gave in to the pleasure of our lovemaking. He held me firmly down on his body until I could feel the last remnants of his release spurting inside of me.

Breathing hard, he kissed me and bit my lip while slowly lifting me up and setting me down on the floor. My legs were like Jell-O, so I slid down the wall to a sitting position while Cooper lifted his jeans and knelt in front of me. Thankfully, the room was carpeted so I didn't have to worry about cold, hardwood floors against my ass.

"I take it you liked that?" he asked, fixing the top of my dress to cover up my breasts.

I smiled lazily. "No ... I loved it."

Taking my hands, Cooper pulled me to my feet and then buttoned his jeans with a melancholy look on his face. "Since we're alone, I'll go ahead and tell you about tomorrow. My family's coming into town and I would like for you to be there with me."

"Why am I sensing that you're not happy about that?" I asked.

"It's because I'm not. My mother and father aren't exactly the easiest two people to get along with. If I do something right there's always something else that I do wrong. I could never please them, so I gave up trying."

I couldn't imagine living like that. My parents were always supportive and they still were. I didn't see them much, but I at least tried to call them a couple of times a week.

"Is it just going to be your mother and father tomorrow? Are they staying at your house while they're in town?"

"No," he answered, glancing down at the floor. "They're staying at my uncle's house. That's where we will be going tomorrow afternoon."

His uncle's house?

"I didn't know you had family in North Carolina? Why didn't you tell me?"

"Because," he murmured softly, "it's not something

everyone needs to know. I'm only telling you because I trust you."

"What is he? Our mayor or something?" I teased.

"No, he's much closer to you than that … he's our coach. Joel is my uncle."

Eyes wide, I stood there and stared. I definitely didn't see that coming.

"So now that you know I'm sure you can figure out the rest. Needless to say, my career was over until my uncle pulled some strings and got me on the team. Without him, I'd be sitting on my ass drugged out of my mind and drunk." He paused for a second and blew out a sigh. "Also, without him, I would have never met you. I owe him so much."

Taking his face in my hands, I kissed his lips softly and felt his arms snake around my waist, his deep blue gaze melting me where I stood. "I owe him a lot, too. I'll be happy to go with you tomorrow, not only because you asked, but because I want to. Your parents may not see all of your accomplishments and support you, but you'll never have to worry about that with me. I'm on your side … always."

His lips turned up into a devilish smirk. "That's what I like to hear. All right, love, we need to get back before our dates come searching for us. Lara and I will follow you and Luke back, and then I can come stay with you if you want."

"I'd like that," I said as he opened the door.

But first, I needed to talk to Luke.

Luke was quiet the whole car ride home and I knew it was because Cooper and Lara were close on our tail. It almost felt like something was going on that I didn't know about. It wasn't until we pulled into my driveway that Luke finally spoke, "Tonight wasn't exactly what I thought our date would be like. There's no use in fighting, is there?"

Luke turned his emerald green gaze my way, and for the first time ever I didn't see any humor in his expression. "I'm so sorry, Luke. I guess it just wasn't meant to be."

Sighing, he leaned over and kissed me on the cheek. "Are you absolutely sure this is what you want? You don't even know this guy. You've known me for years."

"It's not always about that," I said. "Sometimes things just happen."

He scoffed, "Yeah, and sometimes things change."

"What's that supposed to mean?"

Luke shook his head and sighed. "Nothing, Kate. I'll get over it eventually." Taking my hand, he kissed it and let go. "I'll be around if you ever need me."

My heart ached for him because he *was* my friend and I'd hurt him. He was Luke Collins, though. He'd be back in the playing field before tomorrow.

Chapter 20

COOPER

Each second we got closer to my uncle's house, the more I regretted ever even considering letting Kate join me. She already knew a lot from what she'd read in the papers, but there was so much more that only certain people knew ... those people happened to be my family, especially my parents. They had no qualms about rehashing them all with me, but I could only pray they showed some manners with having Kate there.

My family had always been accustomed to money and success. One way or another, whether it be in business or sports, each generation had all excelled in something. I was the first one to put that legacy in jeopardy.

"Cooper, are you okay?" Kate asked, placing her hand on my leg.

Taking her hand, I lifted it to my lips and kissed her knuckles, one by one. "Yeah, I'm fine. You know, it's not too late to take you back home."

She scoffed, "Please, I can handle your parents, Cooper. Honestly, how bad can it be?"

"You have no idea," I grumbled.

If she only knew how fucked up they were. Other than my uncle, I didn't really know much of my family on the eastern side of the United States. They were scattered from Virginia all the way down to Florida.

"Well, if it gets too bad we can tell your parents to go to hell and leave, right?" she asked. "They can't expect to make you feel inferior and you sit there and take it. I'm sure you love your parents, but I for one am not going to listen to them downgrade you."

"So you don't care if they approve of you or not?" I asked curiously.

She shook her head. "No, I don't. The only person that I want to approve of me is you. Would you care if my parents didn't like you?"

"Actually, I would," I replied. "If they didn't it wouldn't be the end of the world, but it'd be nice to know they thought I was worthy of you. Do you think you'll ever introduce me to them?"

Smiling, she tilted her head the side and bit her lip. "Hmm … we'll see. I'll think about it and let you know. They retired and moved to a cabin in the mountains, so it's not like I get to see them that much. I'm pretty sure they'd like you."

Kate looked amazing in her little blue sundress and her golden hair in waves down her back. As far as looks went, she would definitely be accepted by my family, but Kate didn't come from wealth. My mother would see Kate as being after only one thing … my money. The only woman they'd ever accepted was Claire. Then again, I'd never been serious about another woman since her; hence, the reason why they'd never met anyone else.

When we pulled up to my uncle's house, there were about fifteen cars parked in and around the massive sized yard. I could hear them all laughing in the backyard, so after taking a few deep breaths, Kate and I walked down the path that led straight to them.

Please don't let my family screw things up, I mumbled silently to myself.

Opening the gate, I walked through first with Kate following along behind me. Joel had a massive sized pool where a handful of kids and teenagers, who were most likely my cousins, were swimming while the adults all congregated on the deck, eating and drinking.

My mother was up there chatting away with a lady who I had no idea who she was. In fact, I didn't recognize anyone other than my parents and my aunt Sadie; she was my uncle's wife, and she always reminded me of Catherine Zeta-Jones. She used to love it when I'd tell her that.

"Are all of these people your family?" Kate asked.

Putting my hand on her back, I slowly led her across the yard. "I think so. I don't recognize a lot of them, but then again I hadn't seen my family on this side of the country in years."

"Which ones are your parents?"

I pointed in the direction of my mother and father. "Okay, the woman with the short, brown hair and wearing the yellow top is my mother. She may look sweet, but she's not. My father is the man beside her with the gray hair, wearing the green polo shirt. As far as sports go, his father was the grandfather I told you about that got me into football. My father, on the other hand, pursued a career in golf. It's strange because I can't play golf worth a damn."

"Well, if it makes you feel better I can't play it either," she laughed. "Both of my parents play, but I was never coordinated enough to get it. The only sport I was good at was track. I love to run. Now is your uncle Joel your mom's brother or your dad's?"

"My dad's," I told her. "Can't you see the resemblance?"

"Cooper, darling," my mother interrupted, holding out her arms to give me a hug.

She wrapped her small arms around me and squeezed tight. "Mother, it's good to see you," I lied. "How long are you in town for?"

She smiled and glanced over at Kate. "Your father and I will be here until tomorrow night. Who's your lady friend?"

Before I could introduce Kate, she did it herself. Holding out her hand, she grinned and said, "Hi, I'm Kate. It's nice to meet you."

"A friend, huh?" my mother chimed, taking her hand. "Well, Kate, my name's Jackie. Joel told us Cooper was bringing a friend, and I must say I'm kind of shocked because he doesn't really do the friend thing." She batted her eyes and glanced up at me smugly. "Shall we go say hello to everyone else?"

"Lead the way," I told her through gritted teeth.

Kate squeezed my arm and leaned in closer. "Just breathe, Cooper. I'm not taking anything she says to heart."

Everyone up on the deck smiled and greeted us warmly as we approached, including my father. "Son, it's good to see you. You were amazing in the game yesterday."

"Thank you, but the majority of the success was with

144

the whole team." Putting my arm around Kate, I nodded over at my father. "Kate, I'd like you to meet my father, Richard."

Kate smiled and held out her hand. "It's nice to meet you, Mr. Davis."

"Likewise," he said, taking her hand, "but please … call me Richard."

"All right, everyone, the food's ready," Joel shouted, taking the chicken and steak off of the grill. When he saw me and Kate, he waved the tongs in the air. "Thank you for coming you two. It's been a never ending party here since last night after the win."

"I'll bet," Kate shouted happily. Starting the season out with a win had to be a good feeling for him. With Evan and the other members of the team, I was surprised they hadn't had much success with winning; they were all great athletes.

At the tables, I pulled out a chair for Kate to sit and took the one beside her. My parents both sat down across from us, staring curiously back and forth. "So, Kate what do you do for the team? Joel didn't specify. Are you one of the cheerleaders?" my mother asked.

Kate smiled even though I knew she hated it when people thought she was one of the cheerleaders. "No, I'm not a cheerleader. I'm one of the team physicians, Mrs. Davis. I've been working with Cooper to help manage his shoulder injury. I think he's one step away from being perfectly healed."

Lifting her brows, my mother pursed her lips and glared at me. I knew exactly what she was thinking, and by the look in her eyes she assumed I was up to my old tricks.

"And you and my son are just … friends? Is there not

a policy about relations between the staff and the players?"

Before Kate or I could say anything, Joel took a seat at our table and cut in, "Actually, I've never enforced such a thing because I feel my staff and my players are adult enough to handle their own personal lives. Second, Kate has been helping Cooper by doing physical therapy exercises for his shoulder. It's not what you're thinking."

"So it's not like last time?" she asked, glaring at me.

"No, it's not," I hissed low. "Things aren't like that here."

"Well, I sure hope not. I would hate to see you ruin someone else's life. Hopefully, this one is smarter than the other."

Out of the corner of my eye, Kate's head immediately turned my way. Her unease was palpable, and I could feel a black cloud settling over me. I thought my parents would have seen the change in me, but obviously they were too oblivious. Why the hell did I even try to make them happy, to make them proud of me? It was never going to be enough.

The truth is … I honestly didn't give a fuck anymore.

Rising from my seat, I didn't say a word as I took one last look at my mother and father before turning my back on them. I wasn't going to argue, and I sure as hell wasn't going to fight with them. I was done hoping they'd somehow see the good in me. I had changed for the better, and it was all because of Kate … and being away from them. Joel was my family now, and as long as I had Kate, I had everything I needed.

My parents could go to hell.

Chapter 21

Kate

After what Cooper's mother said, I literally thought he'd lose it, especially after the week he had with lowering his pill dosage. Instead, he stood up quietly and turned his back before walking out of the gate and up to the front of the house.

"Cooper! Come back," Joel shouted, getting up from the table. Cooper kept going, so I took that as my cue to leave as well.

"Kate, I am so sorry for this," he apologized. "I'm the one who thought he should come. I should've known better."

Jackie scoffed, "Please, he's just sulking. He'll come back." She smiled over at me as if she didn't just put down her own son right in front of me; like it was no big deal. "Do you mind bringing him back, dear? I'm sure he'll listen to you."

All manners aside, there was no way I could be civil to that woman after what she just did. Scooting the chair back, I got to my feet and glared at her. "I'm sorry, Mrs.

Davis, but I'm not going to do that. Cooper's a great man and he works hard. I've seen some of the struggles he's gone through, and I've been watching him work past them. The last thing I'm going to do is sit here and listen to you belittle him."

To Joel, I turned and smiled. "Thank you for letting me come, Joel. I'm sorry we couldn't stay longer."

Joel nodded, and turned a lethal glare to Jackie. "I understand Kate. Next time, I'll invite you and my nephew over when we have fewer guests."

Turning on my heel, I stalked off toward the gate. "Don't you even want to know what happened to the last doctor my son screwed around with?" his mother yelled.

I almost faltered—my heart thundering in my chest—but my pace didn't slow and I kept going. "No, I don't," I shouted back. "And if did, I wouldn't want to hear it from you."

What the hell was she talking about?

As soon as I stormed through the gate, hidden from prying eyes, Cooper pulled me into his arms and crushed his lips to mine. I melted into his embrace and held on tight, but when he let go, his gaze was unsure, guarded.

"I'm so sorry for bringing you here, Kate. Thank you for what you said. I just wanted to make sure I kissed you before I took you home."

"Why is that?" I asked. "You couldn't wait that long?"

He held my face in his hands and sighed. "No, it's because there's something I need to tell you and I don't know how you're going to handle it."

"Is it about what your mother just said?"

Nodding, he took my hand and led me up the path to

his car. "It's not something I'm proud of, and I had hoped you wouldn't find out this way."

The look in his eyes scared me. I knew he had skeletons in his closet, just like everyone, but something in his gaze had me worried. *It couldn't be that bad, could it?*

"Okay," I drawled out slowly, "but let's get out of here. I really don't want to see your mother again because if I do I'm liable to lose the southern charm you love so much about me."

"I think I'd like to see that," he admitted with a gleam in his eye. "My mother hasn't had someone put her in her place in a really long time. Not even my father stands up to her. I wanted to tell her to fuck off so bad, but I didn't."

Quickly, we both got into his car so we could leave before anyone tried to stop us. "Why not?" I asked. "If my mother talked to me like that just to be a bitch, you better believe I'd put her in her place. There's such a thing as equal respect. You're an adult and you need to be treated as such. Just because she's your mother doesn't give her the right to treat you as someone of less importance."

As soon as Cooper backed out of the driveway, we both breathed a sigh of relief, glad to be away from there. Every time I tried to say something, his phone would ring. Obviously annoyed, he shut it off and angrily threw it in the backseat. "Kate, before I tell you anything I want you to do something with me. It's something that I should've done from the beginning."

"Sure," I replied nervously. He wouldn't look at me, which made me even more nervous. "It's not *that* bad, is it?"

He nodded and finally glanced over at me. "Kind of. There are a lot of things I've done that I shouldn't have, and I regret every single second of what I did. I just don't want you to see me differently, and I'm so afraid you will."

"Cooper," I whispered, taking his hand that was balled in a tight fist. "It'll be okay. Nobody is perfect and we all make mistakes. I don't scare so easily."

Ten minutes later, Cooper turned down our street. Instead of taking me home, he stopped at his house. He didn't say a word as he opened his garage and pulled his car inside. His garage had a bunch of boxes piled in the corner, but other than that there wasn't much else. Since he hadn't been in town long, I figured he hadn't had time to unpack.

When I got out of his car, Cooper saw me looking at the boxes and said, "I haven't really spent much time unpacking. You'll see what I mean when you come inside. One day I'll get to it."

"Yeah, if you stop spending all of your time with me," I teased. "Do you want me to help you?"

Before he opened the door, he turned to me and placed his hand on my cheek. "I would love for you to, but first you need to decide if it's something you *want* to do."

The door he led me through opened up to his kitchen, which seemed to be fairly unpacked. There were boxes stacked on one side of the counter, but he at least had a basket full of fruit and some of his appliances set out on display. His living room was the same way, with boxes here and there, but he didn't stop to let me see. Instead, he led me up the stairs on down the hallway until we reached his bedroom.

Inside, he had a king-sized bed with a navy blue comforter and pillows, and the room smelled just like him, all masculine and woodsy. "Okay, what I'm about to show you is going to come as a shock, so please don't freak out on me."

Hesitantly, he walked over to a set of dressers and pulled out one of the drawers. Carrying it over to the bed, he flipped it upside down. I couldn't even begin to describe what I felt in that next moment. I was confused, shocked beyond belief. Bottle after bottle of painkillers toppled out of the drawer and onto his bed; it had to be at least a hundred bottles or so of nothing but little white pills.

"Oh my God," I choked, putting a hand over my mouth. "How did you get all of this? Or better yet, why do you have all of this?"

I picked up one of the bottles; it was filled to the hilt with hundreds of pills. There had to be thousands among thousands of them in his grasp. Cooper picked up one of the bottles and took it to his bathroom. Breathing heavily, he opened it up and slowly tilted it, letting each and every pill fall into the toilet.

"Before I tell you what happened, I need you to know that I'm not going to make excuses. I was stupid and there was a time when I sunk to a new low. The story was kept out of the papers because I spent a lot of money keeping it secret."

Bottle after bottle, I watched Cooper take them into the bathroom and flush its contents, his face a stony mask of regret. "Cooper, just tell me," I begged. "I don't like seeing you like this."

Angrily, he grabbed a few more bottles and dumped them. "The doctor my mom referred to was a woman I was fucking, Kate. She lost her medical license because of what we did."

"What did you do?" I asked nervously.

Swallowing hard, he flushed another bottle of pills and came to kneel before me, his voice pained and raw. "The deal was that if I slept with her she'd give me a bottle of pills. It was payment for what I did for her."

Eyes wide, I gasped and glanced at all the bottles, then up to him. "Holy shit," I cried.

"Yes, I know, you don't have to say it," he said, cutting me off before I could say anything else. "It's disgusting and I'm sure you're wondering why the hell I did it?"

Grabbing a few more bottles, he held them in his hand—his chest heaving up and down in anger—and it was like everything within him finally snapped. His arm reared back and he threw them against the wall, hard, scattering pills everywhere. I yelped, jumping back in surprise. Turning his back on me, he faced the window and fisted his hands in his hair.

"All I wanted was the pills, Kate. At that time in my life everything was a fucking disaster. The girl I thought I'd spend the rest of my life with left me for someone else, and then not long after that I got injured. You saw what my parents are like, so you know they weren't supportive. All they cared about was when I'd get better to get back on the field. When Oakland didn't want me anymore, that was the last straw. The pain meds helped me cope with it all."

"Who was your doctor?" I asked. "How did you even get that set up to exchange pills for sex?"

Releasing a heavy sigh, Cooper sat on the edge of the bed and kept his back to me. "I'm not going anywhere, Cooper," I promised. "Just answer the questions." When he didn't say anything, I got up and stood in front of him, tilting up his head with a hand to his cheek.

His blue gaze penetrated mine … so sad and distraught. "Are you sure I haven't scared you off yet?"

"Not yet," I answered wholeheartedly. "It takes a lot more than that to scare me off."

He scoffed, "Well, sit tight because I'm not done yet. My doctor had been my regular physician for years. She was a friend of my parents, and I knew a lot about her personal life. I knew she had problems with her husband, so one day when I was getting low on pills I decided to seduce her. I didn't want to, but I knew she'd give in. Over time I used my advantage with her to ask for the pills. Her husband eventually found out and turned her in, along with filing for a divorce as well. So needless to say, she lost her license and her husband all in one day. When he threatened to go to the press, I paid him off … and her along with him."

Lowering his gaze, he took my hands and kissed them gently. "That's what happened, Kate. As of tonight, I'm not taking any more of these pills. I don't care what kind of withdrawals I go through. I just want this part of my life over."

"You know what will happen if you do that. It's not going to be easy, Cooper," I replied, trying to reason with him. "It's not a smart thing to do."

"I don't care, Kate. It needs to stop … now."

There were still tons of bottles on his bed, so I took a deep breath and picked one up, taking it to the bathroom. "What are you doing?" he asked.

Dumping the pills into the toilet, I threw away the bottle and grabbed another one. "I'm helping you, Cooper, because that's what I want to do. I'm not going anywhere.

If this is what you really want to do, then you're going to need as much support as you can. I'm not going to leave you."

Cooper jumped to his feet and wrapped his strong arms tightly around my body. "You have no idea how much this means to me, Kate. I don't understand why you're even doing it. You deserve someone so much better."

Leaning up on my tiptoes, I closed my eyes and kissed him gently on the lips. "I deserve you, Cooper. I thought it would be quite obvious why I'm helping you. You should already know why."

"Yes … but one day I want to hear you say it."

Chapter 22

Kate

The next morning was brutal.

I knew something was wrong when I woke up drenched in not my sweat, but Cooper's. He lay there shivering, but his skin was warm to the touch. He had already gone through some symptoms last week with reducing his medication, but it was nowhere near what he was experiencing now. I had no idea how long it was going to be like that either.

"Cooper," I murmured, wiping the dampened hair off of his forehead. His eyes were closed, but I knew he was awake. Wrapping my arm around his stomach I kissed his bare bicep and rested my cheek against his skin. "Cooper, you can do this. You just have to work through it. I know it feels like you're sick, and I'm sure you're body hurts like hell, but it *will* pass. The best thing to do is to keep busy and keep your mind clear."

"How … long … will this last?" he muttered, his teeth chattering as he spoke.

"It all depends. The symptoms can last from five to

ten days."

Groaning, he sat up in bed and put his head in his hands. "Fuck! How am I going to do this? I didn't realize it was going to be this hard."

Last night, I wanted to tell him how difficult it was going to be, but I didn't want to discourage him. He had been so hell bent on stopping that I had no choice but to support him. Taking Cooper's hands, I pulled them away from his face and kissed his lips. "I have faith in you, Cooper Davis. You're the NFL's star quarterback, and not to mention, you're one hell of a star in bed. There's nothing you can't do, and nothing you can't overcome. This is your chance to prove everyone wrong … like your parents. Show them that nothing can bring you down and that you *will* succeed."

Squeezing my hands, he glanced up at me with his crystal blue gaze. "You believe in me that much?"

I nodded. "And I always will. Right now, you need to get ready for practice. I'll be there every step of the way."

"What if I can't do this, Kate? I feel like complete and utter shit, and all I want to do right now is hit something. I feel angry, agitated. My teeth hurt from gritting them so hard and my heart is pounding so fast it feels like it's going to explode." He closed his eyes and hung his head. "What if I do something to hurt you? There's so many things going through my mind right now, and none of it's good."

"Like what kinds of things?" I asked nervously. "The only way you're going to hurt me is if you do something to hurt yourself."

"It's nothing like that, Kate."

"Then what is it? You know you can tell me."

Aggression and agitation were two of the main side effects to withdrawals, and I could see it in the tenseness in his body that his concerns were not of hurting himself … but actually hurting me.

Slowly, Cooper lifted his head, his eyes feral and possessive as he trailed them down my body. I swallowed hard and licked my lips, my heart thundering in my chest. "Are you sure you want to know?" he growled, pushing me back onto the bed.

When I nodded, he spread my legs with his knees and pushed his hard cock against me. Looking down at my breasts, he bit his lip and squeezed my breast hard, making my nipple pucker. "Seeing you in my shirt and in my bed makes me so fucking horny I can't stand it. I know you're mine, but all I want to do is fuck you so hard that you won't want to think about another man. I want to see my marks on that perfect skin of yours, I want to flip you around and grab a handful of your hair while I fuck you from behind."

Groaning, he sat up on his knees and angrily fisted his hands in his hair. When he looked down at me his eyes were wild, feral. "You see, Kate. I feel the angst inside of me and all I can focus on is fucking you senseless. I don't want to hurt you, but the longer you're here the more I want you. Maybe it's best that you leave."

I wasn't afraid of Cooper, but there was one thing I knew for certain … he wouldn't hurt me. The stuff going through his head would subside, and in a man with his sexual nature I knew it would only intensify once he got off the pills. Pain pills were known to subdue the libido, and now that it was out of his system it would no longer be a hindrance. It wasn't a hindrance before; except now it was a whole new ball game.

I would do anything to help him, and if it meant letting him have his way with me then I'd let him. "I'm not leaving you, Cooper. If you want me, then take me. There's one thing about me that you may not know … I don't break easily. Do what you have to do to get your mind off of everything. If that means you have to have sex with me ten times a day then so be it."

For once, a smile spread across his face, but it didn't last long. "You're serious, aren't you?"

Now it was my turn to push him down on the bed. I lifted the shirt off my body and tossed it onto the floor, along with my underwear. The tip of his cock protruded out of his boxers, so I grabbed him firmly with my hand and flicked my tongue across it.

"Does this answer your question?"

Fisting his hands in my hair, he held on tight as I sucked him hard, moving my mouth up and down the length of his cock. A little rough sex wouldn't hurt, and if I was truly honest with myself I was actually kind of looking forward to it.

Chapter 23

Kate

Five Days Later

The past few days went by in a blur. It was almost as if Cooper's mind was in another world, struggling to come back. I didn't know what I was bargaining for when I agreed to this, but it was all worth it to see the smile on his face when he slipped out of bed this morning. My Cooper was back, and it was over.

"Love, you awake up there?" Cooper yelled from downstairs. "Breakfast is almost ready."

While he'd slept during the past couple of days, I'd snuck off to my house to grab some clean clothes and document everything that happened in my notebook. From the way he woke up this morning all happy and relaxed, I started to believe that he *did* let his mind retreat to another place. During practice, everyone thought he was sick. They'd kept their distance, and even threatened to kick his ass if he didn't go home and get rest. I didn't dare tell anyone what was going on, not even my brother or Joel.

Thankfully, I was going to be able to put the ending words in my notebook: *Mission Accomplished.*

Putting on one of my long-sleeved T-shirts and pajama pants, I quickly used the bathroom and washed my face … only to gasp when I looked at myself in the mirror. Even though it felt good while Cooper did it, I had red marks all up my neck from the stubble of his beard. He hadn't shaved all week, but I prayed the redness went away before the game tonight. September had finally come, but it was still hot outside and the last thing I wanted to do was wear a turtleneck. I had makeup, but I didn't exactly want to douse my neck in foundation.

The marks on my arms and legs were another story. I had hoped they would go away before he saw them, but now that he was back to normal I knew he would see them if he got me into bed. When I got downstairs, Cooper smiled and scooped me up into his arms. My body was so sore I cringed, but bit my lip to hold in the gasp.

"Thank you for standing by me this week, Kate. I can't tell you how much it means to me. I'll admit, it's all kind of a haze and I don't remember too much, but in the center of it all you were there. Your voice was what I heard."

"Well, I told you I wouldn't leave you," I replied wholeheartedly. "Do you think you're ready for the game this afternoon?"

Cooper scoffed, "Of course, I am! Except I wanted to ask you if you wouldn't mind if we skipped the after party tonight. I know this week had to be hard on you, and I thought it would be a good idea if I made it up to you."

"What did you have in mind?" I asked, smiling from ear to ear.

"Well, I was thinking that since we hadn't been out on an official date since we started seeing each other, I figured it was time we let the world know we're together. Are you ready for that?"

"Only if you are," I teased. "You know that if your women fans see us together you might lose some of them. When you're not accessible you're not as appealing to them anymore."

He gazed at me incredulously. "I don't care about that, Kate. I don't want any other woman … I want you. I want them all to know that you're mine. Now let's eat and get ready for the game so I can show you off."

"Shouldn't it be the other way around? I'm not anything worth showing off, Cooper. I'm not like the models or the rich girls you were seen with out in California. You're probably going to get hell for being with me."

"No, I'm not," he scoffed. "If anything, *you* are going to get hell. That's why I want to make sure this is what you want before we start really going public. This is your chance to turn back."

I leaned up to kiss him gently on the lips. "I told you before and I'll tell you again … I'm not going anywhere." That was a promise.

Chapter 24

COOPER

For once in my life I wasn't in any pain. My shoulder felt the best it had ever been since I injured it and I had Kate to thank for that. I never realized how much better I'd feel by getting clean.

We were in the locker room getting ready to run out and take the field when Evan came up beside me and said, "You look like you're feeling better today. I must admit the guys and I were worried that you'd flake out on us. You weren't looking too good this week."

"Yeah, I wasn't feeling good at all," I replied cautiously. "But I think I'm better now."

"Great! Then you and Kate can come to the party tonight. It's going to be at Derek's."

"I can't," I told him, before he could walk away. "I have plans to take your sister out tonight."

Evan had his back to me, but he turned around slowly and waltzed back over to me. "So you're choosing my sister over the team tonight?"

"Yes, I am. Is that a problem?"

He stared at me for a moment, but then laughed and slapped me on the arm. "Nope, not at all. There's going to be strippers at the party tonight, so I guess it's a good thing you're not going to be there. I'd hate to kick your ass for drooling over them when you have my sister, especially since Luke seems to not stop talking about her. I didn't want to ask you when you were sick because you literally looked like you could rip someone's head off, but he told me about this letter you found. You didn't write it, did you?"

"What? Hell no, I didn't write it. Kate chose me before the note even got written. Why would I even do that?" I asked incredulously.

Evan shrugged. "I don't know, but Luke says he didn't either. If he didn't then that means someone else did. I'd like to know who. Whatever's going on it involves my sister and I don't like it."

"And you believe that Luke didn't do it?" I asked.

He didn't think twice before responding, "Yes, I do. Luke can be many things, but he wouldn't lie to me about this. He was the one who came to me. Do you mind asking Kate if she thinks it could be anyone else?"

Sighing, I hung my head and closed my eyes; I knew I should have just told her. "That might be a problem. I never told her about the letter."

Evan's eyes went wide. "Why not? Luke figured that was why Kate's ignored his calls this week. He thought she was mad at him. I think she needs to know."

Now more than ever I thought so, too. If Luke wasn't the one who put the note on my car, then who did?

"I'll tell her later tonight after we go on our date," I told him. "I don't want to ruin the evening by telling her before then. Now all we need to do is figure out who put it on my car. Is there anyone else who has a thing for your sister?"

Evan shrugged. "I'm not sure. She's only ever around the team, so if it's someone who likes her it could be one of the others. Tonight after your date ask her if any of the guys have been coming on to her. It might give us an idea on who it could be."

"And if it happens to be someone on the team?" I asked.

"Then we kick his ass," he replied, cracking his knuckles, "just like we're going to do to the Seahawks this afternoon. Don't worry, though, we'll figure it all out. Right now we need to get our heads in the game."

Easier said than done when I wanted answers.

The time had come for the game, and now a new worry had fallen in my lap. I hadn't thought more on the note until now, and as I watched each and every single player walk out of the locker room, I couldn't imagine that one of them would stab me in the back. If there was one thing I knew for certain, I had to keep my eyes open.

We were up by six points in the fourth quarter with only one minute left to spare. It was anyone's game so we couldn't celebrate yet. The call was for me to reverse the play to our running back and have him pass it off to Evan. The only problem I had with that play was that there was too much room for error. My uncle was going to kick my ass, but I had to go with my instinct.

Our full back, Ashton Blake, was one of the fastest runners we had, and that was what I needed at the moment. If we went with our current running back and counted on him to pass the ball to Evan we'd be screwed. I would rather just pass the ball to Evan myself and be done with it, but the Seahawks knew that Evan was my prime choice. I had to switch it up.

"It's coming to you, Ash," I whispered low as I passed him to get into position.

He nodded once and I knew I only had one chance to make this play. Once into position, I glanced at our line quickly and yelled, "Blue 24, Blue 24, Hut, Hut, Hike!"

The second the ball snapped to me, I waited for Ashton to get in the clear, blocking out the yells Joel spat my way. Once I threw it, I didn't get to see Ashton catch it because the moment the ball left my fingers my body slammed into the ground by a giant Seahawk tackling me to the ground. The breath was knocked out of my lungs and they burned as I gasped for air.

What the fuck? That hurt.

Screams and cheers erupted through the stands, and when I turned my head to look at the score I hollered as well. As soon as the other player got off of me, I jumped to my feet and ran down the field toward Ashton. All of the players surrounded him, including my uncle who was ecstatic and cheering along. Kate, however, ran toward me.

"Cooper, are you okay? How's your shoulder?" she asked worriedly.

Lifting her in my arms, I held her tight and kissed her. "It's doing great. Don't worry about me, love."

She laughed and shook her head. "I don't know about that just yet. Joel wasn't too happy with the play change."

We both turned to look at Joel who had the biggest grin on his face. "Well, maybe he's happy now, but just a few minutes ago he was pissed."

Taking her hand, I pulled her along beside me and off the field. "Well, how about we get out of here before he has a chance to yell at me. That could take all night, and I promised to take you out on our first date. I can't have him ruining that."

Kate looked back at the screaming mass on the field and picked up her pace. "I agree … let's go!"

Chapter 25

Kate

While I changed for our date, Cooper stayed downstairs and watched television. After about twenty minutes of rummaging through my clothes, I settled on a thin, white long-sleeved lacy top that was still summer looking but perfect for September. The bruises on my wrists were close to being gone, but I wanted to keep them covered for a little bit longer. Tonight once we got back I just had to make sure the room was a little dark before we had our fun in the bedroom.

If Cooper saw them I knew it would tear him apart to know that he hurt me even though it didn't actually *hurt* me. Hastily, I picked out the skirt I wanted to wear and danced around my room in my bra and underwear, singing my favorite Bruno Mars song. Thankfully, Cooper was downstairs with the television on so I knew he couldn't hear me.

However, when I turned around, my eyes went wide and I gasped. Cooper stood there, leaning against the door frame with a smile on his face. Quickly, I clasped my hands behind my back hoping to hide my wrists, but I wasn't quick enough; he saw them. His smile immediately vanished while his gaze stayed frozen on my arms, but my wrists were behind my back.

"Cooper," I whispered. "It's not as bad as it looks."

Gritting his teeth, he slowly walked toward me; cautiously, like he expected me to cower away from him. Gently, he took my face in his hands and tilted my head to each side, clenching his teeth harder with each mark he found on my body. There were a couple of places where he sucked too hard, and needless to say, it resulted in hickeys. I didn't like them being visible, but I used makeup and my hair to hide them; that was an easy fix.

His fingers grazed over my arm so lightly that it tickled, making chill bumps fan out across my skin. Once he got to my elbows, he pulled my arms out from behind my back and sighed heavily, his gaze full of agony.

"What the fuck, Kate? I did this that first night, didn't I? I knew I shouldn't have let you stay."

Dropping to his knees, he kissed both of my wrists and hung his head. "Fuck, fuck, fuck. Kate, I am so fucking sorry."

"Cooper, it's okay," I assured him. "I'm fine, I promise."

He shook his head quickly and growled, "No, you're not because if you were you wouldn't have tried to hide what I did to you. The thought of hurting you makes me so goddamned sick. I promise I'll do anything to make this up to you, just tell me what to do and I'll do it."

Slowly, I bent down on my knees and took his face in my hands. Refusing to look up at me, he kept his gaze on the floor and I soon realized why when I felt warm tears fall across my fingers.

"You already made it up to me, Cooper, by fighting your addiction. If you promise to stay clean that's all that matters. Knowing I helped you through your tough times is what's important to me. I didn't want to leave you."

Finally, Cooper gazed up at me, his eyes red and pained. "Please tell me you forgive me for this, Kate. You know I never wanted to hurt you."

"I know, and there's nothing to forgive," I whispered, tears falling down my cheeks. "I'm so proud of you for pushing through it. I know it wasn't easy."

Nodding quickly, he got to his feet and pulled me over to my bed, holding my hands gently in his. With his weary gaze on my wrists, he thumbed the bruises gently and murmured, "Do you want to know why I don't ever want to hurt you? Why it kills me that it was my hands that did this to you?"

"Why?" I whispered, holding my breath.

Sighing heavily, he lifted his gaze and placed both hands on my cheeks, wiping away my tears. "It's because I love you, Kate, and people aren't supposed to hurt the ones they love. The last thing I want is for you to hate me for what I did."

Mouth gaping open, I sucked in a ragged breath and held it while my heart beat out of control. *Oh my God, he just said he loved me!* Thankfully, I was sitting down because I wasn't expecting those words to come out of his mouth. I knew I had strong feelings for him, but I didn't realize how strong they were until now. I could never hate him, but there was one thing I knew for certain … I loved him, too.

"Cooper," I breathed, holding onto his wrists. He still

held my face in his hands and stared at me longingly, waiting for my next words. "For the longest time, I never thought I'd feel this way ever again … but I do. I love you, Cooper. I know we're not supposed to hurt the ones we love, but it's inevitable. No one's perfect, but we learn from our mistakes and we grow. This brought us closer together because you trusted me and let me see you at your lowest. It takes a lot of courage to do that."

A slow smile spread across his lips, and I leaned over and kissed him. Chuckling lightly, he teased me with his tongue, tracing my lips lightly. "So where do we go from here, love?" he asked.

With a grin on my face, I slid off the bed and put my shirt and skirt on. "I say, we go wherever it leads us, and right now we need to go on our date … I'm starving. I'm sure Lara will rush our order if we go to The Carolina Tavern."

His eyes lit with humor and he smiled. "Well, what about dessert? Will we be getting that as well? I seem to recall there being a massive selection there the other day."

"Oh, you'll get dessert," I told him, "but it's not going to be at the restaurant."

"Well, then what are we waiting for, love? Let's go."

Taking my hand, he led me out of my room and down the stairs. Even though he had a smile on his face, I could still feel the turmoil brewing underneath the surface. Hopefully, by the end of the night I could convince him enough that I was fine and that everything would be okay. I didn't want him to hurt anymore.

Chapter 26

COOPER

I wished there was a way to turn back time and do things all over again. I would've gotten my shit together and stopped taking those pills a long time ago. Kate spent all week trying to cover up what I did to her and all because she didn't want to hurt *me*. How the hell did I get so lucky as to have someone like her love me?

"You're not going to get drunk and pass out on the bathroom floor this time, are you?" I joked as we walked inside of the restaurant.

She smacked me on the arm. "Ha-ha, very funny. No, I don't plan on drinking a single thing while we're here other than sweet tea."

Just inside the door, Lara stood off to the side, surveying the dining room. When she saw me and Kate walk in, she smiled and sauntered over. "Hello, Kate, how are you? I haven't seen you in a while. Usually you come by a couple of times a week."

What was she talking about? Lara's seen Kate a lot over the past couple of weeks.

"Yes, I know," Kate replied. "I've been so busy this past week that I hadn't had a chance to come by. Are you doing well?"

"Much better, thank you." Turning to me, she grinned and held out her hand. "I take it you're Cooper Davis. I'm Summer … Lara's sister, or twin as it will. By the look on your face I figured you thought I was her."

I took her hand, but I couldn't seem to get over the fact that she *did* look exactly like Lara. They didn't talk the same, but they definitely looked the same. Sheepishly, I confessed, "Okay, yeah I thought you were her. It's nice to meet you though, Summer. I love your restaurant."

She laughed lightly. "Thank you. Lara and I get confused as each other a lot, but once you start talking to us most people realize that I'm the sane one. Lara is a little more outspoken and outgoing than I am." Fetching two menus, she motioned for us to follow her. "She's in the back so I'll grab her for you. Do you know what you want to drink?"

She led us to a table in a quiet corner and set down our menus. "I'll take a sweet tea," Kate said.

I'd never tried it, but I figured I would give it a shot. "I'll do the same."

"Have you ever drank sweet tea before?" Kate asked curiously.

I laughed. "No, but I figured I would try it since I'm living in the South now."

"Okay, you two, I'll get you your sweet teas," Summer chimed.

After she left, Kate opened her menu and looked down at the selections. "After you retire from football, do you think you'll always stay around here or would you want to move back to California?"

"I'm not sure. It all depends on what's going on in my life at the moment. Like I told you before, I can work for the West Coast branch of M&M Architectural Design, or I can actually stay in Charlotte and work for the owner that's in charge of the East Coast. Either way, I would still be working for the same company. It's just a matter of where I want to be."

She nodded as if satisfied with my answer and looked down at the menu. "What about you?" I asked. "Do you think you'll ever go back to school and finish up?"

Sighing, she glanced up at me and shrugged her shoulders. "I don't know. I would love to, but then I would have to leave the team to finish up. I love my job and I don't want to lose it."

"What about the money? Wouldn't you make so much more if you were an actual physician instead of an assistant?"

"I would, but it's never been about the money with me. I never once thought when I was growing up that I wanted to be a doctor just to earn a bunch of money. I wanted to help people, to make a difference. That's all that matters. One day I'll go back, but right now is not the time."

Summer came by and dropped off our drinks before heading to another table. I picked up my glass and stared at it for a second before taking a huge gulp. It actually wasn't that bad, maybe a little too sweet. It was going to take some getting used to, but I liked it.

"Hey, guys, how are you?" Lara asked. Wearing a white shirt and black pants she actually looked like a waitress with her hair in a ponytail and stains on the apron.

"Do you know what you want to eat? I'm sorry it took me so long to get out here to you. We're a little shorthanded."

Kate waved her off. "No worries. We were just sitting here talking anyway. I think I'll do something different tonight and try the salmon. I figured a change might do me some good."

Lara's eyes went wide when she looked over at me. "Wow, I don't know what you've done to her, but this is a first. I've tried a gazillion times to get her to eat something different. Do you know what you want?"

"What would you suggest?" I asked her. She worked at the restaurant , so she had to know what the best was.

Narrowing her eyes, she bit her lip and looked up in concentration. "Okay, let's see. I think I would have to go with the prime rib. It's amazing and our cook is fabulous. Do you want to try that?"

Taking Kate's menu, I handed them both to Lara and nodded. "Yes, please, that sounds great."

"Easy enough, guys. It'll be out shortly."

Now that I really took a good look at her, I could definitely see the difference between her and her sister. They had the same color of hair, but their eyes were different. Lara's were more wide and full of life; Summer's were gentle and sophisticated. I could definitely tell Summer was the responsible one out of the duet.

After Kate and I ate and talked about random things, it was time to head back home. "So when do you want to start unpacking your things?" Kate asked. "It'll feel more like home if you do."

I took her hand and kissed it. "I already feel at home, love. However, if you want me to unpack I'll start on it tomorrow, but of course, you'll have to help me. Maybe we could even convince Lara to help."

Kate laughed and shook her head. "You know, the first day when I dropped you off at your house, Lara told me she saw us. She asked me if I made you brownies as a housewarming present."

"And why didn't you?" I asked, lifting my brows. "That would've been very southern of you."

Slyly, she winked and grinned wide. "Oh, don't worry, you'll get your brownies. It just so happens that I have everything we'll need to make them tonight."

"Will there be whipped cream involved?"

She nodded.

"What about hot fudge?"

"Definitely," she insisted.

I didn't have to ask her about cherries because I knew what would make the perfect topping to roll around with my tongue. My cock was already hard just thinking about it.

Chapter 27

COOPER

An hour later, the brownies were in the oven while I watched Kate clean up the mixing bowls. With her back turned to me, I opened her refrigerator and took out the whipped cream and the jar of fudge.

Giggling, Kate didn't even turn around when she asked me, "What are you doing, Cooper?"

"I'm just getting things ready for my appetizer."

I put the jar of fudge in the microwave and heated it up for a few seconds so it would be warm and runny. Once that was done I'd be ready for her.

Coming up behind her, I pulled her away from the sink and turned her around. Face flushed, she smiled when she could feel my cock pushing up against her stomach. "What exactly do you want?" she asked huskily.

Without speaking, I undid the button to her skirt and let it fall to the floor before lifting her shirt gently up and over her head. "You, my love, are going to be my pre-dessert. Once I have you undressed, I'm going to lay you out on the table and taste you."

Shivering, her body broke out in chills as I undid her bra and slowly lowered her underwear to the floor. Gently, I picked her up and laid her out on her kitchen table, her golden hair fanning out behind her and over the sides.

"When am I going to get the chance to do this to you?" she teased as I fetched the chocolate and whipped cream.

"Soon, but not tonight. Tonight is all about you, love."

After shaking the can of whipped cream, I released just a tiny bit on her lips and licked it off before spreading them apart with my tongue. She moaned into my mouth and held me into place with her hands on both sides of my face.

"Are you ready for more?" I asked.

"Yes."

Her lips were red and swollen, just the way I liked them, but I had other places on her that I wanted to kiss before going back to that mouth of hers. Arching her back, she moaned when I sprayed the cold whipped cream around her breasts on down her stomach. Next, I drizzled some of the hot fudge onto her taut nipples and watched her squirm as the heat intermingled with the coldness of the cream.

Removing my shirt, I took a moment and just stared at her; the way her body curved gracefully, and the smoothness of her skin. She had a natural beauty to her that I had never seen in another woman ... and she was mine.

As soon as I leaned over and licked a portion of the whipped cream, she jumped and giggled. "I take it this is your first time being splayed out on your table?" I teased.

"Um … yes. I'm not really experienced when it comes to this kind of stuff."

Chuckling low, I swiped my tongue across her chocolaty nipple and groaned, "Well, it looks like I'm going to have to change that."

Her breathing picked up faster the more I teased her with my tongue and lips. My cock hurt so bad that I had to unzip my jeans to give it space. I wanted so fucking bad to make love to her right there on the table, but I knew it wouldn't be comfortable for her.

One half of her body was clean from the chocolate and whipped cream, but I still had the other side. Sucking on her nipple, I trailed my fingers down her stomach to in between her legs. She opened them further, and it was just the invitation I needed. Her body was hot and slick when I slid a finger inside of her, teasing her by rubbing my thumb across her clit. I loved how she was always so ready and turned on for me. It felt good to know that I could make her feel like that.

"Does it feel good when I suck your nipples and tease you between your legs?" I asked.

She moaned and arched her back, pushing her breasts higher, "Yes … oh, yes, it does. Please don't stop."

I wasn't planning on it. With another finger, I gently pushed it inside of her and instantly felt her tighten against them. I knew she was close and I was going to take her all the way. Faster, I rubbed her clit with my thumb, sucked harder on her breasts, and thrust my fingers in and out of her. Her labored breathing grew more rapid just as she tightened her legs around my hand and rocked her hips, screaming out her pleasure. Breathing hard, I waited for her to calm down before slipping my fingers out of her.

"That felt good," she rasped. "What are we going to do now?"

At that time, the timer for the brownies went off so I left her on the table and pulled them out, setting them on the stove. "We're going to take a shower, love, and then I'm going to make love to you the way I should have this week."

She sighed. "You did make love to me, Cooper."

Picking her up in my arms, her body was like liquid fire as I carried her up to her room. "I know I did, but this time it'll be different … I promise."

When I got her upstairs to her room, I set her down on her bed and waltzed into her bathroom so I could let the shower water get warm. With her gaze half-open, she bit her lip and watched me as I dropped my pants to the floor and slid my boxers down. Slowly, she got up from the bed and followed me into the shower.

I couldn't stop from touching her, her breasts, her nipples … her ass to pull her closer to me. Taking her soap, I skimmed it across her chest and down her stomach to wash away the rest of the stickiness of the whipped cream and chocolate. The second she reached down and wrapped her fingers around my cock, I thought I was going to lose it. Jerking in response, she chuckled as she lowered to her knees and began to suck me off while massaging my balls in her hand.

"Kate," I groaned. "What the fuck are you doing to me?"

In reply, she sucked harder and I almost lost it. "I'm going to come if you don't stop, love." Putting her hands on my thighs, she pushed me back until I landed on the built in seat in her shower. I used to think showers with a place to sit were useless … but not anymore.

Watching her swollen lips glide up and down my cock was such a fucking turn on. Picking up her pace, her head bobbed up and down and I couldn't help but wrap my fingers gently in her hair to feel her move. I wanted to come like that, with her mouth on my dick, but it wasn't the way I needed for it to happen.

"Stop, love," I groaned. "I need you to stop."

With a smile on her face, she slowly got back up to her feet, her breasts right in my line of sight. "You sure do know what you're doing, don't you?" I scolded halfheartedly.

Turning off the water, I grabbed a set of towels that were draped on the rack and dried her off quickly. Once we were semi dry, I carried her to the bed and spread her wide. Her lips, her nipples, and her clit were so swollen that I knew it had to be the same agony I felt within my own body. That feeling before orgasm when everything heightens was the strongest yet euphoric feeling anyone could ever imagine.

Gently, I laid on top of her and pushed inside slowly, feeling her tremble underneath me. I continued with that slow pace, at least until I could feel her tightening around me. As soon as I felt that, I pushed in deeper and a little harder; that was all it took to drive her over the edge. Holding on tight, I thrust as deep as I could go and released inside of her at the same time she screamed my name from her lips.

"I love you, Kate," I murmured across her lips.

Breathless and with a tear streaming down her cheek, she gazed up at me with her gentle, gray eyes. "I love you, too, Cooper. Thank you for helping me realize it was possible again."

"I think I need to thank you for the same thing."

Because without her I would be in the same place I'd been for the past year, and that place was nowhere special.

Chapter 28

Kate

Ring ... ring ... ring.

Groaning, I turned over in bed and looked at my alarm clock. Surely it wasn't time to get up, was it?

2:23 a.m.

Nope, it definitely wasn't. Who the hell would be calling at two in the morning? Reaching for my phone, I had to blink a few times to get the blurriness away before I could read the screen ... it was Lara.

"Lara," I answered curiously, "what are you doing calling me at this time? You know I don't stay up late like you do."

"Yes, I know, and for the first time in forever I actually went to bed as soon as I got home from the restaurant. Hey, listen, someone's prowling around your house. I came down to the kitchen to get some water and I noticed someone snooping around your front door. Do you want me to call the police?"

Shooting up out of bed, I grabbed a pair of shorts out of my dresser and quickly slipped them on. "What? You have to be kidding me? What do they look like? Is there a car out there or anything?"

"What's wrong?" Cooper asked, running a hand through his hair.

"Someone's outside," I hissed low. "I'm getting my gun."

"No, there's no car … oh wait, there is one parked out by the Stewart's driveway," Lara informed me. "I've never seen them drive that kind of car before. It's blue and it looks kind of like a Toyota Camry or something. I can't tell from this far away. I'm going out there."

"No, you're not, Lara. If you go outside so help me God I'm going to kick your ass. Don't be stupid," I warned.

Rushing to my safe, I entered in the combination and pulled out my .50 S&W and a clip of bullets. Cooper jumped out of bed and threw on his clothes before quickly coming to my side.

"Kate, let me have the gun," he said, prying my fingers away from it. When I narrowed my gaze at him, he held up his hands and sighed. "I don't doubt your shooting skills, love, but I'm pretty sure I have more experience. Now let me have the clip."

Huffing, I handed it to him. "I know how to use a gun, Cooper. My dad taught me how to when I was a little girl and I go to the shooting range with him at least once every few months."

"Kate, what are you going to do?" Lara asked.

"I don't know, but when I hang up, call the police and get them out here."

"Okay, just be careful."

As soon as the call was over, I turned my phone on

vibrate and put it in my back pocket. Cooper and I slowly walked down the stairs as quietly as we could, but he went straight to the front door and I went to the very front bedroom so I could look out the window.

Before I could look out, Lara called again.

"They're running to the car, Kate. We need to get the license plate number. I'm going out there."

"Dammit," I hissed, running out of the bedroom.

Cooper must've seen the person running off because he unbolted the door and took off outside with me following, but I stopped once I noticed something strange out of the corner of my eye. Before I could figure out what had happened, Lara bolted out into the street and ran with Cooper down the road.

From where I stood, I could already see that they weren't close to catching the person because it wasn't long before I heard a set of screeching tires and watched as a set of tail lights disappeared down the street. Slowly, I walked around Cooper's car, and that was when I noticed what was wrong. His tires had been slashed, and in the front one there was a knife protruding out of it. The closer I got to that knife, the sicker I felt because it just so happened that I recognized it. *Oh no, please don't let it be his,* I screamed in my mind. Bending low, it didn't take long to see the set of initials that were engraved on the hilt. I knew they were there because I was the one who had it engraved for his birthday … it was Luke's.

No, I screamed in my mind. Luke hadn't caused any problems since I made my decision. Why would he do such a thing?

By the time Cooper and Lara made it back to the house, the police finally pulled up. "Did you get the license plate number?" I asked.

Cooper shook his head. "No, it was too dark. They had too much of a head start." It was then he looked down and noticed that the tires on his car had been slashed. "What the fuck?" he growled.

Lara came to my side and put her arm around me, shaking and breathing hard. "We have never had anything like this happen in our neighborhood."

When the officer got out of his car, he shined his flashlight around my yard and approached us. "I'm Officer Stilwell. What's going on here tonight?" he asked, looking back and forth at all three of us. He was pretty muscular, with a shaved head and blond goatee, and probably around my age or maybe slightly older.

"Well, Officer, it was probably about twenty minutes ago when Lara," I said, pointing to her, "called me and told me that she saw someone lurking around my house. They had a car parked up the road and it looked to be something like a blue Toyota Camry or something along those lines. We didn't get a license plate number or anything."

"I see. And who lives here?" he asked, pointing to my house.

I lifted my hand. "I do. My name is Kate Townsend."

He nodded and pointed to Cooper. "And you are, sir?"

"I'm Cooper Davis. I live in that house over there," he said, pointing to the one beside Lara's.

"And I'm Lara Jacobs. I live next door."

"Did any of you get a good look at the person? Were they male or female? Did they steal anything?"

We all shook our heads, but then I pointed to the car.

"They didn't steal anything, but they did slash Cooper's tires."

The officer shone his flashlight around the car until he got to the knife. "Do you have any enemies, Mr. Davis? Or anyone that you've pissed off recently." Pulling out a glove from his pocket, he took the knife out of the car and inspected it.

Cooper laughed halfheartedly. "I'm sure I have plenty of enemies, Officer, but I can't think of anyone that would want to do this." He glanced at me quickly and I could tell he was lying. He knew he had pissed off Luke. *I wonder why he's not saying anything.*

"Do any of you know someone with the initials of LC?" Officer Stilwell asked, holding up the knife.

Lara gasped, putting her hand over her mouth. "I take it that means yes. Care to tell me who?"

Nervously, Lara glanced over at me, leaving me no choice but to tell the officer what I knew. "It's Luke Collins, Officer. That's his knife."

"And how do you know it's his?"

"I know it's his because I bought it for him for his birthday. I had his initials engraved into it."

Fuming, Cooper crossed his arms at the chest and mumbled something to himself. He was pissed and I couldn't blame him. I had no idea Luke would ever do something like this and leave the evidence behind.

Officer Stilwell walked around the car, shining his flashlight this way and that. "It looks like we need to pay Luke Collins a little visit. Do any of you know why he would do such a thing?"

My gaze went straight to Cooper.

"Ah, I see," Officer Stilwell said. "I take it he didn't

get the girl."

Spotting something on the ground, he shone his light onto it and picked it up. Cooper walked around his car and looked down as well.

"Does this mean something to you?" he asked Cooper. "It says this is your second warning. When was the first one?"

Marching to their side of the car, I glared down at what the officer had in his hands and then up to Cooper. "What is that? What does it mean by second warning?"

Cooper sighed and hung his head. "I was going to tell you tonight, but then we got distracted. There *was* a first warning last Saturday."

"Was it just a note that time?" Officer Stilwell asked.

"Yeah, but it was on my car in *my* driveway, not Kate's. It said to stay away from her and that it was my first warning. That's all it said."

"Why didn't you tell me?" I snapped, interrupting them.

Sighing, Cooper came up to me and gently took my hands in his. "Because he's your friend and I know you care about him."

Officer Stilwell took the note and the knife to his patrol car and bagged the evidence. "All right, I'm going to take this stuff to the station and find out where Mr. Collins is at. As soon as we find out what's going on, we'll get in touch with you. Before I go I'm going to need your phone numbers."

He handed us a notebook and pen, so we all three wrote our numbers down. "If Luke did this, what will you do to him?" I asked, handing him the notebook.

"There's probably not much we can do other than

make him pay for the damages and charge him with a misdemeanor. Now if he tried to harm you or anyone else here then the charges would be different. The only problem with these types of scenarios is that the issues tend to escalate. The first warning was a note, this time it was slashed tires. What's it going to be next week?"

"I understand," I said with a nod. "You have a point."

"If you want my advice, I'd stay away from him until we get to the bottom of this. We don't want anyone to get hurt."

Before getting into his car, he turned to Cooper and smiled. "Good game, by the way. I would've told you earlier, but I didn't think it was appropriate while surveying your damaged car. Glad to have you in our city, though."

Cooper chuckled. "Thank you, Officer. I'm glad to be here."

As soon as he left, Lara threw her hands up in the air, her eyes wide. "Please tell me you don't think Luke did this," she argued.

Clueless, I shrugged and leaned into Cooper's body for comfort. I didn't like what was going on one bit. "Lara, I honestly don't know what to think. It doesn't make sense, that's for sure."

"And as much as I don't like the guy," Cooper stated, "I don't think he'd be stupid enough to leave a knife with his initials on it. Something's not right here."

I nodded. "Agreed, but what's going to happen if something worse happens next week?"

Cooper rubbed his hands down my arms to warm away the chills before holding me tight against him. "And that, love, is what I'm worried about."

Chapter 29

Kate

I barely slept once everything was said and done, and now that it was midday I thought we would've heard something from the police. My brother hadn't called, which was a shock since I was sure Luke would've called him to tell him what was going on.

"What do you think is taking so long?" I asked.

Cooper sighed and joined me on the couch while I impatiently flipped through every channel. "It takes time to find people, and they probably had a lot of questions to ask him."

I had a lot of questions to ask him. It took all I had not to pick up my phone and call him myself.

"What if it wasn't him? Is there anyone on the team that doesn't like you or would want to play a cruel joke like this?" I asked.

"I can't think of anyone. The only person that really makes sense is Luke, but then again given the circumstances I'm starting to doubt it's him."

Ring ... ring ... ring.

My heart thumped in my chest, and when I looked at my phone it was a number I didn't recognize. "Hello," I answered nervously.

"Ms. Townsend?"

Immediately, I recognized the deep, baritone voice from last night; it was Officer Stilwell.

"Yes, this is she."

"This is Officer Stilwell. I wanted to call and give you an update. Unfortunately, we have yet to find Mr. Collins. No one seems to know where he's located, not even his family. Do you know when the last time you spoke to him was?"

"It was last Saturday," I told him, "when he dropped me off at my house after our date. He had tried calling this week, but I never answered."

"Okay, thanks. We're still trying to hunt him down, but in the meantime, if you see or hear from him we need to know. Also, there were several fingerprints we detected on the knife and right now they're being examined. We should have the results of those by tomorrow morning."

"Thank you. I'll let you know if we hear anything."

As soon as we hung up the phone, I called my brother since he was Luke's best friend; surely he had to know where he was. "Kate, what's up," he answered, yawning into the phone.

"Hey, do you know where Luke is? Have you talked to him or the police for that matter?"

"The police? Why would I have talked to them?"

"It's because they're looking for Luke. We're not sure, but we think he might have slashed Cooper's tires last night. The knife I gave him was stuck in one of the tires."

Evan fumbled with the phone. "You can't be serious? This is a joke, right?"

I sighed. "I wish it was. Have you talked to him?"

"No, I haven't talked to him in a couple of days. He said he was leaving to get away from everything and that's the last I heard from him. He's probably at his cabin. If I can't get in touch with him I'll drive up there."

"Thanks, Evan. I just want to find out what's going on," I said.

"Yeah, me too," he said before hanging up the phone.

Cooper put his arm around me and squeezed. "Anything?"

"Not yet. The police can't find Luke, but they also said they found other prints on the knife. I'm sure I have a set on there, but there could also be a ton of other prints as well. I don't see how that's going to help. Evan's going to try and find him; however, in the meantime all we can do is wait."

"I can think of something we can do while we wait," Cooper teased, burying his nose in my hair.

"You're insatiable. Is that all you think about?"

Chuckling, he grabbed me around the waist and tossed me on the couch, covering me with his body. "Actually, I was referring to unpacking my house, love. However, if you want to do something else, I'm pretty sure I can rise to the occasion."

Already he was hard and ready between my legs, but there was so much on my mind I couldn't begin to think about sex. "I tell you what," I began, "why don't we unpack some of your boxes, and tonight you can *rise* as much as you want. How does that sound?"

Sighing, Cooper's smile slowly disappeared and his

gaze grew wary. "I know you have a lot on your mind, Kate. It'll all get figured out soon, okay? Just try not to worry so much."

It was hard not to when stuff was happening to the one you cared about. What if it got so bad that he didn't want to have anything to do with me anymore?

"What if things get bad, Cooper? It's all because of me that you're going through this."

Eyes wide, he shook his head quickly and held my face firmly in his hands when I tried to look away. "Look at me, Kate." Releasing a heavy sigh, I lifted my gaze and stared into his crystal blue eyes. "Nothing and no one is going to keep me away from you. Do you think I care about my tires or my car? None of that even compares to you. I'm not going anywhere … I promise. Now let's get out of here."

Swallowing hard, I held back the tears and nodded quickly. I passed the test by staying with him during his hard times, now it was his turn to try his luck during mine.

Chapter 30

Kate

Over the past six hours we'd gotten through a bulk of Cooper's boxes and put everything away, but we still had a ton more to do. I was ready to make a night of it just to stay busy. Cooper went to take a shower while I offered to clean the kitchen after finishing his famous grilled chicken dinner. Finally, the call I'd been waiting on came through … it was my brother.

Heart pounding, I rinsed off my soapy hands and dried them before grabbing for my phone. "Evan, what's going on?"

I could hear someone arguing in the background, and I knew it was Luke by the sound of his voice. "Dude, calm down," Evan snapped at him. Then to me, he said, "Sorry about that. He's kind of pissed right now."

"Where are you?"

"We're on our way to your house. He's angry because I wouldn't let him use my phone to call you."

"Where's his phone?" I asked curiously.

"Somewhere out on in the woods. That's why no one

could get in touch with him. He lost it out on the trails when he went out riding on his bike."

"Evan, you can't bring him here," I warned. "The police are looking for him."

"They've already let him go. As soon as I found him at the cabin and told him what was going on, we immediately left and I took him to the station. His alibi was solid, Kate. He hadn't been in town in three days." Luke fumed some more in the background. "All right, I have to get off of here before dumbass makes me wreck. We'll be there in five minutes so you can talk to him."

Quickly, I finished up the dishes and bolted out of Cooper's house. By the time I got into my driveway, Evan and Luke were pulling up in Evan's black Toyota Tacoma. Luke bolted out of the truck first and rushed over to me; his blond hair matted to his head and his jeans and navy T-shirt covered in mud.

"What the hell is going on, Kate?"

"I should probably be asking you the same thing," I said, glancing down at his dirty clothes.

"Well, I had just gotten back from riding when I saw Evan's truck in my driveway. When he told me what was going on, I jumped in his car and told him to bring me back."

Evan scoffed, his nose turned up in disgust. "Yeah, it wasn't fun riding back with him stinking up the truck and covering everything with mud. He's definitely going to clean that shit up."

Luke rolled his eyes. "I wanted to get here as soon as I could. I didn't want you thinking I had anything to do with what happened. You didn't, did you?"

Sheepishly, I hung my head and shrugged. "I don't

know what I thought," I told him truthfully. "On one hand I knew you weren't the type to do something like that, but on the other it *was* your knife. I gave that to you. I thought it might have been your way of showing me how pissed at us you were."

Lifting my chin with his hand, Luke shook his head and sighed. "I loved that knife, Kate. I didn't want to tell you that I lost it, but it appears now that someone took it. I was afraid I'd hurt your feelings by telling you I didn't know where it was. Usually, I keep it in the center console of my truck, and now the police are going to dust for prints to see what they can find."

"What made you want to leave in the first place, Luke?"

Casting a glance in my brother's direction, he blew out a nervous breath and pulled me further away so my brother couldn't hear. "You did," he answered. "I knew that if I stayed I would see you and Cooper out together, and I didn't want to get pissed off more than what I already was. At first, I wasn't that angry, but then I had time to think. I didn't understand why you would choose him over me. We were always so close and I thought I could use that to my advantage." He paused for a second and bit his lip before saying, "Look, I don't think it's safe for you to be around Cooper."

I heard the low growl from Cooper's throat before I could even speak. "And I don't think it's safe for *you* to be around her."

Glancing over Luke's shoulder, I saw Cooper scowling with damp hair, wearing a pair of khaki shorts and a white T-shirt. Luke huffed and turned around, gritting his teeth. "All I'm saying is that whoever is after you is coming to Kate's home. What if this person goes after her next? The first warning said to stay away from her; that's not something to joke around with."

"Don't you think I thought about that?" Cooper snapped. "Believe me, that's the last thing I want, but leaving her by herself worries me more. That's obviously what this person wants. Well, they're not going to get it."

"It looks like you're missing the other point," Luke scoffed. "Whoever is doing this is making it look like I'm the one responsible. They're trying to pin this shit on me. They obviously want me away from her, too. So the question is ... who? What exactly are we dealing with?"

Evan cut in the middle of Luke and Cooper and came to my side. "You don't think it could be Scott's family doing this, do you?"

The thought did cross my mind, and Scott's mother did vandalize my car two years ago, but I hadn't had any other incidents since then. "I don't think so," I told him. "If it was them they would come after me, not the guys."

Nodding, he agreed, "Yeah, that's true. Can you think of anyone else? One of the guys on the team maybe?"

I shook my head. "I don't know. I'm completely clueless."

"Maybe you should stay at my house then?" Evan recommended. "That way if someone does go after Cooper you won't be in the crossfire."

"I think that's a great idea," Luke agreed.

Cooper scoffed. "Yeah, you would."

"Guys, that's enough," I snapped, glaring at them all. "I'm staying here and that's final. Evan, you know I can take care of myself. I have an arsenal in my safe and I know how to use every single gun in there. I'll be fine."

My brother rolled his eyes. "Why are you so stubborn?"

"Because I get it from you," I teased. "Anyway, the police are going to have fingerprints tomorrow. Hopefully, that'll help them shed some light on who's messing with us. It'll all be over then."

Deep down, I had a feeling it wouldn't be that easy.

Chapter 31

Kate

Cooper and I rode together to practice since his car still sat in my driveway with flattened tires. My stomach was in knots all night because I couldn't help but wonder if any of those prints on the knife were going to be someone on the team. I didn't want to imagine any of the guys doing something like that.

"Kate?"

Jumping in my seat, I turned around and Brianna was there, stretching her legs. "Oh wow, I had no idea you were behind me."

She laughed. "That doesn't surprise me. You've been too busy looking at Cooper to notice. You know, Lindsey was pissed when she found out you two were like seriously dating."

I'm sure she was, I thought to myself. Over my shoulder, I could see out of the corner of my eye that Lindsey was glaring at me. When I looked at her, she turned her head quickly and pretended to do something else. Why were women so petty sometimes?

198

"She'll get over it," I said.

"Do you want to run with me? It looks like the guys are about to run around the track, too. Maybe we could show them up today."

Chuckling, I tightened up my laces and joined her. At least if I did something to occupy my time, it would be less stressful than waiting for the phone to ring. Placing my phone in my bag, I zipped it up and set it with everyone else's.

"All right, let's go."

We took off around the track, and before the guys could catch up to us, Brianna blew out a breath and said, "You know, ever since you started dating Cooper I think you've become a hot commodity around here. Now the guys know that you'll date a football player. I've had at least two of them this past week ask how serious you and Cooper were."

I gasped. "And what did you say?"

"Well, it's not like I could tell them anything," she scolded. "You haven't exactly told *me* how serious you two were."

The guys were about to catch up to us, so I had to ask quickly, "Who were they, Brianna? Which ones asked about me?"

She looked over her shoulder and smiled. "Derek was the first one to ask. I'll admit I was kind of bummed be-cause I thought he was going to ask *me* out. We've been kind of talking here every now and again, but I guess it was to get info on you."

"Oh, Brianna, I'm so sorry. I could definitely see you and Derek together. He's such a sweet guy. Who else asked?"

Derek was definitely not one I would've imagined asking about me, let alone anyone else. My brother threatened them all when I started working for the team.

"Let's see … there was Jaxon. I'm surprised he hasn't faked an injury just so they could be alone with you."

Cooper ran up to my side and discreetly smacked me on the ass. "Mind if I run with you ladies?"

"Sure, but don't get upset when you can't keep up," I taunted playfully, blowing out the air in my lungs. My legs were already on fire and I knew without a doubt that he could keep up.

Derek came up and squeezed himself in between me and Brianna. "I know I can keep up. You know, Kate, I've been getting this really sharp pain in my calf recently. It's not that bad, but sometimes the pain shoots up my leg and it hurts like a bitch. Do you mind taking a look at it?"

I snuck a glance over at Brianna and she mouthed the words, 'I told you so' to me. Slowing my pace, I looked up at Derek and nodded. "Yeah, as soon as we're done I'll take a look at your leg."

When we got to the end of the track, Cooper smiled at me and walked away with Brianna so I could talk to Derek. "Do we need to go to the locker room?" he asked.

"No," I blurted out, maybe a little too loudly. I laid out a few towels on to the bench so it wouldn't be so hard, and pointed to it. "Here is fine."

He looked around and focused on Brianna and Cooper before lying down, stomach first. "Okay, which leg is it?"

"My right one, back here," he said, pointing to the upper back part of his thigh.

I massaged his leg, trying to gauge if it was a hamstring strain, and never once did he squirm or complain. "Are you sure I'm in the right spot?" I asked.

Sheepishly, he looked at me over his shoulder. "Don't be mad at me, but there's something I wanted to ask you and I didn't know of any other way to get you alone."

Removing my hands, I placed them on my hip and glared down at him. "Please don't tell me you lied about your leg so you could ask me out?"

Derek bolted upright and shook his head. "No, that's not it at all."

"Really? Then what is it? Because that's not what Brianna said. She told me you were asking about me and Cooper."

Closing his eyes, he groaned and ran his hands through his hair. "Shit, I knew I shouldn't have done that. When I tried to talk to her the other day I froze up, and when I looked away I saw you and Cooper. To cover up my fumble I asked how serious you two were. I wasn't meaning it that I was interested in you, but I guess that's how it came off. She's going to think I'm a fucking idiot."

Chuckling, I sat down beside him and elbowed him in the side. It was a relief to know he wasn't interested in me. I liked Derek, and the last thing I wanted was to think he had anything to do with what happened to Cooper; especially when they seemed so close.

"She's not going to think you're an idiot. I'm almost positive that if you asked her out she'd say yes."

His eyes sparkled when he peered over at her. "You think?"

"Oh, I know. Although, I never took you for the shy type."

He snorted. "Yeah, well, it's kind of hard not to be

around Brianna. She's different from the other girls. Over time you just want a change … a woman that doesn't want you for your title or your money. It's hard to find that sometimes."

"I don't exactly have that problem since I'm not famous or anything, but I know what you mean. Brianna is a beautiful girl, inside and out, and the sweetest one at that. That's why I choose to spend my time with her."

Derek smiled as he watched Brianna talking to Cooper, her hands waving animatedly in the air when she spoke; she loved to talk with her hands. "That's how I knew she was a genuine person," he said, glancing back at me. "I knew you wouldn't be around her if she wasn't."

Before Cooper and Brianna headed back our way, I stood up quickly and said, "Ask her out, Derek. I know she's single, so get to it before someone else beats you to it."

"Is your leg better, pansy?" Cooper joked, slapping him on the shoulder.

Smiling wide at Brianna, I winked and pushed her toward Derek. "He's all better now … I think. He just needs to stretch his legs out a little more. Brianna, you're good at that, so why don't you show him how you do it?"

"Okay," she stammered awkwardly, glancing back and forth between us all. Grabbing my bag off the ground, I took Cooper's hand and led him to the stands so we could take a break. I pulled out a protein bar and a bottle of water and handed it to him.

"What was that all about?" he asked, nodding toward Brianna and Derek.

Opening a bottle of water, I took a sip and broke off a bite of my protein bar. "Well, Brianna happened to tell me that Derek and Jaxon had asked how serious you and I were. I thought that was kind of strange since no one has ever shown interest in me. Anyway, I talked to Derek and got that situation all sorted out. Jaxon, however, has never really shown interest in me. Do you ever talk to him?"

Cooper shrugged and glared at him on the field. "Not really. He tends to stick to himself. I'll talk to him and see how he acts around me."

"Don't do it yet," I pleaded. "Let me talk to the police first about the fingerprints. I would hate for you to scare the poor guy and him not have anything to do with this."

"Has anyone called you yet?"

"I'm not sure," I remarked hastily, rummaging through my bag. As soon as I found my phone, I noticed I had two missed calls. They were both from the number Officer Stilwell called me from yesterday.

I had a voicemail to listen to, so I punched in my password and hoped my heart would stop its incessant pounding so I could hear the message.

"Ms. Townsend, this is Officer Stilwell. We have the results from the fingerprints and I really think you should come down to the station so we can discuss matters further. One of our lead detectives, Sam Lennox, has been brought in and he wants to talk to you as well. If you would please give me a call back so that I can arrange a time for all of us to sit down and talk that would be great."

My fingers shook as I dialed his number and waited for him to pick up. "What did the message say?" Cooper asked.

Impatiently, I tapped my foot up and down, waiting on Officer Stilwell to answer. "He said they had the results from the fingerprints, and also something about bringing in one of their detectives … Sam Lennox, I believe."

Finally, Officer Stilwell picked up the phone. "Officer Stilwell," he barked, catching my attention.

"Good morning, Officer Stilwell, this is Kate Townsend. I'm returning your call."

"Yes, Ms. Townsend, as you already know we have the results. Is there any way you can come down to the station to discuss what we found. It's extremely urgent that you get here as soon as possible."

An immediate sense of dread crept over my spine and through to the pit of my stomach. By the sound in his voice, I knew something was wrong. "Um … I can be there in twenty minutes," I said, trying to keep my voice from shaking.

"Sounds good, Ms. Townsend. I'll tell Sam that you're on your way."

I hung up the phone and started toward my car while Cooper kept his pace beside of me. "I have to go, Cooper."

"What did he say? Did they find out anything from the prints?"

"He said they had the results and that it was extremely urgent. He wants me to go in and talk to them right away. He's bringing in a detective named Sam Lennox. I have no clue what that means."

Cooper closed his eyes and sighed. "I think I do," he murmured regretfully. "I'm coming with you."

"Cooper, you can't just skip out on practice."

Following me to my car, he opened the passenger's side and climbed in. "Sorry, love, but I'm going. I don't give a shit if I get reprimanded. I refuse to let you go through this alone when it concerns me as well. We're in this together, Kate."

Taking a deep breath, I started up my Jeep and gripped the steering wheel so tight to keep my hands from shaking. I wished I knew what was going on.

Chapter 32

Kate

When we arrived at the station, Cooper and I were led to the back by a young deputy who didn't look a day over eighteen; he had perfectly combed over brown hair and a boyish looking smile. I couldn't imagine seeing him take on a hardened criminal in a fist fight, but as I'd learned before … looks could deceive you. The deputy stopped outside of a closed door and I finally had a chance to see the name on his uniform; it was Alex Whitman.

"You can go right on in, Ms. Townsend. They're expecting you."

He nodded at both me and Cooper before continuing on his way. Meanwhile, we stood frozen outside of the door. Cooper pulled me close and rubbed his hand soothingly down my back.

"Are you going to be okay?" he asked.

Blowing out a shaky breath, I wrapped my hand around the door handle and nodded. "Yeah, I'll be fine. I just want to get this over with. The last time I was at a police station was two years ago."

Even though Alex said we could go on in, I still knocked and waited a second before opening the door. Inside, Officer Stilwell—dressed in his crisp police uniform—sat in front of a large mahogany desk that was scattered with a million pieces of paper. Behind the desk was a man, who I figured was Detective Sam Lennox. He looked to be in his late thirties with closely cropped dark brown hair. Instead of wearing a uniform, he was dressed in a Little League baseball T-shirt that had the word 'coach' in the upper right corner.

Both men stood from their chairs and shook our hands. Sam was the one who spoke, "Good morning, Ms. Townsend and Mr. Davis, I'm Sam Lennox. Thank you for coming by so quickly." He motioned toward the other two chairs. "Please, have a seat."

Cooper and I sat down, and so did Sam and Officer Stilwell, both tense and on edge. Opening up the file splayed in front of him, Sam clasped his hands together and took a deep breath. "Ms. Townsend, before we start, I'm sure you already heard that we've spoken to Luke Collins and everything came up clear for him."

I nodded. "Yes, he came by my house last night."

Sam nodded and leaned forward on his elbows, glancing back and forth between me and Cooper. "I figured he would considering he was anxious to get out of here and talk to you. Even though his alibi came back conclusive, I still wanted to check around to see if he had any friends that could've vandalized Mr. Davis' car on his behalf."

"Did you find anyone?" Cooper asked.

Sighing, Sam looked down at the file and pulled out a piece of paper. I couldn't tell what was on it, but when he peered up at me there was an insurmountable look of concern in his gaze. "Ms. Townsend, there were a few prints that showed up on the knife, including yours, but I know that's because you were the one who bought it. However, there was the tiniest bit of a print that we detected, and it happens to be someone you know."

Cooper reached over and took my hand, squeezing it tight. "Who?" I asked.

Almost reluctantly, he slowly handed me the paper, but before I looked down I took a deep, shaky breath. The second I glanced down at the paper I gasped as everything came tumbling down around me. It was definitely someone I knew, and someone who hated me more than the devil himself.

It was Scott's mother … *Marianne Easton.*

It'd been two years and she still hadn't let me live down what happened to her son. I continued to feel guilty over losing Scott, but I wasn't going to let her torment me anymore … or Cooper for that matter. I let the phone calls slip by and let her grieve by calling me names and cussing me out because I thought it would help her come to terms with what happened. Obviously, that wasn't the case.

Handing the paper to Cooper, I clenched my teeth and glared at Sam. "Please tell me you have her in custody. I'm done letting that woman ruin my life."

He shook his head. "No, that's where our problems come in. I'm familiar with your past with the Eastons and what happened two years ago. Has she tried contacting you at all recently?"

I scoffed, "For the past two years I would get phone calls right around the time Scott died. As you can probably see in the file, the anniversary of the date was two weeks ago."

"Yeah, I noticed that. After we got the results we tried to contact her, but got in touch with her daughter instead. Apparently, she's been missing for a couple of weeks now. She said it wasn't unusual for Marianne to take off for a few days, especially around this time of year."

The woman had seriously lost her damn mind. "So what happens now? Are we supposed to sit around and wait for her to do something else to us?"

"What about a restraining order?" Cooper cut in.

"We can do that," Sam advised, "but she's not going to know there's a restraining order. From what I read in the file, and from what the daughter has said, it appears there's been a lot of issues with Marianne's health. Emily is on her way to Charlotte in hopes that she can find her."

"Great," I groaned sarcastically, "now there'll be two of them in the same city who hate me. They've made my life a living hell for the past two years. I thought in time it would all stop, but it didn't." Closing my eyes, I sighed and leaned over on my elbows so I could rub my tired eyes. "Are we done here or is there something else you need from me?"

"Actually there is," Sam mentioned hesitantly. "Although, I'm not too sure you're going to like it. Emily asked if there was a way she could speak to you when she got here. She told me it was important to the case."

I snorted and got to my feet. "I'm sorry, Detective Lennox, but I refuse to talk to her. She's just as bad as her mother. I usually try to see the good in people, but when it comes to them they can go to hell for all I care. I can't let what happened in the past control my life anymore."

"I understand, Ms. Townsend," Sam agreed. "Until we find Mrs. Easton I want you to be careful out there. We don't know what she's capable of, or what she has planned, but we will find her."

Cooper got to his feet and put his arm around me before acknowledging Sam and Officer Stilwell with a nod. "Thank you, gentlemen. We'll keep our eyes and ears open."

It looks like I'll be sleeping with one eye open.

Chapter 33

COOPER

Two Days Later

"Why do you think she's targeting you?" Kate asked, circling her fingers up and down my bare chest.

It had been two days since we found out it was Scott's mother who was trying to tear us apart. She still hadn't been found, but we knew she was out there plotting her next move. We both decided that staying together as much as possible would be our best bet. If Marianne wanted us apart she wasn't going to get it.

We had just eaten dinner and Kate decided she wanted to watch a movie. It just so happened she picked out Oklahoma, which was a musical my grandmother watched constantly when she was still alive. When she would watch it that was my grandfather's excuse to take me outside and pass the ball around so he wouldn't have to hear it. Unfortunately, I didn't have that option this time.

Tilting her chin up with my finger, I bent down to kiss her lips. "My guess is that she doesn't want you happy with anyone, love. Maybe she thinks you don't deserve to be happy," I told her. "Did you ever try to date anyone after Scott?"

Shaking her head, her hair tickled the skin on my chest as she lifted her gray gaze to me. "No, I never made time for it. You and Luke are the only ones I've gone out with recently."

"Then there's our answer," I stated. "She never had a reason to come after you until now. I bet if you would've started dating someone before, all of this would've happened sooner."

She laid her head back on my chest and groaned. "Ugh, you're absolutely right. I never thought about that."

"Do you want to watch another movie? Or do you want to do something *else*?" I asked, hoping she'd get the hint.

For the past two days she'd been so stressed over everything going on that every night after dinner she'd basically pass out. I had missed holding her and feeling her touch to the point where I honestly came to the conclusion that I had a problem. I *was* addicted to her and I needed her … bad.

Giggling, she hopped off of the couch and took off her shirt, her perky breasts peeking up over the top of her bra. Fuck, I wanted to taste her, to feel her beneath me; two days was two days too long. Slowly, she peeled off her shorts, which only left her in her sports bra and thong.

Smiling, she said, "I need to take a shower first before we do anything else. Do you care to join me?"

With my cock as hard as a rock, how could I refuse? "You're damn right I do. Go get the shower running and I'll be right there, love."

I heard her steps pattering up the stairs, and it wasn't long before the shower water turned on, but unfortunately, the doorbell rang as well. It was most likely Lara, and I was about to send her on her merry way. However, when I answered the door … it wasn't her.

It was a woman with really short blonde hair—probably in her mid-twenties—dressed in a pair of blue jeans and a yellow tank top. In her hand was a file, and on the label it read Scott Easton.

"Who are you?" I asked, narrowing my gaze at her.

She swallowed hard and cleared her throat, her voice desperate when she spoke, "Look, I know I'm not sup-posed to be here, but I didn't know what else to do. I'm Emily Easton. I really need to talk to Kate, please."

"Why? So you can make her life miserable the way you and your mother have done for the past two years? Fuck that. You need to leave … now. She doesn't want to see you, and she made that perfectly clear to the police."

Tears began to stream down her face and her lips trembled. "If I could change the way I acted I would do it in a heartbeat. My mother needs help and I've been trying to find her, but I don't know where else to look. I need you to give this to Kate," she cried, handing me the file. "If I had known the truth, I know things would've gone differ-ently. Please tell her I'm sorry and that I regret every mean thing I said to her. She was the one who actually saved my brother in the long run."

Turning around, she started off down the driveway, wiping her tears along the way. I had no idea if I should believe anything that came out of her mouth or believe what was in the file. For all I knew it was something to try and fuck with Kate some more.

Flipping through my texts, I found the one from Mason with Sam's number in it. Quickly, I called it, hoping Kate would still be up in her room.

"Sam Lennox," he answered.

Quickly, I rushed to the opposite side of the house. "Sam, this is Cooper Davis. Emily Easton just showed up at Kate's house and dropped off a file for her to look at. Do you have any idea what it could be? I would look myself, but I don't feel right doing that. Kate will be pissed as hell at me if she finds out I called Mason to help her out."

Sam chuckled. "Yeah, I figured that was the case so that's why I didn't mention anything about that the other day. Mason said you were a close friend of his wife's, so I figured you were a good guy if he thought highly of you. Anyway, I was about to call Ms. Townsend and give her an update. I just finished validating the contents in that file to make sure everything's legit. Please make sure she reads it. It's not something she's going to like, but it'll shed some light on the whole situation."

"Have there been any leads on Scott's mother?" I asked.

"Not yet, but we're working on it. When we get a lead it's like she's one step ahead. I'll keep you posted though."

As soon as I hung up, I could hear Kate's footsteps coming down the stairs. "Cooper, where are you? The water's getting cold up here."

With the file in my hand, I met her at the bottom of the steps and watched as her smile slowly disappeared into a mask of confusion. "What is that?" she asked, sweeping a glance toward the file.

"It's for you, love. Emily Easton dropped it off and

wanted you to take a look at it. She said she was sorry for all that she's done and that you really need to know what's in the file."

Kate scoffed, "And you believe her. It's nothing but lies coming out of her mouth. I don't want to read that garbage."

Snatching the file out of my hands, she rushed off toward the kitchen. When I caught her, she was about to throw it in the garbage, but I held out my hand, stopping her. "Don't throw it away, Kate. I called Sam while you were upstairs and he confirmed everything that's in the file. Whatever's in there is true."

Blowing out a heavy sigh, Kate closed her eyes and pulled the file tighter against her body. "Do you know what's in it?" she asked.

Rubbing her bare shoulders, I shook my head and bent down toward her ear. "No, love, I don't. Why don't we go upstairs and take our showers? Then we can both sit down and look at it together."

She nodded her head and started up the stairs, holding the folder against her chest. I had no clue what was in it, but I knew whatever it was wasn't going to be easy. I just knew I needed to be there for her like she was for me.

Chapter 34

Kate

The tan folder sat on my bed for about an hour while I stared at it in complete silence. What if Emily gave Sam a totally different file than she gave me? Sam didn't give Cooper specifics on what was in there, so we didn't know the truth either way, and it was too late in the evening to call him and ask. Cooper kept quiet beside me, tracing his fingers along my arms and my legs in hopes that it would help calm me down. Nothing worked.

"I'm scared, Cooper," I finally admitted. "I want to know what's in here, but in a way I don't."

Cooper sat up on the bed and pulled me into his body, placing a leg on each side. "I know you're scared, and believe me, I was scared when I stopped taking my pills because I thought I wouldn't be able to handle it. But I had you with me to help me through it. Now, I'm here to help you through this. Open the file, love, and let's find out what's going on. Scott would want you to know the truth."

His last comment was all it took. Scott *would* want me to know the truth, especially if he could see the way his family had treated me over the past two years. Sliding the file toward me, I hooked a finger underneath the cover and flipped it over. Taking a deep breath, I blew it out slowly and gazed down at the first piece of paper. It was Emily's phone number and a simple phrase of 'I'm sorry' written on it.

The next document that came up was a medical bill with Scott's name on it. Flipping through all of the papers, I saw that they were all medical forms, a ton of them. "Why would she show you his medical bills?" Cooper asked, reading them over my shoulder.

I looked through more papers. "I'm not sure, but there's a lot. There has to be something that tells us why. All of these bills are for CT Scans, MRI's, and other types of tests. I don't get it."

"Did you know he was going to the doctor a lot?"

My throat tightened and I shook my head. "No, I didn't. He must've gone to them when I was in class."

By the time I got through all of the medical bills, I came across a DVD in a see-through orange case with my name on it … in Scott's handwriting. Swallowing hard, I held it in my shaky hands as a tear rolled down my cheek. *What could possibly be on it?*

"Do you want to see what's on it?" Cooper asked softly. "I can step out of the room if you want to watch it alone."

Wiping the tears away, I sucked in a nervous breath and took the DVD out of the case. "No, I need you in here."

I put the disc in my DVD player and turned on the television. My heart raced and thumped so hard I thought I was going to be sick; especially when I pressed the play button. At first the screen was blue, but then it changed to Scott's bedroom at his house. It was the same room I found him in.

Immediately, the tears poured down my cheeks and even more so when Scott sat down in front of the camera with the sweetest smile on his face. He had on his favorite Metallica T-shirt, along with the navy blue baseball cap I got him when I went to a medical convention in Chicago. The date on the video read that it was February of 2011. No wonder he looked so different; it was when things with us were perfect and we were happy. It wasn't until a couple of months after that when everything started going downhill.

"Scott," I whispered, tracing the lines of his face with my fingers. Cooper was still on the bed behind me while I sat on the floor, staring at what used to be the love of my life. It was like the whole world moved in slow motion until I heard the first words come out of Scott's mouth.

"Kate," he murmured sadly. "I don't even know where to begin. Hell, I don't even know why I'm making this video, but the therapist I spoke to said it might be a good idea to do this since I'm not exactly the type of person to express my feelings. It's strange that I can say them to a camera, though. I ... I don't think that makes any sense, but whatever I guess."

"I didn't even know he was seeing a therapist," I cried, peering over my shoulder at Cooper. He didn't say a word as I sat there and sobbed; he just listened. *What kind of therapist was he seeing?* I wondered.

Chuckling, Scott looked down at his desk and shook his head, his smile slowly disappearing to a flat line. "I know you're going to have so many questions, and I'm hoping I'll be able to answer some of them, but first, I just wanted you to know that I love you. I love you, Kate, and even when I die I will always love you." He paused for a second, taking a deep breath and then another. When he finally looked up at the camera, a tear escaped the corner of his eye and landed right on his desk.

"You see, Kate … there's something I need to tell you."

Biting his lip, he stared right at the camera. It was as if he was looking directly at me with those warm hazel eyes that I loved so much. I held my breath and waited on him to tell me, but he didn't. Instead, he huffed and shot up out of his chair.

"Fuck, I can't do this."

Immediately, the camera went blank and that was it, but then it started right back up and the date claimed that it was two days later. This time he was shirtless, and his blond hair was tousled like he'd just woken up.

"Good morning, Kate. I did some thinking the past couple of days while you've been busy studying for your exams, and I realized that there's so much in your life I'm going to miss. Do you hear that sound in the background?" he asked, putting a finger to his lips. I listened closely and it sounded like running water … and me singing.

"Oh my God," I whispered hoarsely. "I'm there. He's filming while I'm there."

"Yes, that's you singing, Kate. Every morning when you'd get up at the crack of dawn to get ready for school, I'd lie in bed and listen to you. You always thought I was asleep, but I wasn't. I promise to get to the important stuff soon, but I figured I would show you first why my life has been better with you in it."

In the background, the shower water stopped running and I could hear myself sliding the shower curtain over. Scott raced back over to the bed and climbed under the covers while I snuck out of the bathroom and grabbed the set of royal blue scrubs I had hanging on the closet door. Once I had them on, I crept out of the bathroom with my towel on top of my head, and tiptoed over to the bed to kiss Scott gently on the cheek.

Cooper joined me on the floor and put his arm around me, and as soon as he touched me I broke down again. "I used to kiss him on the cheek every single morning like that before going down to eat breakfast. I always thought he was asleep. All that time he pretended and I had no clue."

As soon as I left the room, Scott got right back up and went back to the camera, his eyes full of love and adoration. "I love it when you kiss me like that every morning. Okay, now it's my time to get ready for work."

He turned off the camera and again it started right back up with a collection of other days. They were just snippets of us laughing together, me dancing and acting stupid, and some of when I was so engrossed in my studying that I didn't notice he was filming me. It was all precious moments we shared as a couple when all I thought I had to worry about was passing my exams and finishing school.

"You looked so happy back then," Cooper murmured in my ear. "I can tell you loved him."

Smiling, I wiped my eyes and nodded. "I did. Does it bother you to watch this?"

Cooper held me tighter and kissed my forehead. "No, love, it doesn't. I'm seeing a side of you I've never seen before. It's amazing that he wanted to show you this so you'd know how much you meant to him."

"It's weird seeing us together like this. Things were so different back then; I was more carefree. You know, I never thought I would love anyone again after what happened to him. I didn't want to let anyone get close and then lose them like that. It was a pain I don't ever want to experience again."

"And you won't have to," Cooper promised. "I'm not going anywhere unless you decide you don't want me anymore."

Gazing up at him, I smiled through my tears and wholeheartedly stated, "And that's not going to happen."

After about five more minutes of various clips, Scott came back on, only this time more serious … more intense. It was five months later than the original date when the video started. Scott's cheeks had sunk in a little more and he had lost weight. It wasn't much, but I could see it in his face and in his arms.

"Kate, you have no idea how hard it was to put this video together. The more I watched our time together, the angrier I started to become. I thought I could get through this without getting upset, but the more I see things, the more I don't want to lose them. I didn't want to have to tell you this, and for some reason I thought maybe this would all end up as a bad dream. That I would wake up one day and it would all be okay. You would finish up school, we'd get married and have kids, grow old and die together; except none of that's going to happen for me."

Taking a deep breath, he blew it out slowly and cleared his throat. "Kate, you know how you've been nagging me to go to the doctor because I've been sick? Well, I finally did a few months ago and had some tests done. It turns out that after all of this time of procrastinating, I sealed my own fate. If I would've gone sooner like you told me to, I might have had a fighting chance."

Gasping, I moved closer to the television, never taking my gaze away from Scott. What was he saying?

"I'm dying, Kate. I have gastric cancer and it's already spread. The doctors say I only have a few weeks left, but if I start chemo I can probably prolong it for another month, maybe even a few months." Biting his lip, he closed his eyes and squeezed them tight, not looking at the camera when he spoke his next words.

"I know you're going to kill me, but I denied the treatment. Why would I want to spend the last few weeks of my life sick and weak from chemo? I'm already in enough pain as it is, and thankfully, the doctors have given me some pain meds to help the discomfort in my stomach. It's been so fucking hard to keep this to myself, but I know I must. Please forgive me, Kate. I knew that if I told you it would draw attention away from your studies, and the last thing I want you to do is worry about me when you're trying to get your medical degree. Deep down I want to be selfish and just tell you so that you'll spend every last waking moment with me. I don't want to die alone, and I know you've been getting frustrated with me because you think I've been pulling away. Trust me, it's the last thing I want to do, but I've had no choice. It's hard pretending that I'm fine when I'm dying on the inside."

Covering his face with his hands, his shoulders started to shake as he sobbed silently. I cried along with him while Cooper held me tight.

"I thought he was cheating on me," I said softly.

"When we stopped making love, I thought it was because he wasn't interested in me anymore. I had no clue it was because he was in so much pain. I engrossed myself more into my studies and tried to overlook his aloofness, but I should've paid more attention to him instead of being too scared to find out the truth. I wish I was there for him toward the end."

Cooper put his hand on my cheek and turned me to face him. "He didn't give you the chance to be there for him. You would've given up everything to be with him and he didn't want that. He was looking out for you, love."

The camera shut off and then started up one last time with the date of record being the day before I found him dead. It was the hardest part of the video to watch because I knew without a doubt that after his final words it would be the moment he decided to take his life. He was wearing the same red T-shirt and jeans that I found him in on the morning of his death.

His eyes were tired and weak; his face pale and drawn. It was amazing how sickly he looked and I didn't even notice it back then. I loved him more than anything, but I was blind. I wanted to see him the way I'd always seen him, and I failed to acknowledge that something was completely wrong.

"Kate," he whispered hoarsely. "My time has come, darling. I can feel my life holding on by a thread. This will be the last time I get to speak to you, and I want you to know how proud of you I am. Whatever you do, please don't hate me when you watch this. You have to know that I wanted to preserve my life for as long as I could and still maintain some sort of normalcy. I wasn't supposed to live as long as I have, but I honestly believe that being with you gave me that extra time. I wrote you a letter, and of course, I couldn't say all of the things I wanted to, but that's why I did this video. I'm going to miss you so much. The thought of leaving you behind is the one thing that keeps me here, but the reality is that I have no choice. It's the end for me, and the beginning for you. Follow your dreams, Kate."

Before he could shut off the camera, he looked into it one last time, and it was as if he was finally at peace. I reached out and touched the screen, tracing every single line of his face. For so long I didn't have the answers I needed, and now I did. I just wished I had known, so I could've been there for him and taken care of him.

"I love you," he whispered, and after a few seconds of staring into the camera he was gone. There was no more …

I love you, too, Scott. Always.

Chapter 35

Kate

I watched Scott's video over and over until the sun rose the next morning. My eyes were swollen and sore from crying all night, but my heart felt ten times lighter. I got the answers I needed from Scott, but there were still answers I needed from his family.

Emily Easton was one of the last people on earth I wanted to see, but in order to get closure I had to. The team had an away game this coming weekend in Arizona, and our flight to leave was scheduled for early afternoon. Cooper and I had already packed our things, and since we had the morning to ourselves, I knew it was time I faced Emily.

"Are you sure this is what you want?" Cooper asked. "You could always wait until we get back home on Sunday night."

I dialed the number Emily had left on the piece of paper and waited for her to answer. "I have to talk to her," I told him. "As much as I don't want to, I know I need to. It's time to get everything out in the open. Once I speak to her I'll finally be able to put all of this behind me and really move on with my life."

"Hello," Emily answered, her voice soft and trembling.

"Emily, it's Kate. Can you come over this morning? I need to talk to you."

She gasped, "Sure. Should I head over there now?"

"Yes, that would be great," I said. "I'll see you when you get here."

Quickly, I hung up my phone and laid it on the dresser. The last time I saw Emily was at Scott's funeral, and I still remembered the way she glared at me in disdain. I wasn't allowed to sit with the family during the service, nor was I even acknowledged as someone special in Scott's life. The scars of that day would never go away, and I planned on making sure Emily knew exactly what it felt like.

About twenty minutes later, I heard a familiar sound coming down the street … it was a sound I didn't think I'd ever hear again. Rushing to the window in the spare bedroom, my heart almost fell to the floor when I saw Scott's black Ford Mustang pulling into my driveway.

"She's here," Cooper called from the kitchen. "Do you want me to let her in?"

Hurrying to the door, I stopped him by placing my hand on the door before he could open it. "No, I'm going to talk to her outside. I don't want her inside of my house after everything her family has put me through. I still don't know if I trust her."

Cooper nodded, his blue gaze full of concern when he stared down at me. Taking his face in my hands, I smoothed my thumbs over his stubbly cheeks and kissed him gently on the lips. "I know things have been crazy the past couple of days, and once this is over I'm going to make it up to you … I promise."

He smirked and bit his lip. "I'm going to hold you to that, love. As soon as you get back in we'll eat breakfast and who knows what else." Cooper kissed me on the forehead and went back to rummaging through the refrigerator. "I'll keep my eye on you. If I notice anything strange I'll come out there."

Before walking out the door, I took a deep, calming breath and held my head high. "Thank you. Hopefully, it won't come to anything like that."

The doorbell rang, but I decided to go through the garage door and meet her out front. When I turned the corner, I saw that she stood by the door, fidgeting on her feet nervously.

"Hello, Emily," I announced, startling her.

Quickly, she turned around and grabbed her chest. "Hey, you scared me. I didn't know you'd be coming up behind me. How are you?"

"Better now," I said, crossing my arms at the chest. "After last night a lot of things finally cleared up for me, but I still have a lot of questions."

Emily slowly crept down my front steps and approached, making sure to keep adequate distance. Emily was a petite woman with short bright, blonde hair and reminded me of a life-sized version of Tinker Bell. When Scott introduced me to her, I told him that she looked like the fairy, and ever since then he had always called her by that nickname. I called her that too, at least on up until his death.

Emily sighed and crossed her arms at the chest as

well, mirroring my stance. "What do you want to know?" she asked.

Not wasting any time, I went straight to the point. "Why is your mother still messing with me when it's obvious that I wasn't the reason for Scott's death? You all blamed him being miserable on me."

Nodding quickly, she lowered her head and sniffled. "Yes, I know we blamed you, and I can't begin to tell you how sorry I am for that. I found out about Scott's illness a couple of weeks ago, and when I tried to tell her she wouldn't believe me. Right after that was when she took off."

"Why did it take two years to figure out what happened?" I asked incredulously. "That doesn't make any sense."

Defeated, Emily sighed and flung her hands in the air. "I know it doesn't make any sense, but after Scott died we had all of his things packed up and put away. None of us knew that Scott was sick, and since we were living in Ohio at the time we never saw him. He always sounded exactly like himself when he called to check in with us. Mom was too heartbroken to go through it all, and I was too busy trying to take care of *her*. It wasn't until recently when I decided to start going through his things. I regret not doing it sooner, at least maybe then it would've spared all of us the senseless heartache."

Sniffling, she wiped away her tears, but kept her gaze on the ground. "You see, my mother fell apart after Scott killed himself; it was like every single thing she lived for just vanished. I thought with having me by her side it would help, but I wasn't Scott. I wasn't her favorite. After she basically shunned me, I couldn't help but hate you, too. My life has been nothing but hell for the past two years."

"Yeah, well so has mine," I snapped. "You're not going to get any sympathy from me. It wasn't exactly fun listening to you and your mother call me on the anniversary of his death and bitch me out for taking everything away from you. Did it ever occur to you that I loved him and lost just as much as you did? For the past two years I've felt nothing but guilt over what happened. I didn't think I was worthy of anyone's love until Cooper came into my life."

"And I think that's what set my mother off," she confessed, lifting her tear-filled emerald gaze to mine. "There were times when she'd just disappear for a few days and then come back home. She would never tell me where she went, but I figured it out when I looked at her bank statements. Every so often she would travel here to Charlotte. My only guess was so she could spy on you."

Gasping, my eyes went wide. "Spy on me? You can't be serious?"

"Trust me, Kate, if I had any other clue I would tell you. My mother's lost her mind. That's why I tried to call you a couple of weeks ago to warn you. She doesn't want you to be happy. Now that she's seen you with Cooper and that other guy, she's been doing anything and everything possible to destroy that. Did you not listen to the message I sent you?"

"No," I huffed, "I didn't. I thought you were calling because it was the day Scott died. I was expecting to hear another guilt trip come out of your mouth, so I threw my phone against the wall and shattered it. I honestly didn't want to listen to your message."

"I understand, but I tried to warn you that something was wrong. I knew my mother would get to the point where she'd snap, and it didn't help when she found the brochures to these rehab facilities I wanted to put her in. She needs help, Kate. I haven't been able to control her, and I don't know how far she's going to go this time."

"Whatever she does," I said, placing my hands on my hips, "she's not going to get Cooper away from me. I refuse to let her bring me down any more than she already has. I'm done letting her grief rule my life."

Sadly, Emily smiled and nodded her head. "I feel the same way." Reaching into her pocket, she pulled out a set of keys and handed them to me. "Here, these are for you. Scott left you his car, along with some other things that I also brought. I'm sorry it's taken so long to get it to you. My mother refused to let anyone send you the things he'd left."

Oh my God. After all of this time, I had nothing of Scott's in my possession. I felt so disconnected to him because I was denied any of his belongings … not even a simple T-shirt he wore so I could remember his scent or the pictures we took together.

Mouth gaping open, I gasped and reached for the keys with tears streaming down my cheeks. "Thank you for doing this. You have no idea how much this means to me."

"You're welcome, Kate. I owe you so much for what you've done for my brother, and what I put you through the past two years. In the trunk you'll find the title for the vehicle and all of the paperwork. Scott had it all put in your name a long time ago. Don't worry, though; I've kept it maintained and paid the taxes on it. I'm pretty sure I could be arrested for withholding it from you, but I'm hoping you'll find it in your heart to forgive me. Also, there's a box in there that has your name on it. I never opened it, so I don't know what kind of surprises he had in store for you."

My lip trembled as I slowly walked over to Scott's car; it was his baby. It still looked shiny and new like the day he bought it. I was with him that day, and he drove us all the way to the Blue Ridge Parkway so we could have a picnic. Then he drove all the way back so that I could spend the night studying. His spontaneity was one of the things I loved about him.

Smiling, Emily came up beside me and placed a gentle hand on the hood of the car. "I'm going to miss this thing, but I know Scott wanted you to have it." She looked down at her phone and held it tight. "If you don't have any more questions for me, I'm going to call a cab to come pick me up and take me back to the hotel. I'm actually leaving to go back home tomorrow. I can't afford to take off anymore time from work."

"Are you sure?" I asked. "Cooper and I can drive you back to the hotel."

I knew I didn't owe her anything, but it took guts to confront me and say that she was sorry. As much as I wanted to be a bitch and not care, it wasn't in my nature to do so. She was Scott's sister and he loved her.

Emily shook her head and opened her phone. "No, but I appreciate it. Cooper didn't seem too happy when I showed up last night." After searching through her phone, she dialed one of our local cab companies and asked them to come pick her up. When she hung up, she smiled at me one last time before walking to the edge of my driveway and sitting down on the ground.

I didn't want to leave her alone, so I sucked up my pride and joined her. We sat like that for fifteen minutes, waiting on the cab to come while talking about all of the times Scott made us laugh. It felt good to finally talk about him; it was like I could feel his presence all around me.

As soon as Emily left, I opened up the trunk to Scott's car and Cooper finally joined me. There were two boxes—one with my name on it—along with Scott's favorite baseball bat. "Um ... why did she leave without taking her car?" he asked curiously.

I lifted one of the boxes out of the trunk and passed it to him. "It's actually Scott's car. He gave it to me."

"Really?"

Grabbing the other box and the bat, I shut the trunk and followed him inside the house. "Yeah, Scott's mother refused to give me the things he left for me. That's why Emily brought them since they belonged to me."

"So I take it everything went okay? I was expecting to have to go out there and separate you two," he joked.

I laughed and shook my head. "No, it was actually pretty civil. She thinks her mother *is* trying to sabotage us so that I won't find happiness. That's why she's coming after you. We need to be careful, Cooper. I don't know what all she's capable of."

Cooper set the box in his arms down on the coffee table in the living room. Taking mine from me, he set it down as well. "Kate, I don't care what that woman does to me. Whatever happens, she's not going to succeed in tearing us apart. That's the last thing you need to worry about, love. I'm not going anywhere."

Biting my lip, I sidled up to him and ran my fingers up and down his chest. "Well, that's good to hear. However, I seem to recall us having a little bit of time before our flight leaves. Did you ever figure out what you wanted to do?"

Cooper growled low in his chest and grabbed my ass, holding me against his hardening cock. "I'm sure I can come up with something." Trailing his lips down my neck to my collarbone, he then grazed his teeth along my earlobe and whispered, "You know it's been a couple of days, love. Being able to touch you right now makes me feel like I'm going to go in-fucking-sane. I've wanted to make love to you so bad that I've basically walked around with a rock hard dick for the past two days. Please tell me you want it as bad as I do. I need to hear it in your voice that you want me to fuck you … to make love to you until your body only recognizes the pleasure that *I* can give you."

Lifting me in his arms, he carried me up the steps, and waited on me to answer as he laid me down on my bed. His heated gaze penetrated me further and deeper than any amount of lovemaking ever could. I could feel it between my legs as my clit throbbed in anticipation. Just the slightest bit of movement would set me off, and I knew the first second he touched me down there I would scream.

"Yes, Cooper," I whispered huskily. "I want you to take my body and fuck me as hard and as raw as you can so that I can feel you in the deepest parts of my body. I want that delicious ache between my legs to remind me that you dominated me, body and soul."

His fingers gripped on to the waistband of my shorts and he forcefully yanked them down before throwing them across the room. Gasping, I knew I was in for a wild ride when he ripped away his shorts and spread me wide. His thick cock glistened on the tip, so I grabbed his ass and squeezed, using my force to bring his body closer. He straddled my chest, and I licked the tip of his cock, swallowing the salty drop down my throat. While he thrust himself between my breasts, I kept my mouth on the tip of his cock, sucking hard. Cooper trembled for a second before pulling away and lifting my shirt and bra over my arms in one swift movement.

Grabbing my breasts in both hands, he squeezed them hard and bent down to take a firm nipple between his lips. Already I could feel my orgasm building, and as soon as he thrust his cock inside of me I let go.

"Cooper," I screamed, digging my nails into his shoulder. "Oh my God."

Keeping up his pace, he chuckled and pushed harder, faster. "I love it when I can make you come that quickly. It's so fucking hot to know that I turn you on."

Oh, and he definitely turned me on. Just a simple look from those blue eyes of his could drench my underwear in a heartbeat. Harder and harder he pushed until I could feel his cock pulsing inside of me, going deeper as he swelled larger. My insides clenched tighter, milking him with my body until he finally let go and released that delicious warm liquid inside of me. My arousal came hot and swift just in time to feel the last remnants of his release coating me with his desire. I loved it, I wanted more … and so did he.

"Now that I fucked you hard," he growled, "I'm going to make love to you slow. Your pussy knows that I was there and it'll feel it for the next couple of days, but now your heart needs to feel the rest. I want each time I make love to you to make your heart feel like my love will last not only a couple of days … but forever."

Slowly, he lowered himself back onto my body and gently glided inside of me, in and out. Fast fucking could drive me insane with its intensity, but there was something about making love slow that drove me wild.

"I love you, Kate," he murmured in my ear. "I never thought it was possible to love someone so much."

A tear streamed down the side of my cheek and I nodded. "I know the feeling," I whispered softly.

Chapter 36

Kate

We made it to Arizona in one piece, but I made sure before we left to tell Lara to keep an eye out on mine and Cooper's house. I didn't have time to look in the boxes that Emily brought me; after our lovemaking we were already running out of time to get to the airport, so we put them in my room. The first thing I planned on doing when we got back was open them.

Now we were on our way to the University of Phoenix Stadium in hopes of winning our third game for the season. However, Cooper could tell I was a little on edge. Saturday's weren't exactly my favorite day, considering it'd been the choice day for Marianne Easton to wreak her havoc. I was just waiting on something to blow up in my face.

"Relax, Kate, it's going to be fine. Nothing's going to happen out here," Cooper promised.

Evan was the one driving us around in one of the Cadillac Escalades that was rented for us while in Arizona. The only people in the vehicle were: Evan, Derek, Brianna, Cooper, and me. My brother already knew what was going on, but I explained it to Derek and Brianna so they wouldn't be lost.

"Please tell me you're not honestly scared of this woman?" Derek teased. "I thought you were more badass than that, Kate."

Since he was in the front seat, I smacked him on the head. "I'm not afraid of her, jackass. I'm afraid of what she's capable of. The woman's lost her mind. What if she followed us out here?"

"Then you kick her ass," he explained incredulously. "It's very simple."

Cooper smacked him on the head this time. "Derek, shut the hell up."

Sadly, Brianna sighed and squeezed my shoulder. "I'm sorry you have to go through this, Kate. I know it can't be easy on you. I'm sure the police will find her soon, though. There are only so many places you can hide."

I truly hope so.

When we got to the stadium, everyone filed out of the cars and headed inside. It was hot as hell in Arizona, and it actually made me miss the humidity in North Carolina. I didn't think that would ever be possible.

"All right, love, you better cheer me on today. Why don't you get out there and dance with the girls," he teased, smacking my ass. "I think you'd be sexy as hell in those little skirts."

"I tell you what," I began sarcastically, "how about I borrow Brianna's outfit and wear it for you behind closed doors. The last thing anyone is going to want to see is my uncoordinated ass dancing around on the field."

237

Cooper chuckled and put his arm around me, pulling me close so he could whisper in my ear, "Well, that may be so, but I have to say you're pretty damn coordinated in the bedroom. You can't be all that bad shaking your ass on a dance floor."

"Kate, let's go," Brianna called, waving at me. "I need you to check my ankle before we go out there. It's been swelling off and on."

Taking my chin, Cooper kissed me gently on the lips and then on the cheek. "Get going, love. I'll see you out there."

"Okay, but make sure you play hard."

Turning on my heel, I sauntered off toward Brianna, who rolled her eyes at us. Unfortunately, Cooper wasn't done. "What's my reward if I do?" he asked, drawing the attention of everyone around. His grin was so contagious that it was hard not to smile back.

"I don't know. Why don't you win the game and find out?" Winking, I turned around and continued on my way. The place we were staying at was one of the most beautiful resorts in the Phoenix area. I was pretty sure I could figure out something to reward him with. Our private hot tub would be a good place to start ... or better yet, I had another idea that would work just fine.

As soon as I sat down on the bench, Joel came over and sat beside me. "Are you all right, Kate? Over the past week you've been a little on edge. Do you need to take some time off? I'm sure Andrew wouldn't mind taking on your players as soon as he gets back from vacation. Thankfully, no one has had any problems other than Cooper with his shoulder."

"No," I blurted out, eyes wide. "With everything going on it's just been a little stressful. I promise I'm fine."

Frowning, he nodded and patted my shoulder. "Okay, I believe you. If you feel you need your space, will you let me know?"

"I will," I told him honestly.

When the time came for the players to come out, I got to my feet and cheered for Cooper when he came into view. He winked at me and smiled, full of confidence and power. The guys all looked to him for guidance, even my brother, and Evan was a natural born leader.

Before the first play even began, my phone vibrated in my pocket. As soon as I looked down and saw that it was the detective, my stomach twisted up in knots. Hopefully, they found Scott's mother.

"Hello," I answered, raising my voice so he could hear me above the screams all around me from the fans.

"Ms. Townsend, I wanted to call and give you the good news. Marianne Easton turned herself in today. She admitted to vandalizing Cooper's car and breaking into Luke's truck to steal his knife."

"Really?" I asked skeptically. "Why do I feel like I'm missing something here?"

"Well, she says she's tired of running away from her problems. She'll be charged with a felony, breaking and entering, and slapped with a few fines along with paying to have Cooper's car fixed. That's all we can get her with at the moment. She's not going to serve any jail time, but she is heading back to Ohio tomorrow afternoon. I know you have to be excited that she's getting out of our town."

"So it's all over?"

"I believe so," Sam said happily. "Thankfully, it didn't turn out as bad as it could. I've seen people do some really stupid shit in my line of work. I take it from the noise in the background that you travelled with Cooper to the away game?"

"Of course. I have to watch my team win," I told him.

Sam chuckled. "Yes, and I hope they do. I'm getting ready to turn on the television and watch it. Look, I don't know if you've thought about this, but did you ever decide if you wanted to issue a restraining order against Mrs. Easton? If you want my honest opinion, I think you should get one. That way I can scare her pretty hard before she leaves. If she gets anywhere near you we can throw her ass in jail."

"Then let's do it," I agreed automatically. "I don't trust her, nor do I trust Emily, but I don't think Emily is the problem."

"All right, I'll get everything going with the paper-work. Enjoy the game, Ms. Townsend. Now you can rest easy."

"Thank you, Sam. If you need anything else from me just give me a call." As soon as we hung up, I couldn't stop smiling. It was like a huge weight had been lifted from my shoulders and I could finally breathe. I couldn't wait to tell Cooper the good news, especially after he dominated the field with his impressive throws. The crowd was going nuts.

When the first quarter finally ended, Cooper was able to come in for a few minutes to take a break. "Okay, so are you smiling because we're kicking ass, or are you really just that happy for some reason?" he asked, giving me a quick kiss on the lips.

"Both," I squealed. "Marianne turned herself in! Not only is she going to have to pay to get your new tires, but she's going back to Ohio tomorrow with a bunch of fines and two felonies attached to her name."

Cooper hooted and swung me around in his arms. "Thank God, the bitch is going back. Now we can put her shit behind us and move on. It's all going to be over now."

Hopefully, with her going back home Emily could get her the help she needed. Even though she had turned herself in and faced a felony on her permanent record, I still didn't know if I believed it was over. Maybe a restraining order would be good to have … just in case

Chapter 37

COOPER

We won!

When I played for Oakland I never felt such pride in my teammates like I did for Carolina. They worked so hard and never really got noticed until now. Hell, I never even noticed them and my own uncle was the coach. They weren't a part of the division I was in, so Oakland never played them, and if they did it was only on rare occasions. I could only hope that I'd get to play against them at least one time before I retired. I wanted to show them that they made a mistake in letting me go.

"Dude, we have to celebrate tonight," Derek shouted, clapping me on the shoulder. "We're going to go to a couple of bars, you want to go?"

I had some celebrating to do, but it wasn't going to be with a bunch of drunk football players at a night club. I smiled and said, "Sorry, man, but I have better things to do."

Derek scoffed, "Yeah, I get it. You're choosing a girl over the guys."

Evan walked by at just that moment with a smirk on his face and bumped into him, making Derek lose his balance and fall onto the bench. "It's not just any girl, cocksucker, it's my sister. If he's going to blow us off then I can forgive him if he wants to spend that time with Kate. She's worth it. Maybe you should consider doing the same with Brianna since she's finally decided to go out with you."

"Would you?" Derek countered, looking more serious. The locker room was pretty much empty now that all of the guys were excited about going out for the night and celebrating.

When I first met Evan, my impression of him was that he was going to be an arrogant jackass like so many of the guys I'd played with before. The more I got to know him, the more he reminded me of Kate. They almost had the same morals and same ways about them.

Evan threw on his shirt and turned back to Derek. "Shit, if I was lucky enough to find a girl that was worth it I would ditch you guys in a heartbeat. I typically don't attract those, though. The only girls I seem to get are bitches like Lindsey. Maybe one day."

Kate's voice echoed through the locker room, "Knock, knock. Are you guys almost ready? Brianna and I have been waiting out here for forever. I'm starting to think you guys gossip more than the cheerleaders."

"Ha-ha," Derek joked sarcastically, but to us he lowered his voice and asked quietly, "How do you know when a girl is worth it?"

Evan and I both glanced at each other and grinned before I smiled back at Derek. "You just do," I said. "I knew the first second Kate opened up her mouth and spoke to me."

She loathed me at the beginning, but I knew without a doubt that she was worth every second I spent thinking about her.

"I heard the guys were going to a strip club tonight. Are you sure you don't want to go?" Kate announced from the bedroom.

We ordered in room service instead of going out with some of the guys and were about to take a soak in our own private hot tub. I had already changed into my blue swimming trunks while Kate locked herself away in our bedroom to change into her bathing suit. The moment she walked out wearing a skimpy black bikini with her golden hair hanging loose down her shoulders, the last thing on my mind was a fucking strip club.

My hands paused on the champagne bottle while I watched her walk toward me with a sly tilt to her shiny red lips. She knew what she was doing … and so did my cock when all of the blood decided to rush to its aid.

"Is that new?" I asked, gazing up and down her smooth bare skin. "Because you didn't wear that one when we had our little pool rehab session."

She snickered and reached around me, grazing her breasts against my chest as she grabbed the champagne bottle. Uncorking it, she poured me and her both a glass and smiled. "No, it's not new. I just never felt comfortable wearing it until now. I've always been a little too modest, I guess. Don't get me wrong, I like to wear sexy things and I know I have the body for it, it's just I don't like to flaunt it." She took a sip of her champagne and slightly opened her lips, grinning seductively. "But you know, I don't mind doing sexy things for you."

"Really?" I growled. "Like what?"

Licking her lips, she traced her tongue along the rim of her glass and took another long sip. "You'll see."

With her lips wet from the bubbly liquid in her glass, I lowered my mouth to hers and tasted her, sucking the remnants of the champagne from her bottom lip.

"You know," I began, murmuring across her lips, "one of the things I love about you is that you take care of yourself. You don't have to show off your body so people know how sexy you are. A woman who respects herself is sexy as hell. However, I must admit … there's nothing wrong with a dirty girl from time to time."

She finished the rest of her champagne and held out her glass for more. "A dirty girl, huh? Give me a couple more glasses of champagne and I'll get down and dirty for you. Now that things are finally getting better, I feel like I should celebrate by doing something I've never done before. You up for it?"

My cock throbbed in anticipation; I was definitely up for it.

Taking her hand, I put it on my shorts so she could feel how hard she'd just made me. Kate bit her lip and smiled. "Okay, I tell you what. Go have a seat on the couch and I'll be right there."

When I tried to take the champagne bottle, she shook her head and took it. "You'll get more of it, but the next time you take a sip it'll be off my body. Now go," she commanded.

Once I sat on the couch, my dick was so hard it fucking ached. Kate came back in and set the bottle of champagne on the table beside me before plugging in the iPod dock across the room. She scrolled through her phone and set it in its place, keeping her back to me the whole time. Her body began to move, gracefully and seductively, as a song started to play over the speakers; the song was none other than "Pony" by Ginuwine.

"I thought you said you couldn't dance," I groaned as she straddled my waist, thrusting her hips up and down my cock.

Grabbing her breasts, she squeezed them hard and pinched her nipples while throwing her head back, moaning. "Correction," she breathed, her body trembling. "I can dance, I just don't do it in front of people … only you."

"Well, then I guess I'm lucky."

Her body moved perfectly to the music and all I wanted to do was hold her down on top of me and plunge inside of her. She untied her bathing suit top, and as soon as her breasts fell out, I wrapped my lips around one and sucked … hard.

I looked up at her biting her lip, her eyes glassy and heated. "Are you thirsty?" she asked breathlessly.

Hell yeah, I was. Her nipples tasted sweet like the apples she always smelled of. I could suck every inch of her body and never get enough. That was how bad my addiction to her was.

"I'm always thirsty for you, love."

"Then open your mouth," she commanded.

She took the bottle of champagne and held it over my lips while I sucked it down in gulps. "Why don't you pour it over your tits and let me drink it that way?"

Smiling wickedly, she leaned back and tilted the bottle to where it only trickled down her chest. It flowed over her nipples at just the right amount for me to suck it down perfectly. "How does that feel?" I asked. "I've always heard that champagne makes the nipples tingle and heightens pleasure. Is it true?"

"Oh, yes," she agreed. "We definitely need to do it again in the future."

"We can do it as much as you like, love."

The song still played, enticing me with its tune and words. All I wanted was for her to ride me as hard and as fast as she could, and to feel her glide across my cock with how wet she was. I could feel the heat between her legs through my shorts, and how drenched she was when she allowed me to graze my fingers through the edge of her bottoms.

"Pull your shorts down a bit," she murmured. Slowly, she untied her bottoms on both sides and pulled them off while I slid my shorts down as far as they could go.

Rubbing her slick heat across my cock, her swollen clit made my mouth water and I wanted so fucking bad to throw her down on the couch and fuck her with my tongue. It was almost like an animal instinct inside of me that wanted to claim her … possess her. I had never felt this way about any woman, not even Claire when she was the only woman in my life for so long.

"I want you to make love to me, Cooper," she moaned.

Taking her face firmly in my hands, I pressed a hard kiss to her lips and held her tight. "I will do whatever you want me to, love."

Gently, she lowered herself onto my body, keeping

her gaze on mine the entire time. She closed her eyes for only a second, but when she opened them they were shiny and bright with tears.

"What's wrong, Kate?"

Keeping up her pace and clenching her body tight all around me, she shook her head and let the tears fall. "Nothing's wrong, everything actually feels right. For once I feel … complete."

"So do I, love," I told her. "So do I."

I wiped away her tears and lifted her in my arms, our bodies still connected. Outside on our private deck there was a large hammock-style bed that swung in the breeze. It was the perfect place to make love to her; to watch the moonlight as it grazed across her skin and shone in her eyes. Before, I never cared where I had sex with women. Hell, give me a bathroom counter and a condom and I was ready to roll. Not with her, though … not with my Kate. She deserved to be made love to under the stars with someone that would do absolutely anything for her. I would walk through the fires of hell just to be with her one last time.

I laid her down on the hammock and covered her body with mine, entering her slowly. The hammock rocked back and forth, swaying in the breeze as I made love to her, and kissed every inch of her body. When she let go, her body tightened all around me and she screamed out my name just as I released inside of her, letting my own self go. It was the perfect ending to a perfect day. We won the game, Scott's psycho mother had been found, and I just made love to the one woman who saw past my flaws and chose me.

Things were finally looking up for me … or so I

thought.

Chapter 38

Kate

Mine and Cooper's peaceful night of sleep felt like it ended abruptly when the pounding on the door woke us up. We were still outside—naked and in the hammock—swinging back and forth.

"I guess we better get up and get some clothes on," I murmured, chuckling as I tried to get out of the swinging bed. "We're not running late, are we? Our flight doesn't leave until lunch time."

Cooper yawned and crawled off the hammock. "No, it's still early. It's probably Derek or your brother. Let me throw on my clothes and I'll get it."

Even though we had a private deck, it still felt weird walking around outside naked. Rushing inside, I grabbed my phone, noticing that I had several missed calls and the time was only seven o'clock in the morning. *How did I not hear the phone ring?*

Another loud bang sounded on the door, making me jump. "Damn, whoever that is they're going to piss off the people around us. It's only seven in the morning," I groaned.

By the time I threw on a pair of my flannel pajama pants and slipped on one of my camis, Cooper opened the door. In rushed Joel, wearing a wrinkled white T-shirt and jeans with a Carolina baseball cap … and in his hand was a newspaper of sorts. With his lips set in a firm line, his face was bright red and angry as hell. I'd seen him like that before at practice when one of our team members got arrested for a DUI.

Cooper watched him cautiously and so did I, afraid to speak. Thankfully, Cooper was brave enough to go head to head with his uncle. "What's wrong, Joel? You don't look so good."

Joel threw the paper on the small kitchen table and pointed to it. "Why don't you take a look? I don't think you or Kate are going to be happy with what I saw this morning. Not to mention, the whole goddamned world is going to know the reason why I got rid of my last quarterback for you."

I gasped and rushed toward the table to pick up the paper, but Cooper beat me to it. His gaze was on fire, his body coiled like a snake. With his teeth clenched tight, I waited on him to explode just like Joel, but all he did was close his eyes and carefully put the paper back on the table.

"Cooper," I whispered, "what's going on?"

He sighed and covered his face with his hands before running them angrily through his hair. "I'm sure you'll figure that out when you read it. I have to get out of here for a while."

Turning on his heel, he stalked off toward the door without acknowledging me. I immediately rushed to follow him, but Joel sidestepped in front of me and stood in my way. "Kate, let him go. He's going to need his space to cool down after this. Trust me, he's a Davis … I know."

"Cool down? What the hell is going on?"

When my gaze finally found the article on the table, I didn't need to ask any more questions. It was all staring at me right in the face. The paper wasn't even a reputable one, like *New York Times* or anything … no, it was one of those gossip magazines that liked to talk shit about anyone and everything in the celebrity world. It was like porno for gossipers that wanted to get the down and dirty scoop on who was cheating on who, or who was secretly dating who. The article on Cooper, however, wasn't anything like that.

"I'm assuming it was Scott's mother who took all of these pictures?" Joel asked.

There were pictures of me and Cooper at Joel's house when we were invited over there for the dinner before we left in haste. The article exposed every dirty secret about Cooper imaginable. Now the world would know about Joel being his uncle, the deal he made with the doctor, and what he did to supply his drug habit. It was all there for the taking and now everyone would know. Setting the paper down, I couldn't even stomach to read the rest.

"You know that once the guys see this they're going to have a lot of questions. I wanted to save this embarrassment from Cooper, but now it's all going to come crashing down on him. I'm afraid of what he'll do. I know how he's handled his stress in the past, and I don't want to see him get that low again. "

In my heart I knew Cooper wouldn't fall back on his pain meds to deal with the stress. I hated that others couldn't see how far he'd come. He was stronger than that now.

"He's not going to go back to that," I stated whole-heartedly. "You have to believe me. If I thought he had a problem I would tell you. You know I would."

I would never let Cooper's drug problem slide by if he was still addicted to them. Even though we were in-volved, I would never jeopardize the team by letting him stay.

Sighing, Joel nodded and took a seat at the table. "I believe you, Kate, it's just we've started the season out so great and now this has happened. He's probably most up-set about what they said about you."

"About me?" I gasped. "What would be said about me?"

Frantically, I skimmed over the rest of the article until I saw my name. Once I turned the page, I choked in horror, angry tears welling in my eyes. "Oh my God. Why the hell would they write that?" Falling back into one of the kitch-en chairs, my hands shook as I read the rest of the article, struggling to take in a deep breath. Again, my past had been misconstrued and made to look like I'd be the end of the famous Cooper Davis.

Suddenly, it dawned on me. That was why Scott's mother turned herself in. She didn't need to send a third warning because I was staring at the fucking thing. The rest of the article was about how Cooper needed to stay away from me since I was known for making my boy-friends so miserable that they killed themselves. They even put a picture of Scott in the paper and described how he overdosed on pills, hoping that Cooper wasn't next.

It also went on to mention that Cooper's standards

had lessened since he went from a successful woman like Claire O'Briene, to his many one night trysts with famous celebrities and models, finally ending with someone like me who couldn't hack it as a physician since I dropped out and decided to be a physician's assistant.

"How did you find this?" I asked, gritting my teeth. If I ever saw Scott's mother again, I was going to slap the shit out of her. I thought she had gone too far with slashing Cooper's tires, but this was way worse.

"They're everywhere, Kate. When I went down to the lobby to eat breakfast, I saw one lying on a table with Cooper's name in plain sight. Knowing it's one of those stupid gossip magazines, I didn't think much of it until I saw the pictures. Do you think it was Scott's mother who did this?"

"I have no doubt," I huffed, glaring down at the article. "Cooper's gone through so much shit the past couple of weeks and it's all because of me. What if he gets tired of it and doesn't want to deal with it anymore?"

Joel tapped me on the chin with his finger, wanting me to look up at him. "Then you'll have your answer, Kate. I love Cooper just like a son, but if he gives up that easily then it's his loss. You deserve someone who will fight for you no matter what. Besides, he's kind of used to the tabloids running his name through the mud. You should've known your name would be dragged through this as well by getting involved with him."

Unfortunately, I didn't think anyone would waste their time talking about me.

"Thanks, Joel," I murmured sadly. "We'll deal with it somehow. I just wish I knew what to do."

Joel got to his feet and pushed his chair under the table, tenderly squeezing my shoulder before walking toward the door. "Well, there's nothing we can do about it here in Arizona. Why don't you get your things packed up? I'm sure Cooper will be back soon. I'll talk to the team once we're all together back home."

After Joel took his leave, I walked around the suite in complete silence while all of the memories from the night before replayed in my mind. I did my first strip tease, and slept outside under the stars for the first time in my life as well. I held those memories close to my heart while I packed up our things.

He had already been gone an hour, and I was beginning to think he wasn't going to come back in time before we had to leave for the airport. I didn't want to leave without him, but I would if he needed more space. For the first time in my life I was happy, and I didn't want to lose it.

I was determined to do whatever I had to do to keep it that way.

Chapter 39

COOPER

As soon as I left the suite, I knew who I needed to call. There was only one person in the literary business who was widely known and could get shit done … Shelby Dawson, a.k.a. Paige Monroe, the well-known journalist. Before I injured my shoulder, she had interviewed me for a ten page spread in the illustrious *Physique Sports and Fitness Magazine.*

I didn't want to call her on a Sunday, but I had no choice. Scrolling through my contacts, I finally found her number and dialed it, taking a seat on a secluded bench out in the courtyard of the hotel.

"Hello," she answered.

"Shelby, hey it's Cooper Davis. How are you?"

"Well, I'll be damned. I'm doing great, how are you? Did Bryan call you or something? I told him I was going to get in touch with you tomorrow."

"Uh … no, he didn't," I replied skeptically. "Why were you going to call me tomorrow?"

She laughed. "I guess it was fate then. Bryan wants to

do a follow up article on you now that you've transferred to another team. Would you be up for that?"

Wow, I believe it was fate. Now I could get my own story out there and redeem both Kate and myself.

"I would be honored," I told her. "I think that's actually what I need right now."

"Great, I know it has to be a change for you being over in North Carolina instead of California. My husband and I bought a house in Nags Head just recently. We can always do the interview out there if you want instead of you coming out this way."

"I would like that," I said. Kate could come with me and we'd have a whole weekend away … that was if she still wanted to be with me after today.

"So what may I ask is the reason you called if Bryan hadn't gotten to you first?" she asked curiously.

"Do you happen to know anyone who writes for *The Star Report*?"

She scoffed, "Unfortunately, yes. I know a couple of the journalists. Why do you ask? They didn't do another article on you, did they?"

"I wish I could say they didn't, but they did. Now everyone will know that the only NFL team that wanted me was the one coached by my uncle."

She gasped. "Is that even true?"

"Yes," I sighed, "it is. The truth is that no one wanted me after my injury. My uncle took a chance on me and brought me on. Believe me, it was an embarrassment for my family to know that I had fallen from grace."

"No, you didn't. You're brilliant out on the field. Why do you think my magazine wanted to interview you? Do you honestly care what others think, especially TSR?"

Angrily, I ran a hand through my hair and huffed, "No, I don't. I'm not going to lie, I used to care because I didn't want to let down my family, but now I couldn't give a shit. The only problem is that the article wasn't just about me."

"Who else was involved this time?"

Thoughts of Kate ran through my mind, and I couldn't shake the fear deep in my gut that there was a chance I could lose her over this. "Shelby, there's a woman I've been seeing and she happens to be one of our team physicians. She's not like all of the other girls you've probably seen pictures of with me in the past. This one is different."

"It sounds like you love her," she said softly.

"More than anything, which is why I need your help. Kate knows everything about me and has helped me face my demons, but she also had some demons to face herself. There's a woman who wants nothing more than to ruin her, and her plan was to come after me in hopes that I'd let Kate go. I'm not going to do that, though."

"Wow, this is kind of complicated, Cooper. Hold on while I look this up to see if I can find the article you're talking about."

I heard her typing over her keyboard keys for a second before her sigh came through over the phone. "Okay, I think I have it. Give me a second so I can read it." It was kind of a long article, but she read it in about three minutes. "Um … this is crazy, Cooper. Is the part about the doctor losing her license over you true?"

"Unfortunately, yes," I said. "And just so you know, Kate's not supplying me with pain meds like they seem to think. She's the one who actually helped me get off of them."

"Now what about the part about the guy named Scott? What's the deal with Kate supposedly sending her boyfriends to kill themselves? I'm assuming this Scott did that."

Gritting my teeth, I bit down so hard on my lip that I could taste blood. "Yes, he did by overdosing on his pain pills. Apparently, his mother went fucking psycho after he died and blamed it all on Kate. We only recently just found out that he had cancer and that's why he killed himself; the pain was getting to be too much for him. He made a video for Kate, and after two years, his sister finally shows up on our doorstep and gives it to her, along with the other stuff Scott left her."

"Oh my God," Shelby cried, "that's heartbreaking. I can't even imagine how upset Kate was over that."

"The story doesn't end there, though," I thundered. "Scott's mother had spent the last couple of weeks coming after me. She left a note on my car giving me a warning to stay away from Kate, and then the next week I got the tires slashed on my car. Obviously, when I didn't agree to stay away from Kate, she went to the tabloids and spilled this story."

"I see," she murmured sadly. "Yeah, the woman seriously needs some help. All right, it looks like the journalist's name is Kevin Layton. He had to have gotten a serious amount of money to be able to write this story."

"Do you know who he is?" I asked.

She groaned. "Yeah, and he's a real piece of work. Don't worry, though … the guy loves me. I'm sure I can get some information from him. What exactly are you looking for?"

"Shelby, some of the things in this story are only things that certain people in my life know. I need to know how this Kevin Layton got it. There's no way Scott's mother could have gotten that information on her own. I spent a lot of money to keep that shit quiet."

"All right, I think I have enough to go on. I'm sorry you and Kate have to go through this. Trust me, I had my own version of this going on a few months ago. It wasn't fun, and it nearly destroyed me. If this woman is coming after you two because her son is dead then what makes you think she's going to stop now? What's her goal? If she wants you two apart and this didn't work, don't you think she's going to come back?"

"Fuck," I hissed. "You're right. She's not going to give up when she sees us together."

"The question is … what are you going to do about it? Is this girl worth your career?"

Closing my eyes, I took a deep breath and hung my head. "She's worth way more than that, Shelby. I honestly don't know what I would do without her. I can't let this psycho bitch tear us apart."

"Then you have your answer, Cooper. No matter what you do, you always need to fight for those you love. I learned that lesson the hard way. Anyway, I'll call Kevin tomorrow and get the information you need. Just be careful, okay. I know from personal experience what desperate people are capable of."

"Thank you," I said to her before saying my good-bye and hanging up the phone.

Desperate people might be capable of anything, but I wasn't afraid of Marianne Easton. She could go to the press with her nonsense and I wouldn't give a shit. I refused to see Kate hurt anymore, and if Marianne Easton thought she got rid of me she had another thing coming.

If Kate still wanted to fight I would give up everything to stand by her side. The only problem now was facing her and finding out her answer.

Chapter 40

Kate

My brother had called about thirty minutes ago, saying he wanted me and Cooper to meet him, Brianna, and Derek in the lobby so we could leave for the airport. When neither Cooper nor I showed up, my brother came to our suite looking for us just like I knew he would.

"What's going on?" he snapped, glaring at me as he walked in. "We have a flight to catch and I'm beyond ready to get the hell out of here."

"Cooper's not back yet. I don't want to leave without him."

Evan's eyes went wide. "Where did he go?"

The magazine was on the table so I grabbed it and shoved it into his hands. "Take a look."

I watched as he read it, waiting on him to say something. When he didn't, I threw my hands up in the air, exasperated. "Well, aren't you going to say something?"

Throwing the paper on the table, he shrugged his shoulders. "What do you want me to say? It's a stupid tabloid magazine. The stuff about you is a joke, and anyone at home who knows you will know that it's bullshit. I know it sucks to see it, but when you decide to date someone as high profile as Cooper you had to know it was a possibility to be in the crossfire. Do you think Scott's mother is the one who's responsible?"

I rolled my eyes. "Who else wants to make my life miserable? If she's trying to break me and Cooper up, she might've succeeded. Once he saw the article he left and hasn't been back. I don't know where he is and he's not answering his phone."

Evan pursed his lips. "I'm sure he'll be fine, Kate." He paused for a second, furrowing his brows and opened his mouth to speak, but then shut it before doing it again. "Is he really the coach's nephew?" he asked curiously.

Glaring down at the paper, I put my hands on my hips and blew out a frustrated breath. "Yeah, he is. He didn't want that information to get out, but somehow Marianne found out and told the people at TSR. I have no clue how."

Evan squeezed my shoulder again before letting go. "Whatever the reason was for him not wanting people to know isn't going to matter. A lot of people aren't going to believe it, and most people aren't going to even care. No one's going to believe that shit."

"I think you're missing the point, Evan. It doesn't matter if people believe it or not, Marianne is going to keep trying to mess with me any chance she gets. I don't know if I'll ever escape from her."

"You don't think she'll ever get tired?" he asked.

"I don't know, but it's too exhausting to even think about it."

Turning my gaze toward the glass door that led to the private deck, I watched as the hammock Cooper and I slept on swayed back and forth in the wind. I wished with all of my heart that I could go back in time to last night when everything was perfect and I thought things were finally going to be different. *I guess it was all wishful thinking.*

From behind, I could hear Evan carrying my bags to the door and setting them down. When I peered over my shoulder, he stood in the doorway with his arms crossed.

"It's time to go, Kate," he commanded.

I'd hoped Cooper would come back in time before we had to leave for the airport, but he still hadn't. I wasn't even sure if he knew what time our flight departed.

"What about Cooper?" I asked frantically. "I don't want to leave him. He's not back yet, and I don't want to take his suitcase if he needs it." It was actually my excuse so that I could stay and wait on him.

"Kate, I'm sorry but I'm not leaving you here. You're coming with me, and if Cooper is smart enough he'll meet us there. Don't get me wrong, I've grown to like the guy, but he's a big boy. He doesn't need you taking care of him. Now come on before we miss our flight."

"Fine," I snapped, grabbing my phone from my back pocket. "If he doesn't answer this time then I'll leave with you, okay?"

Evan nodded and waited on me to call, but it went straight to voicemail. *You have got to be kidding me!* I wanted to scream. Clenching my teeth tight, I slid it back into my pocket and walked silently out the door along with Evan. I was going home … alone.

Before we took off, Evan and Brianna traded seats so that I could have her to talk to. She and Derek seemed awfully cozy when I met them in the lobby this morning; it might've been because she had on one of his jersey T-shirts and snuggled up to him on the leather couch. *At least they were happy.*

We had only been on the plane for two hours, and I grew angrier with each second that passed. *How could Cooper just leave me like that after everything we've been through?* I had no clue if he was okay, or if he really just wanted to get away from me since I was the cause of his problems. All I wanted was for him to talk to me, even if it was just to end things with me.

"Where do you think he is?" Brianna asked softly.

Sighing, I uncrossed my arms and shrugged my shoulders. When I looked down at my skin, I had crescent shaped indentions from where I'd dug my nails into my forearms. "I'm not sure. I guess back in Arizona. I don't understand why he wouldn't answer my calls."

"Maybe he was on the phone," she suggested. "I'm sure he had some people he needed to call. I wouldn't worry about it, Kate. You're probably getting all angry for nothing. This is what Scott's mother wants … you angry and miserable. Just forget about what that stupid article said and move on. It's not worth it."

It was hard not letting it get to me. When you're a celebrity, you have to grow a tough layer of skin because you're always in the spotlight and in the eye of the critics. There's always something negative said about you somewhere. I wasn't used to that.

"I'm going to ruin him, Brianna," I choked, a tear sliding down my cheek. "He's come a long way and it

265

hasn't been easy. His family sucks ass, especially his mother, and I know he doesn't really have someone to fall back on other than Joel. I just don't want to make his life harder than what it already is."

"Yeah, we heard about all of that at breakfast this morning. Derek and the guys were talking about how Coach and Cooper were related. Why was it such a secret anyway?" Brianna asked, turning her body to face me.

"It wasn't really meant to be a secret, but I know Cooper was embarrassed that no other team wanted him. He knew that if the world found out they would see it as a pity trade. He didn't want to have to deal with the snubs and the remarks that he'd get from that. I'm sure he'll have plenty of that to deal with soon."

Brianna took my hand in hers and squeezed. "But you want to know something, Kate? The team doesn't care about any of that. Now, if he wasn't winning them the games I'm sure they'd have a different story, but Cooper is building their confidence and bringing them the wins. They have nothing but support for him. That's all that matters, right?"

Nodding quickly, I looked over at her and smiled even though I wasn't happy in the least bit. "You know, you're right. As long as he has the support of the team I think he'll be fine. I just worry about him."

"I know you do, Kate. It's because you love him and you don't want to lose him."

Closing my eyes, I leaned my head against the seat and took a deep breath, hoping I could keep my lips from trembling. "I do love him, Brianna, and if I lost him I honestly don't know how I could face him every day. I'm miserable just thinking about it, and I haven't even talked to him."

After a while, I slowly drifted off to sleep. Unfortunately, I could still feel the ache in my heart and the chills of feeling alone. Brianna must've put a blanket on me, because eventually nothing hurt anymore and I was warm. Cooper's blue eyes and kind smile was all I could see as I finally entered into the dream world where nothing and no one could hurt me. I was happy there, but that happiness disappeared the moment I was jolted awake by the plane's not so gentle landing and a set of firm arms keeping me in place.

"What the hell?" I groaned, rubbing my tired eyes.

A deep chuckle sounded in my ear, along with his husky whisper, "Oh, it wasn't that bad, love. I couldn't let you fly out of your seat now could I?"

Eyes wide, I gasped and pulled out of the strong set of arms that were reluctant to let me go. "Cooper," I hissed low. "Where the hell have you been?"

He sighed and held my face in my hands. "Look, Kate, I'm so sorry for taking off the way I did, but I had some people I really needed to talk to. I'll explain everything later. Right now, all I need to know is that you forgive me."

I huffed, "I can't right now. I've spent the last six hours pissed off as hell, worried about you, and not knowing if we were okay or not. Excuse me if I can't just forget about all of that."

Cooper's lips turned up into mischievous smile, and I couldn't help but betray my own feelings as I leaned into his touch when he tucked a strand of my hair behind my ear. "I know that, love, but I'm going to spend however long it takes to make it up to you … to make you forget about everything that's happened. None of it's important. You are all that's important to me, and I don't care what Scott's bitch of a mother does to us, I'm not going to let her tear us apart. The question is … are you?"

Leaning forward, he brushed his lips against mine and lingered there until I opened my lips further, basically answering his question with my kiss. At least the plane ride didn't end as horrible as I thought it would.

Chapter 41

Kate

When Cooper and I turned down my street, the first thing I saw up ahead was Scott's car sitting in my driveway. I didn't know if I'd ever get used to seeing it there, or if I'd ever get the nerve to drive it after all this time, but it brought a smile to my face. My memories of Scott would always be exactly that … mine. His mother couldn't take those away either.

On the way home, Cooper told me that he'd called Paige Monroe, who was one of his friends and wrote that amazing article on him in one of my issues of *Physique Magazine.* It was the only redeeming article I had ever read on him, but it also happened to be before he hurt his shoulder and went downhill. Anyway, she was going to find out who spilled Cooper's private information and mine to *The Star Report* people. Hopefully, she'd find some answers soon.

Grabbing one of my bags from the backseat, Cooper fetched the rest and we got out of my car. I couldn't believe that the whole time we were on the plane he was up in first class with Joel. He came aboard late and Joel made him sit up there with him so they could talk. *I wish I would've known he was up there.*

We walked up to the door, but before I unlocked it, I gazed up at Cooper's blue eyes and sighed. "Once we find out who leaked the information to the TSR people, how are we going to go after them? How can they get in trouble if they have freedom of speech?"

"To those I paid off they don't have the luxury of freedom of speech in this matter. They had to sign a disclosure form in order to receive the money I gave them to keep quiet. They talk, they don't get the money. If they took the money and then talked, they would have to pay the money I gave them back times three. So if I find out that it was one of them, they'll be paying me a shit ton of money."

"How much are we talking?" I asked curiously.

Cooper shook his head and smiled. "It's a lot, love. Trust me."

Wow, I can only imagine. I had no idea how much money Cooper has made, but I did know one thing ... I was sure he made more in three months than I did in two years of working. Opening the door, I walked in and carried my bags to my bedroom while Cooper went to the kitchen to fix something to drink. I knew that once I went into my bedroom there would be two boxes filled with things from Scott. I was nervous as hell to open them because I could just imagine there being a sick surprise from his psychotic mother.

While Cooper was downstairs, I figured it was the best time to open them up. Sliding my finger under the tape, the first box I came to was basically things I needed for the car. The title was in there with my name clearly printed in bold letters, but there was also something else attached to it … a note.

Kate,

I know you must be hurting right now with finding out the truth, but I'm hoping you'll take care of my baby for me. Your Jeep is getting old and worn out so I know it's about time to get rid of that thing and move on. I know my baby will be happy in your hands. Make sure to drive her hard and fast sometimes though. She'll get bored only doing the speed limit.

I love you,

Scott

"There is nothing wrong with doing the speed limit, Scott," I half laughed and half cried. With a smile on my face, I folded up the letter and put it back into the box, setting it beside Scott's favorite baseball bat, which I had propped up against my nightstand.

Sitting on my bed, I grabbed the other box and placed it on my lap. Once I had it opened, I looked in to see another box, only smaller in size sitting inside of it. *Okay,* I thought to myself, *this is strange.*

Pulling the smaller box out, I opened it up to find another box, and another, and another, until finally the last one I pulled out couldn't possibly fit a box inside of it.

I was wrong.

My heart fell when inside there *was* another box ... it was a small blue one tied with a white ribbon. Hands shaking, I reached in and grabbed it, tears flowing like hot rivers down my cheeks.

"Oh my God," I cried softly, placing a hand over my mouth. "Scott, what did you do?"

Gently, I untied the ribbon and opened the blue box where a black velvet one sat along with another tiny note. Fingers trembling, I opened up the letter.

Kate,

I bought this ring for you before I found out I was sick. My dream had been to make you my wife before I died, but it would've been selfish of me to ask when I knew our forever wouldn't have been that long. Still, I want you to keep it and someday I hope that you'll find someone that'll love you as much as I do.

Always and Forever yours,
Scott

Closing my eyes, I held the box in my hands and cried until I felt Cooper's arms wrap around my body. I didn't even hear him walk into my room. For the rest of the night, Cooper didn't ask any questions, he just held me tight until I fell asleep.

When I woke up the next morning, I was alone in my bed with Scott's ring glistening in the bright morning sun, except it wasn't in the box … it was on my finger.

Chapter 42

COOPER

"Dude, I can totally see the resemblance between you two," Derek joked, glancing back and forth between me and my uncle, who was down the field talking to Evan. "I don't see how those of us on the team didn't notice it before."

I scoffed, "I can see why. You aren't exactly what I'd call perceptive, Derek."

"Hey, you better watch it, Davis. I'm one of the ones who protect you out on that field. I can easily let someone bypass me and sack your ass."

Chuckling, we both grabbed our bags and started on our way to the end zone where Joel and Evan stood talking. Practice was finally over for the day, but after this weekend's game in Arizona there were a couple of players who were injured and needed Kate's help. I hadn't seen her since this morning before we left to come to practice. I thought she would've kept Scott's ring on, but when she came downstairs to eat breakfast I noticed that it was gone. I didn't ask questions … I just wanted her to know it was all right with me if she wanted to wear it.

Before I could get all of the way down the field, my phone started to ring, so I reached into my bag and grabbed it. It was Shelby.

"Shelby," I answered, "how did everything go?"

She groaned into the phone. "Let's just say you owe me, Cooper. It was the longest lunch date of my life, but thankfully, having an MMA fighter as a husband comes in handy. It tends to strike fear into some."

She laughed for a second, but then cleared her throat and continued, "Okay, so Kevin told me that one of the women he spoke to was Marianne Easton, Scott's mother. I know you already know that. Now here's the part you're not going to like."

Joel furrowed his brows, knowing very well that my body language was coiled tighter than a snake. I could hear my heart pounding in my ears as I waited for the answer to all of my problems.

"Tell me, Shelby," I growled firmly. "I have to know."

My uncle came up to me and put his hand on my shoulder while I waited on Shelby to give me the news. When the name finally crossed her lips, I knew exactly what I needed to do. "Thank you, Shelby. I appreciate you doing this for me."

"What are you going to do?" she asked quickly.

Peering at Joel, I took in a deep, frustrated breath and let it out angrily. "It looks like I'm making a trip out to California."

And it definitely wasn't going to be a pleasurable one.

Sometimes it felt like half of my life had been spent in airports because I was always at one. Even as a child, my family was constantly travelling the world or doing something. One day it would be nice to have roots and just stay there with the occasional travelling here and there.

"Are you sure you don't want me to go with you?" Kate asked. "I don't like the idea of you going alone." She rushed me home after practice so I could pack and get to the airport. The sooner I could get to California, the sooner I could get home. I was glad she drove me because I was too pissed off to even think straight, not to mention, I still hadn't had a chance to get my car fixed.

"I'm sorry, Kate. Trust me, I want you with me, but you don't need to be there. I plan on saying what I have to say and then leaving. I'll be back by tomorrow afternoon."

"Why can't you tell me who you're going to see?" she asked.

I could hear the hurt in her voice, and even in my mind I wanted to believe that everything had been just one huge mistake. I didn't want to say a word to anyone until I knew for a fact that what Shelby said was true. I had to hear it with my own ears.

"I want to tell you, Kate, and when I know for certain that I have the truth I'll call you."

Overhead, the announcement to board my flight echoed over the speakers. Kate's eyes went wide and she jumped in my arms. "Be safe out there, Cooper. I love you."

"I love you, too," I murmured in her ear, wrapping

my arms around her waist. "I'll be back tomorrow."

I held onto her tight and breathed her in as deep as I could before the second and final announcement to board the plane sounded from above. Nodding, she stepped back with wary eyes and smiled. When I bent down to grab my bag, I looked at her hand where I had just put Scott's ring on the night before.

"Why did you take it off?" I asked. "I thought you might want to wear his ring."

Kate looked down at her hand and let out a heavy sigh. "It's a beautiful ring, Cooper, but it doesn't belong on my finger. It might have years ago, but now it doesn't. I'm sure I'll have one there someday. Until then, I'm content with it being bare."

I knew it was too soon to think about marriage with her, but there was no doubt in my mind that if we were still together in the next year that I'd ask her in a heartbeat. Kate wasn't a rush into anything type of girl, and the last thing I wanted to do was scare her off. I'd wait for when the time was right.

"I understand," I told her. Tilting her chin up with my finger, I kissed her gently on the lips before turning around and walking away. I was ready to get this shit over.

Chapter 43

Kate

Through the window, I watched as Cooper's plane took off down the runway before lifting off into the air. I respected that he didn't want to tell me who the other person involved was, but I figured he had his reasons. As soon as I got out to my car, I planned to stop by The Carolina Tavern and get something to eat, but that was put on hold when Detective Sam Lennox decided to call me.

"Hello," I answered.

"Ms. Townsend, it's Sam Lennox. Okay, I'm going to just cut to the chase and let you know. Emily Easton called me today and said that her mother never showed back up in Ohio. I don't know if there's any cause for concern, but until she shows up back home I want you to be cautious. I'm sure you'll tell Cooper for me, right?"

"You can't be serious?" I hissed. *That's not the news I want to hear right now.* "And yes, I'll tell Cooper, but he just left for California."

"I see," he remarked cautiously. "I'll have Officer Stilwell drive by your house every now and again to check it out."

"Thank you, Sam. I appreciate it."

Once I got off the phone with him, I headed over to The Carolina Tavern. When I walked in, my brother and Luke—along with some of the other guys on the team—were sitting at the bar, drinking and eating.

"Can I join you?" I asked, dropping into the seat beside Luke.

From the look on his face I could already tell he'd had one too many beers. "Well, of course, sweetheart. Where's the boyfriend?" he asked, glancing behind me.

"He just left for California. According to the police, I shouldn't be alone, so I figured I'd crash the party."

My brother furrowed his brows in concern. "Why didn't they want you to be alone?"

Behind the bar, Grayson smiled and placed a glass of wine down in front of me. "Thank you," I told him, taking a huge sip. To my brother, I said, "Scott's mother hasn't shown up in Ohio since they let her go. They don't know where she's at again."

His eyes went wide. "Are you shitting me? So she could still be in town?"

I took another sip. "Yep."

"Well, then if that's the case you're staying with me tonight until Cooper gets back. I don't want you alone."

"Evan, that's not necessary," I insisted incredulously.

Smiling, he leaned over the bar on his elbows. "Well, if you don't stay with me then I'll just send Luke over to stay with you. Make the choice, Kate. I'm sure Cooper wouldn't like it if Luke was there all night."

Groaning, I downed the rest of my wine and rolled my eyes. "Fine, I'll stay at your house."

Luke laughed and put his arm around me. "You know, sweetheart, with you not wanting me to stay with you, I'm starting to think you're afraid you won't be able to control yourself around me. Is that it?"

"I can control myself, Luke," I told him, taking his arm and sliding it off my shoulders. "I just don't want to piss Cooper off. I wouldn't like it if he was staying the night with another female."

"Who says he's not?" he asked. "Did he tell you where he's staying? Who he's going to go see?"

I could feel everyone's eyes on me and I choked. In all honesty, Cooper never did tell me who he was going to go see or where he was staying. There weren't too many people who knew of his past, and only one of them came to mind … the doctor he slept with. She was his lover and she lived out in California. What if he went to see her? What if something happened between them?

"You honestly don't know, do you?" Luke asked curiously. "You must really trust him."

I huffed. "Fine, he never told me, but I know that why he went out there is important." I didn't have to look at Luke to know he could sense the shadow of doubt creeping in over my words.

Luke moved closer to me and lightly touched my chin, turning me so I'd look at him. He was dressed in a Red Bull T-shirt and jeans with his hair in perfectly gelled spikes. His eyes, however, weren't lit with mischief like they were two minutes ago, but now full of concern.

He looked around the room at everyone's prying eyes and leaned down to my ear. "Come with me," he commanded, taking my hand.

I followed him through the front door until he stopped

in front of his bike. Taking my other hand, he pulled me in closer and gazed down at me with his emerald green eyes. "Kate, I'm so sorry for putting you on the spot like that. I was just messing with you, thinking you would pick back, but you didn't. I could see it in your eyes that something's wrong. Where did Cooper go?"

I shrugged. "I don't know, but I know it has to do with the *The Star Report* article."

Luke nodded. "Yeah, I heard about that. I didn't want to bring it up unless you did. Who else could be in on it other than Scott's mother?"

"I'm not sure, but I know there are some people that Cooper suspects. One happens to be a woman he used to mess around with."

"As in fucking with?" Luke asked.

Cringing, I closed my eyes and didn't reply. My silence was the answer he needed. "Fuck, Kate, really? And you let him go without you?"

"He didn't want me going," I exclaimed. "What was I supposed to do?"

Luke sighed and pulled me into his arms. "I just don't want to see you get hurt, Kate. Evan keeps telling me to stay away from you, but I feel so protective of you … I always have."

"I know," I whispered, laying my head on his chest. If Cooper had never shown up, I was pretty sure my heart would've eventually belonged to Luke, but it was something I was never going to find out.

Luke held me tighter. "And it kills me that you're going through all of this shit and I'm not the one helping you this time. I honestly thought Cooper would've screwed up by now and you'd be mine." Gently, he kissed me on the forehead before pulling away. "Okay, let's get back in there before they suspect something. I didn't want to talk to you in front of everyone. The last thing they need is seeing me go soft on a girl. I have a reputation to uphold."

Locking my arms with his, I shook my head and smiled. "And that reputation, Luke Collins, is what's holding you back. If you want a girl like me, you aren't going to get it like that."

"Well that's the problem," he said, holding open the door for me. "I haven't met anyone else like you."

"You will, Luke. I promise, when the time is right she'll be there."

"Do you honestly believe that?" he asked, furrowing his brows.

Lifting my hand to his face, I smiled up at him. "With all of my heart," I declared.

Chapter 44

COOPER

After my layover in Dallas, Texas, I had arrived in California around nine o'clock in the morning with no sleep and the worst headache imaginable. The first thing that came to mind was taking a pain pill, but I didn't have any ... I didn't want them. I was ready to get this shit over and get back home to Kate, where I belonged.

No one knew I was going to California and I planned it that way. Once I retrieved my bag—even though I knew I wasn't going to need any clothes in the first place—I went outside and procured one of the cabs that waited along the sidewalk.

"Where to?" the driver asked.

I gave him the address and we were off. My heart pounded and my adrenaline was through the roof the entire car ride to my destination. I only prayed that she was at her house so I could get everything off of my chest and get the fuck out. After this, I was probably never going to go back to California again.

When the cab driver stopped at the edge of the driveway, I handed him a wad of bills and said, "If you stay right here and wait on me, I'll give you double that amount when I get back."

The driver's eyes went wide and his mouth shot open. "Are ... are you serious?" he asked incredulously. "I'll wait for five hours for that. Trust me, I'll be right here. Take your time."

Yeah, I knew he would want to stay. "Thank you," I replied, getting out of the car.

Making sure to grab my bag, I bolted straight to the door. As soon as I got close enough, I banged on it. I'd been to that house many times before and had plenty of memories in it ... most of them involving the cold-hearted woman who answered the door, her eyes wide with surprise. She was dressed in her usual attire of expensive dress pants and blouse, her face covered in two inches of makeup. She may have been in her late fifties, but the woman could easily pass for someone in her thirties.

"Cooper, what are you doing here?" she gasped. "Shouldn't you be in North Carolina?"

"Yeah, well, I came all this way to talk to you ... Mother."

Not waiting for her to invite me in, I pushed the door open and thundered past her into the house. "Why on earth would you come all this way just to talk to me?" she asked, chuckling nervously.

As I glared at the woman who tried to ruin my life, I couldn't believe it took this long to figure out what her problem was. She never loved me, she only loved herself, her money, and the power she held over everyone around her. When I was a child, all I did was strive for her approval, but in reality, she didn't approve of anything. No wonder I was fucked up.

Turning on my heel, I stalked off to the kitchen while my mother followed. "You want to know why I'm here? Take a look at this," I growled, grabbing the magazine from my bag and slamming it down in front of her. "Do you want to tell me why in the hell you gave these fucking leeches the information for this article? For someone who's so concerned about my career, you definitely didn't give a shit when you gave this up."

Nonchalantly, my mother rolled her eyes and fetched a glass out of one of the kitchen cabinets. "I have no idea what you're talking about. Anyone could have given that information to the press." She turned her back on me and filled her glass with water.

"Oh, that's not what I heard. From what Kevin Layton says you were pretty enthusiastic about giving out all of my dirty little secrets. The same thing goes for that psychotic bitch you teamed up with, Marianne Easton."

Dropping her glass in the sink, my mother jerked her body around to face me, muscles tense and eyes on fire. "Yeah, that's right," I stormed angrily, "I know all about it. Did you also know that Marianne had been following me and Kate around, and left warning messages on my car? Not to mention, she happened to slash my tires as well. Now tell me, does that sound like a sane individual to you?"

"She's hurting for her son," my mother spat. "Right now, I know how she feels because you're heading down the wrong path fast."

"What? You're not making any sense. How am I heading down the wrong path? I'm on a wonderful team that's won every single game this season, I've stopped doing drugs thanks to Kate, and I've finally settled down. What more do you want from me?" I shouted.

"I want you to stay away from that girl," she exclaimed. "Marianne told me that her son killed himself, but she thinks Kate had something to do with it. I'm only looking out for you."

I scoffed, "Really? Her son was dying of cancer, Mother. I watched a video of him saying good-bye to Kate and how he was in too much pain to keep living. Kate actually made him happy and *gave* him several more months of living. Marianne should be thanking her. She used you to get what she wanted, and you happily threw me under the bus."

"I told you I was looking out for you. It was the only way for you to see Kate for who she was."

"Since when do you care about *my* well being, huh? And did you not hear what I said just a few seconds ago. *Kate* is the reason why I don't take pills anymore. She's the one who never left my side when I went through withdrawals."

My mother shook her head with a smug expression on her face. "You want to talk about someone who never leaves your side? Let me get my phone and show you exactly how Kate stays by your side."

What the hell is she talking about?

My mother came back her phone and held up a picture of Kate … in the arms of Luke Collins. "Look what Marianne sent me last night. Last night, Cooper. That looks an awful lot like Kate with another man. Are you telling me that she's worth it now when she's let another man grope all over her?"

Seeing Kate in Luke's arms pissed me the fuck off,

but it nowhere near concerned me as much as the fact that Marianne was still in Charlotte and I was in California where I couldn't protect Kate if anything were to happen. I bet Kate didn't know Marianne was still in town.

Unfortunately, my mother wasn't done. "Whatever your reasons are for wanting to date someone beneath you is beyond me. Why can't you find someone like Claire who's beautiful, refined, and from a wealthy family? You have a duty to your family to uphold the name and you're throwing it away. It's an embarrassment."

Eyes wide, I snarled and grabbed her phone, throwing it as hard as I could against the wall, making her shriek and jump back. "An embarrassment? You exposed my personal problems to the world. If anything, you fucked up my career even more!"

Nonchalantly, she blew out a frustrated breath and shrugged her shoulders before looking down at her long, manicured fingernails. "Well, it's not like you're going to be the star you were when you played for Oakland. Joel is a good man, but his team sucks. Why you ever agreed to be on it is beyond me."

You would think hearing those words coming from your mother's mouth would hurt, but I was so far past caring that saying what I did next didn't bother me one fucking bit.

Chuckling, I let my smile disappear into a cold mask, one of complete and utter disdain. "I agreed to be on his team because no one else wanted me, Mother. Since I'm such a huge disappointment to you, I figured I'd tell you the truth. You see, I don't give a fuck if you approve of me or not because everyone back home does. I'm not going to fight for your approval anymore because no matter what I do it's never good enough. I will admit defeat and give up on you."

Holding my hands in the air I said, "I'm done," before walking out of the kitchen straight to the front door.

My mother shouted out behind me, "Where are you going? I thought I taught you better than this, Cooper Holden Davis!"

Shaking my head, I turned around to face her one last time. She would always be my mother, but just because she had that title didn't mean she had worth.

"That's the thing, Mother. You didn't teach me anything. I'll call Dad and tell him good-bye, but I don't ever want to see you again. This is the last time I'm coming here." The look of surprise and horror on her face after that statement would forever stay ingrained in my mind.

"You don't mean that," she chuckled worriedly.

Opening the door wide, I took a deep breath and turned around. "Oh yes, I do. From this day forward I am no longer your son. I don't want to be. You must be one miserable woman to only think of yourself and turn your back on your own family. I hope money makes you happy because in my world it only led to bitterness and pain. I *am* lucky, though … I'm loved by the most amazing woman I know. You need to ask yourself who in this world actually loves you. I can guarantee you there won't be a single person on that list. Good-bye, Mother."

I closed the door with my last words and walked away, never once looking back. It felt good to do what I did, but now it was time to go home … to my real home. The guy in the cab still waited at the end of the driveway, and when I got in I actually had a smile on my face.

"To the airport please," I told him. "I'm ready to get

back home.

Chapter 45

Kate

By the time Cooper called and said he was coming home, I was a complete and utter mess. All night I couldn't help but wonder what he was doing and who he was with. It just so happened that I wasn't near my phone when he called, so all I had to go on was a voicemail. He said his plane would be in at six-thirty tonight, and after working all day—going through the motions like a zombie—I was ready to see him.

When I pulled up at the pickup terminal, I saw him standing there in the same bright blue T-shirt and jeans that he wore the day before. His face was all stubbly from not shaving and he looked tired …exhausted. I knew the feeling because I felt the same way, but when he saw me his face did a complete change.

Opening the car door, he slid inside and immediately grasped my face, pulling me to him and pressing his lips firmly to mine. His tongue opened my lips and he deepened the kiss, not caring about the horns that blared behind us.

"Well, hello to you, too," I chuckled, pulling away from his lips. I wanted to jump right in and ask where he went, but I knew he would get to it soon. Patience was not always a virtue of mine when I wanted answers immediately.

Cooper smoothed his thumbs over my cheeks and over my lips. "You have no idea how glad I am to be back. There's so much I have to tell you. My phone died before boarding the last plane so I had no clue if you knew to come get me. The message I left you was kind of vague, but most importantly I didn't get the chance to tell you that Marianne was still here in Charlotte."

My eyes went wide. "How did you know that? I never got the chance to tell you. Sam called me last night and told me that she never went back to Ohio."

Putting my car into gear, I pulled us out into the slow airport traffic and headed home, sneaking glances at him while I waited on him to answer. He finally turned to me, his gaze narrowed. "So what exactly did you do last night, Kate? Who were you with?"

"I went to The Carolina Tavern, and then stayed over at Evan's house so I wouldn't be alone. Why do you look angry?"

Leaning forward, he let go of my hand and rested his elbows on his knees, sighing. "I know I shouldn't be angry because he's your friend, but Scott's mother had sent a picture of you in Luke's arms. Believe me, it wasn't something I was happy to see, and definitely not happy that she's still watching you."

Oh no!

"Cooper," I murmured desperately, "nothing happened between me and Luke last night. We were just outside talking. I was upset because you wouldn't tell me who you were going to see, and I had so many thoughts running through my head. It was only a hug, that's it."

Cooper immediately sat up and glared at me. "Wait, what are you talking about? What kind of thoughts were you having?"

Keeping my focus on the road, I reluctantly whispered my answer, "I thought you were going to see the doctor you had screwed around with. I couldn't think of anyone else that would want to conspire with Marianne."

"And you what? Thought I'd fuck her or something?"

"No," I gasped, "that's not it." I pulled over to a nearby parking lot and shut off my Jeep. Taking a deep breath, I bit my lip, meeting Cooper's ocean blue gaze. "Cooper, I just couldn't stomach the fact that there was a chance you'd be around someone that you used to be intimate with. Even though I know you love me and wouldn't do anything to hurt me, for the first time in my life I let jealousy take over. You have an extremely scandalous past with lots of beautiful women, and for once I doubted myself. I didn't like it."

"Kate, you are more beautiful and have more worth than any of those women I'd been with. Don't ever doubt yourself with me, okay? And just so you know, it wasn't that woman I went to go see."

Who else could it have been?

"Who was it?" I asked.

Sighing, he laid his head back against the seat and closed his eyes. "It was the one person I least expected … my mother."

I gasped, eyes wide. "Holy hell, you can't be serious."

He snorted. "Unfortunately, I am. After looking at the pictures, I'm assuming Marianne approached my mother after the party somehow. I don't know exactly because I was too pissed off to even ask, but apparently, she told my mother about Scott. They both thought that by exposing our dirty secrets it would tear us away from each other."

"What did you say when she told you?" I asked curiously.

"I told her I was done with her and that I never wanted to see her again. My home is here now anyway … not there. It was never where I belonged."

We sat there in silence for a moment while everything sunk in. *What a bitch!* I couldn't believe his mother would do such a thing. What's worse was that I couldn't imagine how hard it must've been for him to learn the truth.

"Are you going to be okay?" I asked.

Tilting up his chin, he took in a deep breath and closed his eyes. "Actually, Kate, for the first time in my life I think I'm better than okay. I'll never have to listen to my family's negativity about how much of a failure I am, because you know what, I know that I'm not. I believed I was for so long because that's all I heard. Not anymore, though. I have you, I have the team, and I have my uncle. As long as I have you by my side I don't need anything else."

Turning my way, he leaned over and traced his tongue across my lips before nipping my bottom one with his teeth. "Now how about we go home and I show you how much I missed you. After that I'll cook us an amazing dinner because I'm starving. I can't go another minute without having you naked and spread wide in my bed."

"Then hold on tight," I whispered huskily across his

lips, "because the ride home is going to be awfully fast."

A fast ride was definitely what Cooper had in mind as well. He slid his hand down the waistband of my shorts and slipped two fingers inside of me. "Open your legs as far apart as you can, love," he commanded low.

Bending my knee, I propped my foot up on the seat so I could give him more room. "That's good," he murmured, thrusting his long fingers in and out.

I groaned, "This isn't fair, and it definitely isn't safe."

"Oh, don't worry," he teased. "I'm not going to let you come until we get into my driveway."

Breathing hard, I knew I was on the edge, and we still had two miles before we got to our street. There was no way I could hold out, but every time I got close Cooper would slow his pace and my orgasm would ebb off.

"When we get in my driveway, tilt your seat all the way back and I'll finish this for you."

Panting, I turned down our street and put my other hand on the button to tilt my seat back. As soon as I put my car into park, I tilted the seat back and Cooper went into full blast. Thrusting his fingers harder, he aggressively lifted my shirt and bra with his other hand. Instantly, he closed his lips firmly over my nipple, sucking and biting it.

I came immediately, gripping on to his arm while my orgasm felt like liquid fire racing throughout my veins. Chuckling darkly, Cooper slid his fingers out and lifted them to his lips where he sucked them off, groaning the entire time with his heated gaze on me.

"I enjoy the way you taste, love. Now let's get inside so I can make love to you."

We both rushed out of the car, and as soon as we got inside we ripped our clothes off before we could even get to his bedroom. Holding me in his arms with me straddling his waist, he faltered on the stairs and landed on top of me, pushing his way inside. Arching my back because the stairs were cold against my skin, I took delight in the heat between my legs as a distraction. Cooper lifted me up off the stairs and backed me against the wall this time, keeping his cock inside of me and thrusting each chance he got.

"Can you tell I missed you?" he growled, lowering his head to my breasts.

I moaned. "Oh, yes, but I want more."

Finally, we made it to his bedroom and he laid me down on the bed, kissing his way up my neck to my lips. Our bodies moved together slowly, tenderly. With his fingers caressing my cheeks, he kept his gaze on me the entire time we made love.

"I'll give you whatever you want, love. If you want more just say it, and I'll give you more. There's absolutely nothing in this world I couldn't offer you."

"What about your heart?" I asked softly. "Is that something you'll give me one day?"

Rolling his hips harder, he thrust deeper inside of me and held me tight, his eyes never wavering. "Fuck, you're getting so tight. I'm so close."

Arching my back, I let my orgasm go at the same time I could feel his pulsing cock releasing inside of me. He laid his head on my chest for a few seconds to catch his breath before gazing back up at me.

"And the answer to your question, love, is no. I can't

give you my heart one day."

"Why not?" I gasped.

He placed his fingers to my lips before leaning down to kiss me. "Because, Kate, you already have it. I gave it to you a long time ago."

Smiling, I ran my fingers through his hair and placed my hands on his cheeks. "And you've had mine, Cooper. You'll always have it for as long as you want it."

"Then I guess you'll always be mine.

Chapter 46

Kate

I took a shower with Cooper only to realize I didn't have any clean clothes at his house. The last thing I wanted to do was put my dirty clothes back on. "Don't worry, you can wear some of mine," Cooper teased.

Laughing, I towel dried my hair and wrapped it around my body. "Yeah right, they'll fall off of me. While you cook dinner, I'll walk over to my place to grab a set of clothes and a bottle of wine."

Cooper laid out a red T-shirt of his and a pair of black running shorts. When I put them on they were big on me, but I came to the conclusion that I absolutely loved wearing his clothes and he loved seeing me in them.

"I think you look hot like that, but if you must leave to get your own that's fine. I'll get our food started."

Slipping on my tennis shoes, I kissed him quickly and rushed down the stairs and out of his house. My purse was still in my car, so I opened it up and grabbed it so I could find my house keys. My dad always told me that too many keys on my keychain would ruin the ignition on my car;

therefore, I always had a separate set for my other keys. It was actually a pain in the ass.

It was a nice September night, but with the uncommonly cool breeze coming in I knew it was probably the beginning to what would be a cold winter. We didn't have many cold winters and we rarely had any snow, but I had a feeling this one would be different. Once I got to the edge of my driveway, I checked the mail and flipped through all of the envelopes before unlocking my front door.

Setting the mail in the kitchen, I checked the answering machine and wasn't surprised that there weren't any messages on it. No one ever called me on the home phone anyway. Quickly, I rushed up the stairs and slipped into my room, heading straight for my dresser. I pulled out a couple of pairs of pants, T-shirts, socks, and underwear to keep at Cooper's house.

We were always going back and forth, so I figured it would be smart to have a spare change of clothes at his house anyway. However, there was something missing. Staring at the top of my dresser, I realized there was something different about it. It just so happened that it only took a few seconds to figure it out.

"Are you by any chance looking for this?" a voice asked from behind me.

I gasped and froze in place. *How the hell did she get in my house?* Ever so slowly, I lifted my gaze to the dresser mirror. Directly behind me was a woman dressed in a pair of dark denim jeans and a black T-shirt; her hair was short and blonde just like her daughter's. However, in her hand wasn't just the ring Scott gave me … there was also a gun, pointing straight in my direction.

Slowly, I turned around and faced her head on, hands

out to my sides. "Marianne," I said. "What are you doing here?"

She smiled and batted her eyes. "Why, I came to see you, dear. It's been a while and I think it's time for you to pay your dues." She looked down at the ring. "Nice ring, by the way. Is it from Cooper, or that other gentleman I saw you all over last night?"

"It's from neither," I countered.

"My, you sure do get around, don't you?" she spat. "It makes me sick to know my son was in love with a slut. I can't believe you would honor his memory like this … whoring around with two men."

"I am not whoring around," I snapped. "I loved your son and I always will, but what was I supposed to do? I was twenty-three when he died, was I supposed to stay single for the rest of my life?"

"If you still loved him that's exactly what you would've done," she snarled.

Eyes wide, I glared at her incredulously. "Are you even listening to yourself right now? You've completely lost your mind. Scott will always be a part of my life, but I had to move on. He was dying from cancer for Christ's sake. Even if he didn't overdose on pills, the sickness would've taken him shortly after. He wanted to end the pain."

She paced back and forth, mumbling things to herself as if completely oblivious to what I'd just said. "Marianne, did you hear me? I told you Scott was dying from cancer. He didn't overdose on pills just because he wanted to."

It was as if she chose not to listen to me or to reason. She'd completely blocked out anything dealing with Scott's cancer. It was just like Emily said; she didn't want to listen to it.

With her finger on the trigger, she waved it back and forth as tears began to flow down her cheeks. "No, it's lies … all lies. He did it because you ignored him, because he was unhappy. It was all your fault!"

She took a couple of steps toward me and I backed up until I couldn't go any further. Her brown eyes were wild and untamed … if I didn't tread carefully, I'd find myself with a bullet through my skull. *Just breathe, Kate, and figure this out.*

"I watched you off and on for years—living your lonely, sad life—until in rides your knight in shining armor and sweeps you off your feet. I knew Scott's memory flew out the window once he showed up. No one will ever be better than my son." She pointed the gun at me again and I froze, holding my breath. "I want you miserable, the same way I've been for the past two years."

"I'm sorry you've been miserable, and I know you miss him, but Emily—"

Holding up her hand, she scoffed in disgust, "Oh, don't even mention my traitorous daughter. I haven't spoken to her since I left, so imagine my surprise when I see my son's car here the other day. No daughter of mine would turn her back on me like that, or try to send me to a rehab facility that deals with mental patients. She wants to send me off so she doesn't have to deal with me anymore."

"She's only looking out for you," I replied cautiously. "She loves you, and she misses you. I know you miss Scott, but Emily is here and alive, and she wants you to see her the way you saw Scott."

Marianne growled, "Impossible! No one can ever take the place of your first born child. They hold a special place in your heart, but now mine's gone. I didn't even want her, but my husband refused to let me get rid of her. Now that he's gone, I'm stuck with her."

If I ever felt sorry for the woman standing in front of me, I take it all back. How could anyone as sweet and loving as Scott come from such a heartless bitch? I was done trying to reason with her. Right now I needed to get out.

My breaths came out in short gasps as I searched around my room for anything that could help me distract her. There was nothing. She was getting angrier by the moment, and I knew it would only be a matter of time before she pulled the trigger. If I turned and ran she would shoot me in the back and I'd be dead.

Shit, what the hell am I going to do?

In my pocket, my phone started to ring. Immediately, I looked up at Marianne and she snapped, "Don't you dare answer that, or I'll put a bullet straight through your black heart."

"Well, if I don't and it's Cooper," I told her, "he'll be here in a heartbeat. Everyone knows that you're still around and they'll know to come check on me. You may want to kill me, but you'll be signing your own death warrant."

She huffed and waved the gun in the air. "Fine, but you better get rid of whoever it is and make it believable. If you so much as squeal I'll pull the trigger now and seal your fate."

Swallowing hard, I carefully reached into my pocket and pulled out my phone. It was Cooper. Angry and scared, I cleared my throat before answering. "Hey," I mumbled groggily.

"Kate, are you okay? You don't sound so good."

Marianne glared at me and I gritted my teeth, wishing I could find something to hit her with. "Yeah, I'm not feeling so good right now. I think I need to lie down for a while. Can I take a rain check on dinner?"

"Sure," he replied hesitantly. "Why don't I come over in a little while and we can watch a movie?"

I knew he would be persistent.

"No, *Coop*, I'll be fine. I just need to be alone."

Marianne waved her hands impatiently in the air again, wanting me to hurry. It was then I saw Scott's baseball bat leaning against my nightstand. If I could just move over a couple of paces I could get to it. Wouldn't that be irony, hitting her in the head with her own son's favorite baseball bat?

"You're not acting right, Kate. What's going on?"

"Nothing, *Coop*, I swear. I'm just really tired, and I know you're tired too from your flight. I'll see you first thing in the morning, okay?"

"Okay," he sighed. "If you change your mind you know where I'm at."

"I will," I whispered. "I love you."

"I love you, too."

When I heard the final click of the line go dead, I knew it was over. Closing my eyes, I bit my lip until I could taste blood; even more so when Marianne laughed at my expense.

"At least Cooper's mom will be glad she doesn't have to worry about you. There was one thing we had in common … we didn't like you. You see, she knew you weren't good enough for her son, and I knew you weren't good enough for mine. It killed me that Scott chose you over me. Every time I wanted him to come home and visit, he said he couldn't because he was too busy doing something with you. You have no idea what it feels like to be a mother and have your favorite child treat you like second best."

I really wanted to tell her that Scott was a big boy and made his own decisions. It wasn't my fault that he chose me over her. If she wasn't so controlling maybe he would've had a reason to go home. Out of the corner of my eye, I saw a shadow creep up the hallway outside of my door. I didn't dare look for fear that Marianne would look, too. I prayed it was Cooper, but knowing my luck it was probably just a figment of my imagination.

"So what's going to make you happy, huh? Do you want me to break up with Cooper and be miserable for the rest of my life?"

"No, dear," she responded, grinning evilly. "All I wanted was to say what I had to say to you and end it. I honestly thought I'd get more pleasure in ruining you and Cooper, but you two just don't want to stay away from each other. I don't trust you to end it, so now I have to do it myself."

I moved over a step. All I needed was a few more inches and I'd be able to grab the bat. Marianne continued to move closer, waving the gun in the air with her finger on the trigger. She set my ring down on the dresser and slid the piece of paper out from underneath my jewelry box. It was one of the letters from Scott. She had her back to the door, and that was when Cooper came into my line of sight and put a finger to his lips.

Opening the piece of paper, Marianne huffed and said, "I don't know what it is about you and these men, but they fall all over you like you're something special. All I see is a self-involved, spoiled girl who cared more about her schoolwork than taking care of my son, who wor-shipped the ground you walked on. I just don't …"

Her eyes went wide as she read the letter. She imme-diately stopped what she was saying and whispered one word when she got to the end, "Scott."

Everything after that moved in slow motion. Cooper threw something down the hall—making a loud crashing sound—and it captured Marianne's attention for a fraction of a second, allowing me to grab the baseball bat and swing. I didn't get as much force behind it as I wanted, but when it connected with her arm I knew it was going to leave one hell of a bruise, or maybe even a broken bone.

The only problem was that it wasn't enough of a dis-traction for her to drop the gun. When she hollered in pain, she reared back at me, her eyes wild. Before she could lift the gun and aim it at me, Cooper exploded into the room straight for her; except, he didn't get to her in time.

After that … all I saw was red.

The sound of the gun blasted through my ears, and when I saw a spray of blood spurt from Cooper's body, every ounce of fear and terror I felt in my gut made my blood run cold. After that I didn't think … I reacted. Cooper was still on his feet—holding his side—but I was the one closer to Marianne.

My God, I hated her.

Before she could turn around, I took Scott's baseball bat and swung. The sickening thud as I made contact with her skull made my stomach cringe, especially when she landed face first on the hardwood floor. For so long, she hurt me and made me miserable, but now she hurt Cooper. The gun she had in her hand slid across the floor, but it didn't look like she'd be picking it up anytime soon. I hit her pretty hard, but I knew it wasn't a killing blow. Rushing to the gun, I grabbed it off the floor and ran straight to Cooper, who immediately put his arms around me.

"Kate," he murmured, grunting in pain. Crying, I quickly pulled out of his arms and lifted his shirt where he was shot. "It's just a graze, love. It could've been worse."

Realizing it *was* just a graze right above his hipbone, I sighed in relief, but I knew it had to hurt like hell every time he moved. I fetched a T-shirt from my pajama drawer and placed it on his wound, adding pressure. "I need you to put pressure on your wound, okay? I'm going to call the police," I told him, reaching into my pocket for my phone.

"I already called, Kate. Sam should be here any second."

Right about that time I heard the front door slam open and footsteps barreling up the stairs. Sam burst into my room with his gun drawn, followed by Officer Stilwell who lowered his and went straight to Marianne, lying motionless on the floor. He called for a couple of ambulances and for backup while Sam holstered his gun and inspected Cooper's wound.

"This isn't the way I wished it would've gone down, but at least it's over," Sam assured us. "She's not going to bother you again … ever."

"Thank God," I replied, "because next time I don't know if I can stop with just one swing to her head."

Once the ambulances came, the medics loaded Marianne into one in—which Officer Stilwell rode in as well—while Cooper was put in the other one. Before I climbed in, Sam stopped me with a hand on my shoulder. "I wanted you to know that Emily called me this afternoon and told me some things. Apparently, Mrs. Easton was delusional."

Yeah, I kind of figured that out today, I wanted to say.

"There were times when she claimed that Scott was still alive and that he was talking to her, demanding she seek vengeance for his death. There was also an incident up in Ohio when she tried to attack a girl that looked just like you. She wasn't charged with anything so we had no idea that had even happened. They settled it without pressing charges."

"Why didn't Emily say something sooner?" I scoffed incredulously. "It would've been nice to know she was *that* mentally unstable."

Sam sighed and shrugged his shoulders. "I know, but I guess she wanted to believe that her mother would get better. We all hold out hope for the best, right? Anyway, no amount of reasoning with her would've spared you. She knew about Scott's cancer and chose not to believe it. I'm just glad Cooper called and got to you in time."

"Me too," I whispered, looking over my shoulder at the man who risked everything for me.

"Now go and get our star quarterback to the hospital so he'll be ready for the game on Saturday. Just because he got shot doesn't mean he can sit it out," he added with a wink before ambling off.

After climbing into the ambulance, Cooper smiled and patted the bed he sat on. "You know, I think we should christen this ambulance. Don't you think that could be kind of interesting?"

The medic blushed and cleared her throat, keeping her gaze on anything and everything other than me and Cooper. She had to be in her mid to late thirties with short, pixie-cut brown hair and a splash of freckles on her nose and cheeks. She tried to keep from laughing as I sat down on the roll away bed with Cooper.

"Yeah, right! I can see it now in the headlines … *Star Quarterback Makes Daunting Play in the Back of an Ambulance*. I think we've been in the papers one too many times already," I chuckled.

"Not to barge in on the conversation," the medic interrupted, gazing straight at me, "but I'm pretty sure you're going to be in the papers again. Something like this doesn't just happen, especially to people like him," she said, nodding toward Cooper. "Everyone loves him around here, so they're going to want to hear about his heroic attempt to save the girl he loves."

Cooper's wide smile was contagious. He had just gotten shot, but he looked happier than I'd ever seen him. "You see, love. Things are finally looking up for us. I found my redemption and a home here, and you finally have your peace. For once we can live our lives the way we want to and not have anyone hold us back. It's going to be a new beginning for us."

The medic, whose name happened to be Jennifer, shut the ambulance doors and we were finally on our way to the hospital. Thankfully, Jennifer moved up to the front and let Cooper and I have a little bit of privacy. Putting his arm around me, Cooper kissed me on the forehead while I snuggled against his chest. I didn't want to think what would've happened if Marianne had better aim and really injured him. The thought of killing someone had never crossed my mind, but if she took Cooper away from me, I was afraid that nothing would've stopped me from killing her. Thankfully, I didn't have to find out.

"So how did you know to save me?" I asked curiously, gazing up at him.

Sighing, he brushed his thumb across my lips and bent down to kiss me. "You don't ever call me, *Coop*, Kate. I knew something was wrong the second I heard you say that to me. I wanted to ask you what was going on, but I didn't want to run the risk of being heard through the phone. You have no idea how much it killed me to let you go. After that, I immediately called Sam and told him something was wrong. He told me to wait on him before I did anything stupid, but there was no way in hell I was going to waste another second. If I didn't come when I did, I'm afraid it would've been too late."

Skimming a finger across the bandage on his right side, I closed my eyes and squeezed them shut; they burned. When I opened them, tears fell down my cheeks. "Well, you came right on time. I don't know how to thank you, Cooper. You saved me … in more ways than one."

Tilting my chin up with his finger, he stared down at me with his watery blue gaze. "And you saved me, love. For however long you want me, I'm going to spend that time making it up to you … I promise."

"Well, then it looks like you'll be making it up to me for a really long time."

Because I wasn't planning on ever letting him go.

Chapter 47

COOPER

Four Months Later

After everything that happened, Marianne was put away for the rest of her life and even more insane than before she went in. Apparently, the baseball bat to her head didn't knock any sense in her ... it made her worse. One thing was for certain, she'd never see the outside world again and her daughter was finally free of her. Kate hurt for Emily and talked to her about once every week, but there was still some tension that would probably never go away.

My mother, on the other hand, had frequently tried to call me since she found out my team was heading to the Super Bowl. *Yeah, that's right; I'm finally going to the Super Bowl.* What made it even more of an epic event was that our team was playing against the one who got rid of me. There was sure to be some tension there, but I was ready.

I had two weeks until the game, so Kate and I decided

on a little vacation down to Nags Head, North Carolina where the infamous Paige Monroe a.k.a Shelby Dawson Reynolds would interview me for another piece in *Physique Sports and Fitness Magazine.* The interview took a different turn, but I was ready for everyone to know the real me.

Gazing out the window of Shelby's beach house, I watched as Kate walked along the beach with the wind blowing her golden blonde hair behind her. I couldn't take my eyes off of her.

"Are you sure you want the whole world to read this story?" Shelby asked. "It's really personal. It's not easy exposing yourself and letting everyone see inside of you. Although, I do know that people will fall in love with you after they read it."

I chuckled, still gazing out the window. "Yeah, well, I'm sure I'm going to break some hearts coming up soon."

Slowly getting to her feet, Shelby rubbed her swollen belly and came to my side, grinning mischievously at me then out the window to Kate. "Oh yeah, why is that?"

I winked. "Just make sure you watch the Super Bowl and you'll find out. Even if you're in the hospital having that baby of yours, you better turn on the television and watch the game."

Shelby laughed and smacked me on the arm. "Hey, I'm pretty sure if that happens Matt will definitely have the television on while I'm sitting there giving birth. I don't know what it is about men and the Super Bowl." She rubbed her stomach again and smiled. "I'm sure my little tyke will be breaking plenty of hearts when he gets older if he's anything like his dad. It's amazing how things turn out, though. Second chances aren't easy to come by, but yet you got yours."

Yes, I did.

Epilogue

COOPER

Super Bowl Sunday

It was Super Bowl Sunday and the whole city of Charlotte buzzed with raw excitement and energy. Luckily, the game was on home soil, but with that came the added pressure to succeed. Our team was pumped and ready to go; except, I had a different kind of fear skating its way up my spine. We were not only playing my old team for the championship, but I had a special kind of play to do that would change my life forever.

"Are you nervous?" Evan asked, taking a seat beside me. The locker room echoed with laughter and shouts from my team, but I had chosen to spend the last few moments before the big game in solitude.

Taping up my fingers, I smiled and tilted my head toward him. "A little," I confessed, "but I know the team will kick ass out there and have my back."

Evan chuckled and slapped me on the shoulder. "I wasn't talking about the game, but I think you knew that."

Was I that transparent?

He got up to walk away, but then quickly turned around. "Oh yeah, before I go there's someone that wants to talk to you."

"Is it Kate?" I asked, getting to my feet.

He shook his head. "No, it's not her, but he's waiting by the door for you."

Once I was fully dressed and ready, I left my secluded corner and strolled through the locker room, almost going deaf from the guys shouting in my ear. I laughed along with them until I saw who was at the door and my smile vanished. He still looked the same wearing the usual black Oakland jacket with black slacks; his white hair covered by a visor. It was my former coach … William Sanford. I hadn't spoken to him since the last time he told me I wasn't cut out for his team.

"Well, look at you," he announced, extending his hand.

Taking his hand, I shook it firmly and narrowed my gaze. "To what do I owe this pleasure?" I asked dryly.

William held up his hands in defeat. "Okay, I get it, you're still pissed at me and you should be. What I said was wrong, and I wanted to come down here and apologize. You've done really well this season; the team's proud of you."

"Are they now?"

William glanced around the locker room and nodded his head toward the hallway. I followed him out and definitely wasn't expecting the next words that came out of his mouth.

"We'd like to have you back, Cooper. Our manager can pull some strings and have you back on the team by next season. I know you probably want to get back home. That's where your family and friends are."

About that time, Evan and the guys all strolled out of the room down the opposite hallway with Joel pulling up the rear. He glanced over at us, and nodded, his smile melancholy. *Did he know I was being offered this?* Turning his back on us, he followed the team until he disappeared around the corner.

"So what do you say? Are you in?" he asked with a gleam in his eyes.

Taking a deep breath, I shook my head and smiled. "I'm sorry, but I'm going to have to pass."

Eyes wide, his mouth dropped open in shock. "You can't be serious? You actually want to stay here?"

"I do," I admitted wholeheartedly. "My home is here now; this is where I belong. I guess I should be thanking you for letting me go."

William sighed and clapped me on the shoulder. "Well, it was a mistake I'll never live down. All right, if that's your choice I'll leave you be. Just know that the offer still stands. I wish you the best, Cooper, and good luck out there. It's going to be a good game."

Yes, it is.

Once I joined my team out on the field, Joel discreetly sidled up to my side and cleared his throat; he actually sounded worried when he spoke, "So what did you decide? Are you going to go back to them?"

Before I could reply, Evan threw me my helmet and winked; the game was about to begin. Quickly, I turned to my uncle and did something I never thought I'd do out in front of everyone … I hugged him hard.

"You're stuck with me, Joel. I'm not going anywhere."

His arms tightened around my back. "That's what I like to hear, son. Now go out there and show them what you can do. Go!"

I rushed off out onto the field and found Kate immediately. She was in the middle between Lara and Luke—wearing a Cougars jersey with my number—with the biggest grin on her face, waving and cheering my name. Seeing her made me smile, but also knowing Luke was going to hate me after today made me smile even wider.

"All right, boys, this is it," I shouted at them. "Let's kick some ass."

Kate

Half-time approached and the score was tied. The guys left the field to recuperate while the show began in center field. Cooper said that Joel wanted to give them a pep talk during half-time, so instead of hanging out with him like I usually did during the games, I decided to stay with Lara and Luke.

"Don't your motocross races start in the next couple of weeks?" I asked Luke.

All three of us had on Cougars jerseys, but instead of wearing Cooper's number like Lara and I were doing, he had on Evan's.

"Yes, and you promised to come to some of them, remember? I expect to see you at my first one," he insisted boldly.

I nudged him in the side with my elbow. "I'll be there, don't worry. I want to see you win."

"You're damn right."

Once the half-time show was over, we all took our seats and waited on the workers to move the stage off the field. "Guys, I'm kind of thirsty, do you want anything to eat or drink? I'm going to get something really quick before the game starts back up." Lara shook her head, but Luke stood with me.

"I don't want anything," he said, "but I can go with you if you want."

"No, that's fine. I don't mind going by myself. Besides, I don't want Lara sitting by herself. I'll be right back."

Shrugging, he sat back down. "All right, it's whatever you want."

As I started down the stadium steps, my heart stopped and I froze as a voice echoed across the speakers, catching my attention. "Oh my God," I gasped.

"Good evening, ladies and gentleman. Thank you for joining us here at the Bank of America Stadium. I'm Cooper Davis and I wanted to ask that you join me tonight as I do something I never thought I would do. There's someone in the stands that I would really like to bring on this stage, and if you wouldn't mind chanting her name that would be great. Maybe it would get her out here because I'm sure she's probably cussing at me right now for putting her on the spot. Her name is Kate, everyone."

Wide-eyed, I stood there on the steps like an idiot as

the crowd shouted and cheered my name over and over, clapping their hands. "KATE! KATE! KATE! KATE! KATE!"

Lara clapped her hands and pointed straight at me. "There she is everyone!" she yelled.

Cooper chuckled. "Come on, Kate, they're cheering for you, love. Get yourself out here."

Biting my lip, I slowly descended the stairs and made my way out to the field. Cameras flashed all around and I smiled, hoping I didn't look like an idiot. When I got to the stage, Cooper smiled and beckoned me closer. Dressed in his black and blue jersey with his hair mussed from his helmet, he was the sexiest quarterback I'd ever seen.

"What are you doing?" I whispered nervously.

He took my hands and kissed each one before dropping down on one knee. "I think you know, love." The stands went wild as soon as he pulled out the black box from behind his back.

Putting a hand over my mouth, I gasped and cried, "Cooper, are you really doing this?"

He nodded his head and opened the box. "Yes, Kate, I'm really doing this. I love you and I want to spend the rest of my life with you. You know how hard it was for me to change, but yet you stuck by me and always saw the good. You never gave up on me when so many others in my life did. Do you remember four months ago when I promised I would make it up to you for sticking by me for however long you wanted me?"

"Yes," I whispered, "I remember. And I told you that you would be making it up to me for a really long time."

Chuckling, he opened the black box to reveal a round cut diamond ring with blue sapphire side stones; it was beautiful.

"How about I make it up to you forever, love? I don't want to let you go … ever."

Cooper took the ring out of the box and slowly slid it onto my finger. When he got to his feet, he took my face in his hands and bent down so his lips were just a breath away from mine.

"What's your answer, Kate? Will you be my wife?"

The crowd cheered and chanted, "YES! YES! YES! YES!" over and over. With tears flowing down my cheeks, I smiled wide and flung my arms around his neck.

"Yes," I cried. "The answer is yes!"

Lifting me in his arms, he kissed me on the lips and swung me around. "Say it again, love. I need to hear you say it again," he murmured in my ear.

"Yes, Cooper," I whispered back. "I want to be your wife … always, but before we do anything you need to finish this game. Everyone's counting on you to win the Super Bowl for them."

"No," he said, taking my face in his hands. "I'm not winning it for them. I'm winning it for you. It's always going to be for you … forever."

Coming Soon

(A Second Chances Standalone)
~Evan's story~

Keep turning for a sneak peek at what's coming next!
You don't want to miss this!

Note from the Author: As some of you know, I love my MMA fighters. (As seen in Meant for Me and Fighting for Love) Well now I plan on embarking in a new journey that is going to be nothing but hot and sexy, alpha male fighters that'll get your blood racing and your panties dropping. I bring you …

The **GLOVES OFF** standalone series
(A new series based off of characters in my Second Chances fighter books) Check out the list:

A Fighter's Desire – A Gloves Off Prequel
Tyler's Undoing – Book One
Ryley's Revenge – Book Two
Camden's Redemption – Book Three

Coming to the ring this Summer/Fall!

Acknowledments

To my husband, Matt—I love you with all of my heart. My dreams wouldn't have come true without your support.

To my superpower PA, Kim Walker—You have been a lifesaver. I literally would have no hair right now if it wasn't for you. I'm thankful each and every day that I have you by my side.

To the most amazing editor ever—I think I summed it up with that title … YOU'RE AMAZING!

To my cover designer, Regina Wamba—Your creativity astounds me. I'm in love with each and every cover you do for me.

To my readers—THANK YOU SO MUCH! I love and appreciate every single one of you. None of this would be possible without you, and I will eternally be grateful for the rest of my life. YOU ROCK!

About the Author

USA Today Bestselling author, L.P. Dover, is a southern belle residing in North Carolina along with her husband and two beautiful girls. Before she even began her literary journey she worked in Periodontics enjoying the wonderment of dental surgeries.

Not only does she love to write, but she loves to play tennis, go on mountain hikes, white water rafting, and you can't forget the passion for singing. Her two number one fans expect a concert each and every night before bedtime and those songs usually consist of Christmas carols.

Aside from being a wife and mother, L.P. Dover has written over nine novels including her *Forever Fae* series, the *Second Chances* series, and her standalone novel, *Love, Lies, and Deception*. Her favorite genre to read is romantic suspense and she also loves writing it. However, if she had to choose a setting to live in it would have to be with her faeries in the Land of the Fae.

L.P. Dover is represented by Marisa Corvisiero of Corvisiero Literary Agency.

You can find L.P. Dover at:

HER WEBSITE: www.authorlpdoverbooks.com

EMAIL: lpdover@authorlpdoverbooks.com

FOLLOW HER ON TWITTER: @LPDover

"LIKE" her on Facebook:

www.facebook.com/pages/LP-Dover/318455714919114

OTHER BOOKS BY L.P. DOVER

FOREVER FAE SERIES

SECOND CHANCES STANDALONES

STANDALONE (ROMANTIC SUSPENSE)

ALSO CHECK OUT THESE
EXTRAORDINARY AUTHORS & BOOKS:

Alivia Anders ~ Illumine
Cambria Hebert ~ Recalled
A.O. Peart ~ Almost Matched
Julia Crane ~ Freak of Nature
J.A. Huss ~ TAUT: The Ford Book
Cameo Renae ~ Hidden Wings
A.J. Bennett ~ Unintentional Virgin
Tabatha Vargo ~ Playing Patience
Ella James ~ Selling Scarlett
Tara West ~ Say When
Heidi McLaughlin ~ Forever Your Girl
Melissa Andrea ~ The Edge of Darkness
Kelly Walker ~ No One's Angel
Komal Kant ~ Falling for Hadie
Melissa Pearl ~ Betwixt
Alexia Purdy ~ Ever Shade (A Dark Faerie Tale #1)
Sarah M. Ross ~ Inhale, Exhale
Brina Courtney ~ Reveal
Amber Garza ~ Falling to Pieces
Anna Cruise ~ It Was You

Read on for a sneak peek at a couple of new releases coming out!

Tempting SYDNEY

A Tempting Novel, Book 1
By Angela Corbett

Chapter ONE

"IT'S AN EPIDEMIC, Sydney. A freaking epidemic."
Brynn's face was scrunched into a frown as she slid into
the chair next to mine. She put her salad and Diet Coke
down on the table. We were at Soup and Spoon, our favorite lunch spot a block from Easton University campus. I'd
been at the table awhile, my face buried in a book, trying
to study for my law school prep class. So much information was packed into the short summer class that I felt
like all I did was study.

I set the book to the side and took in Brynn's crimson
v-necked tee that showcased her fantastic cleavage,
bootcut jeans that hugged her ass, and thick espresso col-

ored hair that fell in curls all the way to her waist. My hair was long, but I didn't have the commitment required to take care of a mane like hers. She was stop-and stare-gorgeous, though I'd never convince her of that.

"What's the epidemic?" I asked, unwrapping my ginormous chocolate toffee cookie. I'd been saving it as a reward for finishing going through my notes. It's the little things.

"Small dicks." She shook her head in frustration. "Cocktail weenies are bigger than what I've had to deal with lately. I'm going to start making guys tell me their size before I go out with them. I'm sick of wasting my time on tiny weenies."

This should have been shocking, but not much surprised me anymore when it came to Brynn Harper. I laughed, thoroughly amused, as I broke off a piece of cookie. "I guess your date last night didn't go well?"

She threw her arms up in disgust. "No. It didn't. You just don't understand because you haven't been investigating. Just wait, you'll be disappointed."

I considered that as the toffee and chocolate melted together in my mouth. While I wasn't a virgin, sex had never been a big priority for me. I was very goal-oriented. Currently my goals included graduating from my excellent law school at the top of my class, and then moving on to a fantastic law firm, and becoming one of the best attorneys in the country. Pregnancy would hamper those goals. Since no form of birth control was one hundred percent effective, I'd decided to stay away from sex until I at least had my law degree…and maybe forever. It hadn't been too difficult. My experience with sex in the past hadn't been memorable. If history was any indication, I really wasn't missing much.

I raised a brow. "I didn't realize an investigation was underway."

Brynn heaved an exasperated sigh as she dribbled her lettuce with light dressing. "You've known me since we were freshmen in college, Syd. I've been investigating dick sizes for years."

"I thought you were just hooking up. Not taking notes."

She waved me off like I was being ridiculous. "Of course I was hooking up! But it's been impossible not to notice the current state of weenies. The situation is horrifying!" Her eyes were so wide that her long, thick lashes practically hit her perfectly arched eyebrows. "It's all those hormones in milk—I know it. I bet dicks have been getting smaller and smaller for at least thirty years. Someone should study that." She paused, her brows knit together. "I wonder if I could make it a topic for my Master's thesis?"

I broke off another piece of my cookie. "You might want to wait until you actually start grad school before you propose that as your research concentration. It would be bad to get kicked out of the program before you even start."

She rolled her eyes. "You worry too much, Syd," she said, stabbing a forkful of lettuce. "You need to learn to relax."

I nodded. "I will. Once I have my law degree and my dream job."

"'Gather ye rosebuds while ye may'," she said, quoting one of my favorite poems by Robbert Herrick. "You're not really doing that, you know."

I tilted my head to the side, thinking. "We just have two different versions of seizing, Brynn." I pointed to my text book. "Mine involves studying books, not men."

She lifted her hand, opening and closing it as she mouthed the words blah, blah, blah. "My version is *way* more fun. You're going to regret not doing stupid things while you were young and had an excuse." She lifted her eyes, scanning the room and then abruptly stopped, her gaze totally focused somewhere behind me and to the right. "Speaking of *doing* things, the guy behind you is throw-me-down-and-screw-me-now hot."

Brynn had hot guy radar. *That* should be the study of her thesis. We'd done the hot guy assessment routine so many times that it was habit. I waited for her to glance away—which seemed to take a lot longer than usual—counted to ten, and turned slowly, scanning the room in the direction she'd been ogling. My lips parted in a surprised "O" at the man—and he was definitely all man—sitting two tables away. Brynn had reason to stare.

His short, dark brown hair had a little curl to it and was styled like he'd just gotten out of bed. Judging by the shadow across his square jawline, he'd also forgotten to shave. His eyes were what really captivated me, though. I'd only seen such a vibrant shade of blue once before. I'd taken a high school graduation trip to Cancun, Mexico, and thought the colors of the ocean were the most stunning hues I'd ever seen. This guy's eyes were the exact same bright blue. If I'd seen him in a photograph, I'd have sworn they were Photoshopped. His arms strained the seams of the white tee shirt he was wearing, and I had no doubt that everything under his clothes was probably as captivating and sculpted as his face. A matte black, beaded bracelet wrapped around his wrist. Most men wouldn't be able to pull it off, but on this guy, it looked masculine, and just upped his sexy factor even more.

I'd mastered the two second check-out years ago, but this guy had caught me completely off guard. I'd been looking—some might even say leering—for far more than two seconds. Just as I got my wits back, the guy looked up, straight at me. He met my gaze—and held it.

And held it some more.

A flutter started in my stomach. His expression was full of unabashed self-assurance. Clear eyes were trained on me with a brazen focus that made the flutter descend much, much lower. Sparks felt like they were jumping across the room, and my breath caught in my throat. Just when I thought I might pass out, one corner of his lips lifted slightly and he cocked a brow expectantly. I knew how to flirt. And if I was reading him right, he'd just issued a dare to come over—one I wasn't sure I was capable of accepting. I hadn't said a word to him, but it was obvious this guy had almost as much confidence as he had testosterone.

He gave me about five seconds to decide what I was going to do, then tilted his head down, lifting a shoulder in a half shrug that seemed to indicate I'd had my chance and lost it. He stood, grabbing his tray filled with trash left over from his lunch. His jeans hung low on his hips, held up by a wide black belt with a square, distressed silver buckle and I couldn't help but watch him as he walked away. It was a *really* nice view.

"*What* the hell was that?" Brynn asked in a half whisper. Her voice brought me out of my trance. "I think you just had eye-sex with him!"

"Sorry," I muttered, glancing back at her for a brief second so she knew I wasn't totally ignoring her. I watched the guy empty his tray into the trash, and stack it with the others above the bin. Every fiber of my being was willing him to turn back around and look at me again.

Every.

Single.

One.

My fibers failed me. He walked out the door without a second glance. I blew out a disappointed breath. "Sorry, I got distracted."

"No shit!" Brynn practically yelled. "I could feel your chemistry with Blue Eyes from here!"

I waved her off, trying to act like it wasn't a big deal, when really, I was a bit jolted by it. I'd never felt something like that before, especially for a guy I hadn't even talked to. He could sound like a chipmunk for all I knew. And chipmunks were *not* a turn-on for me.

"Well, I bet *he* has more than a cocktail weenie," Brynn said, her eyes bright with teasing. "Why don't you find out?"

The guy passed by the front window and out of my line of sight. I shifted my eyes away from the windows and back to Brynn. "Because that would get in the way of my goals."

She laughed. "You realize you've barely looked at me for the last five minutes?"

I took a drink of my dark chocolate iced coffee. It was my third one today. "I can appreciate nice things without having to try them. He was hot, Brynn. That's all."

She grinned conspiratorially. "Trying them makes it *so* much more entertaining." She leaned back in her chair, contemplative. "I haven't seen him around town or campus before. I wonder if he's a student? Or if he just works around here?"

I'd seen the veins visible through his huge arms, and when he'd stood up, I'd noticed his thighs were pretty darn substantial, too. "I don't know. Maybe he's a trainer at a gym or something?"

She put a finger to her lips. "Maybe…" she paused, thinking about it. "Nah…I bet he does something mountain-manny. Like chopping wood."

I rolled my eyes. She'd been spending way too much time watching stripper movies.

"What?" she said, noticing my dismissal. "I'm just saying he probably has a nice, big ax." She slowly licked her lips and I could practically see the images forming in her head. "And I bet he knows *exactly* how to use it."

That thought made my mind immediately wander to what he'd look like shirtless chopping wood—which would be great if I was home alone in my room, with the secret box only Brynn knew the location to in case of my death so my mom didn't find it and have a stroke over the dirty things her daughter liked—but it wasn't so great in the middle of a restaurant. I quickly changed the subject. "What's the plan for this weekend?" Brynn always had our weekends planned by Wednesday at the latest.

"Party at Collin's."

I sighed. I hated Collin's parties. "I don't know why you still hang out with him. He's like the President of douchebags." Really, he was the President of his frat until we graduated a couple of months ago, and that's pretty much the same thing as being the President of douchery.

She lifted a shoulder in a half-shrug as she pushed her

food away. She'd hardly eaten any of it—typical. "He has free food and beer. Plus, he's a great singer when he gets drunk enough."

I nodded in concession. He really was a good singer, and if I was being honest, he wasn't a bad guy. I just despised frat boys in general…which was a problem since Brynn spent so much time with so many of them. Brynn's phone vibrated and she glanced at the screen. "I have a meeting to go to, but I'll see you at the house later?"

"Sure."

The phone vibrated again. She grinned as she read the text and quickly replied, her fingers flying over the screen.

I eyed her skeptically. "You're not going to a meeting. You're going to hook up with someone."

She flashed a sly smile as she slid her phone into her back pocket and stood. "Well, it *could* be considered a research meeting. I do have a Master's thesis idea I need to gather information for. I'll have to start carrying a notebook, and make a chart."

I shook my head, a little jealous of her spontaneity, and wishing I was a bit more fun as opposed to focused. "Let's hope you find more than a cocktail weenie, then."

She gave me an evil smile and lifted her hand with her index and middle finger crossed as she walked away. I took a sip of coffee, thinking about the current state of my non-social life, and then pushed it to the back of my mind so I could review my notes one more time.

www.ingramcontent.com/pod-product-compliance
Lightning Source LLC
Chambersburg PA
CBHW020225180626
46810CB00006B/2052